Jim Carrey as Andy Kaufman

MAN ON THE MOON

SCREENPLAY AND NOTES BY
SCOTT ALEXANDER & LARRY KARASZEWSKI

AFTERWORD WITH MILOS FORMAN

A Newmarket Shooting Script™ Series Book
NEWMARKET PRESS • NEW YORK

DEDICATED TO DEBBIE AND EMILY

The publisher would like to thank Nancy Cushing-Jones, Cindy Chang, and Bette Einbinder of Universal Studios; Pamela Abdy of Jersey Films; and especially Scott Alexander, Larry Karaszewski, and Milos Forman for their help in preparing this book for publication.

Design and compilation copyright © 1999 by Newmarket Press. All rights reserved.
Text and illustrations (except where noted) copyright © 1999 by Universal Studios Publishing Rights, a Division of Universal Studios Licensing, Inc. All rights reserved.

PHOTO CREDITS
All photographs from the film *Man on the Moon* are by Francois Duhamel.
All photographs of Andy Kaufman and his family and friends are courtesy of the Estate of Andy Kaufman.

The Newmarket Shooting Script Series™ is a registered trademark of Newmarket Press, a Division of Newmarket Publishing & Communications.

This book is published simultaneously in the United States of America and in Canada.

FIRST EDITION

99 00 01   10 9 8 7 6 5 4 3 2 1

Library of Congress Cataloging in Publication Data

Alexander, Scott (Scott M.)
Man on the moon / screenplay and notes by Scott Alexander & Larry Karaszewski. Afterword with Milos Forman.
p. cm. — (A Newmarket shooting script series book)
1. Kaufman, Andy, 1949–1984. I. Karaszewski, Larry. II. Title. III. Series.
PN1997.M25677 A44 1999
791.43'72—dc21   99-051519
CIP
ISBN: 1-55704-400-7

QUANTITY PURCHASES
Companies, professional groups, clubs, and other organizations may qualify for special terms when ordering quantities of this title. For information, write Special Sales, Newmarket Press, 18 East 48th Street, Suite 1501, New York, New York 10017; call (212) 832-3575; fax (212) 832-3629; or e-mail: newmktprs@aol.com.
www.newmarketpress.com

Manufactured in the United States of America.

CONTENTS

Above: Andy Kaufman, on stage with Howdy Doody. *Below:* Jim Carrey, on stage with Howdy Doody.

CONTENTS

Above: Andy Kaufman, on stage with Howdy Doody. *Below:* Jim Carrey, on stage with Howdy Doody.

CONTENTS

Above: Andy Kaufman, on stage with Howdy Doody. *Below:* Jim Carrey, on stage with Howdy Doody.

INTRODUCTION

BY SCOTT ALEXANDER & LARRY KARASZEWSKI

Well, we've gotten away with murder again. *Man on the Moon* is our third anti-biopic—a movie about somebody who doesn't deserve one—a subversive, upside-down tale of an iconoclast fighting the establishment. However, it was almost our second. After we wrote *Ed Wood* in 1992, our lives and careers changed. Suddenly, we were in demand. Studios wanted another strange script about a weirdo, and they would trust us with more creative control than we had previously been used to. So we frantically started scrounging around, examining oddballs we admired or found interesting: Billy Carter, Andy Kaufman, Larry Flynt, Jack Kevorkian . . . they all merited a trip to the library.

For Andy, we watched a terrific documentary, Lynne Margulies's *I'm from Hollywood,* a tribute to Andy's wrestling days. We were tempted, because Andy was absolutely fascinating. We loved the way he bent reality, confusing put-on with fact, and his good and bad sides made for a rich character . . . *but*—we didn't see a narrative. We couldn't find a shape or structure. So many of the moments in his life were bogus—breaking his neck, getting married, nervous breakdowns—that we were bewildered as to their significance. Do fake events count as story? So we abandoned the idea, and a few months later, we sold a Larry Flynt pitch to Columbia Pictures. We spent a year writing the first draft, Milos Forman came aboard and directed a terrific movie, and now it was official: We were the crazy biopic guys.

Not a week went by that we weren't treated to a wacky submission: Preacher Gene Scott, Bob Marley, the Village People, Billy Martin, Linda Lovelace, Buffalo Bob Smith, Charles Manson, Betty Page, George "Superman" Reeves . . . even a guy who wrestled grizzly bears in a robot suit. All these screwball underdogs made for entertaining reading, but nothing quite connected. So we kept ourselves busy writing regular Hollywood scripts, waiting for the inspiration to tackle another biopic. We had to be choosy, because bios are huge undertakings—months of research and interviews, double or triple the usual time commitment.

Then one day a phone call came out of the blue from Danny DeVito. He and Milos Forman had a "secret project" they wanted to discuss. We were ushered into a room with Danny, small talk was dispensed with, drinks were served, and then Danny pitched us his idea: "An Andy Kaufman movie!" We looked at each other in disbelief.

Danny knew Andy from his years on *Taxi*. Danny knew Milos from *One Flew over the Cuckoo's Nest*. One night Danny had regaled Milos with hilarious, bizarre, touching Andy Kaufman stories. Milos was intrigued, and they decided to approach us about writing it. We went back to our office, unsure what to do. We had discarded the idea years earlier—and yet, who were we to contradict Danny DeVito and Milos Forman, who believed this would make a good movie? So we signed on. "Great!" they responded. "We'll sell it to Universal. Let us know when there's a first draft!"

Oops. For the first time in our career, we had taken a job without figuring out the story beforehand. In the past, we always had a three-act structure, a preliminary road map. But this time, we blithely assumed it would just show up.

Starting out, our biggest asset was George Shapiro, Andy's manager. George had saved every single TV appearance and magazine article about Andy. Additionally, and most incredibly, George had hours and hours of offstage Andy on audiotape. Twenty years ago, George had sensed that he was participating in something special and magical, and he had had the foresight to tape-record it. So we had invaluable recordings of Andy with his guard down—goofing, arguing, and always fretting about his career.

Wanting to be completists, we watched, listened to, and read everything. There must have been a hundred hours of TV esoterica, and we bravely trudged through all of it: *Stick Around,* an unsold futuristic pilot; 2 A.M. appearances at the Improv shot on someone's home-video camera; concerts at Transcendental Meditation conventions; New York cable public access; and most incredibly, a once-in-a-lifetime screening of the bootleg director's cut of *Heartbeeps*.

Andy Kaufman's madness started becoming a blur. His act was always about challenging perception, mixing mainstream entertainment with performance art. Soon we fell into the disinformation pit. Our funniest moment was while watching tapes from *Soundstage,* Andy's final TV special. After one skit, a director said "cut," and Andy walked off the set and sat down. We grinned in anticipation. Andy sipped a drink and reviewed his script. We giggled, waiting for the Pirandelloesque twist. An assistant in headphones came over and said they'd be ready in ten minutes. Andy nodded and continued reading. We watched. Andy kept reading. We watched some more. Andy *still* kept reading. We glanced at each other. Where's the joke? This was a typical Kaufman bit, and yet it was straining even *our* patience. The clock ticked, and we began arguing. Larry insisted there was something wrong—this was *not* the show. Scott got indignant— of course this was the bit! Andy *wanted* us disoriented. We just had to stick it out. So we watched Andy sit some more . . . and we then *really* started fighting. Was this funny? Suddenly a bizarre theory emerged: Maybe this wasn't a routine. Maybe this was just uncut raw footage. Dailies. Quickly we fast-forwarded . . . and color bars came up. Pause, and the two of us howled with laughter. We were too far into Andy's deconstructionist style. We couldn't distinguish entertainment from a guy reading a book! We smiled, knowing that if Andy were staring down from heaven, he'd be cracking up, too. He was still pulling the strings.

Because written material on Andy was so slim, we realized that interviews would be the key to understanding him. They're the best source for anecdotes, and we spent months tracking folks down. Almost everyone had fond memories and happily contributed. This produced thousands of pages of transcripts, which we then organized like chapters: "Childhood," "Foreign Man," "Strange Eating Habits," "Meditation." But did we *learn* anything? That took even longer.

George and Danny started us with contacts and phone numbers. Then, like dominoes, an old girlfriend would remember the phone number of a high school buddy, who then sent us to the manager of a health food restaurant. Eventually, dozens of names went into the hopper. George still worked with the family, so Andy's father, brother, and sister each flew out and spent time with us. We sat with *Taxi* co-workers. We talked to numerous girlfriends and extremely chatty TM disciples. People had clung onto any souvenirs— and they shared with us letters, photos, and dusty answering-machine tapes. Some people got emotional, even crying when they saw boxes labeled "Andy" all over our office.

Andy had clearly manipulated his life to create different, discontinuous pieces of himself. Thus, he was an introvert and an extrovert. Some described his all-vegetarian diet. Others related his daily breakfast of bacon and eggs. One girl was led to believe that he was a practicing Orthodox Jew. Marilu Henner found him unwashed and panhandling on a New York street corner. However, key themes came up repeatedly, and we took note—these taught us Andy's essence: dessert, obsessive-compulsiveness, roller coasters, grandmas, street performance. And then, the amusing "theme" that would bubble up at the end of most interviews . . . there'd be a nervous pause, and finally the person would mutter, "You do know that Andy was a, er, uh, oh, how should I put this . . . *ladies' man?*" We eventually figured out what this was code for—he loved hookers.

People spoke about what they knew, and so Andy's family focused upon his childhood and early career days. We realized we'd only have time for a few minutes of this in the film, but we listened to everything, recording hundreds of pages of growing-up stories. It was important to Andy's dad and siblings that we see the innocent Andy, the carefree Andy, the little guy who went off to conquer the world on his own terms. They felt his later career was derailed by indulgent darkness and negativity, and they preferred to remember the nicer stuff. Symbolically, this made a big impression on us. When we finally wrote the script, we tried to keep a balance, maintaining the soft-spoken vulnerability even in the midst of the angriest, crassest periods. (Wrestling, anyone?)

Certain events had such significance that they were related again and again, Rashomon-like, from different players. Hands-down, the firing of Tony Clifton from *Taxi* was the granddaddy of them all, a spectacle of surrealism, a day of anarchy trumping all in the lives of everyone it touched. We heard it so many times (and this story takes a good hour at least) that by the end we begged people *not* to tell us the story. Eventually, we weren't sure whether it even belonged in the script, but we were afraid that omitting it would send the cast of *Taxi* ballistic.

Of everyone, it was Bob Zmuda who gave us the most goodies. Bob was Andy's partner for many years, a gregarious con man with a twinkle in his eye and the holder of all the secrets. Bob understood Andy's art better than anyone, and like a professor of comedy semiotics, he regaled us with astonishingly elaborate detailings of their ruses. Bob is a master storyteller, and sometimes it was hard to separate the embellishments from the truth—but on this project, it didn't matter. The tales were screamingly funny. Sometimes Andy and Bob worked out routines that were headache-inducing in their Machiavellian convolutions, and we questioned how we could possibly do them justice, or even explain them. Check out the Tahoe sequence in this script (which is vastly different from the final film), in which Andy and Bob created untold layers of confusion. The audience is laughing because a man whom they believe to be Andy is absurdly denying he's Andy, while a kook who's also denying he's Andy, and clearly isn't Andy, actually *is* Andy. Who's the joke on? And who's the joke for? Anybody?

Capturing Andy's style was a huge challenge. His stunts worked because of the shock of immediacy. Seeing something in concert, or on live television, makes it seem real. Re-creating a staged "unforeseen accident" in a movie years later will never have the same punch. This led us to our first realization about the script: The film itself would need the structure of Andy's routines, keeping the audience off-balance by constantly pulling the rug out from under them. This flip-flopping would create a dissonance. Sometimes the audience would be included, sometimes excluded, and sometimes lied to, apparently being in on the joke, but then not really. Andy has a nervous breakdown—or did he fake it? Andy tragically dies—but is he dead? Perhaps the genre wasn't even biopic. Maybe it was a puzzle piece, like *Deathtrap* or *The Sting*.

The tone was a house of cards. In our prior scripts, it was important to us that the audience be inside the lead character's head. That's how you create empathy. Yet here, we'd also have to maintain enough distance to fool them.

Once we finished the research, we organized the mountain of material and set about structuring the movie. We have a rule of thumb—don't try to cover the whole life. Pick the years that matter and treat it like a regular movie. Don't make the actor "age." And once you're in the script, don't play up time passing; just let the story happen. We settled on eight or nine relevant years, thereby throwing out the high school and college stories. The movie would pick up Andy right before his big break and follow him until his "death." For a couple of months we shuffled our index cards around, trying to figure out the three acts. But something was off. We didn't know what the movie was about. We didn't know who Andy was. Panic set in. The thousands of anecdotes weren't coalescing into a character, a guy whom we understood. Andy was just a cipher moving through a series of episodes—our greatest fear. We struggled, reading and rereading the notes, looking for our Rosebud, our key to Andy Kaufman. It was hopeless. Freaking, we talked to our agent, floating the concept of refunding Universal our salary. We'd just call it off. He mocked our weakness and told us to get our asses back to work.

In a funk, we rang up Lynne Margulies, Andy's girlfriend the last two years of his life. She was always a key friend to us, a sympathetic shrink. We told her the problem: No matter how much we studied the material, we couldn't figure out the real Andy.

Lynne responded simply, yet provocatively: "Guys, there *is* no real Andy."
And that was it. Lynne had given us the secret to the movie.

Suddenly we saw it. The script would be about a guy with shifting voices and personalities. He was like an onion—layers of masks and subterfuge. But when you peeled off the final layer, trying to get a look at the man inside, there was nothing there. It was anti-Rosebud, and conceptually perfect. Some people just can't be figured out.

Reinvigorated, we got back to work. Soon, a concrete three-act structure fell into place. Page ten—Andy signs with George. He works hard, and End of Act One, Andy becomes famous. Middle of Act Two, Andy discovers his mental instability is a selling tool. He exploits this, but pushes the envelope too far. End of Act Two, Andy's audience turns on him. His career implodes and his life goes into a tailspin. Act Three, Andy announces he has cancer. Nobody believes him, and like the boy who cried wolf, Andy's trickery comes back to bite him.

More simply, Andy creates comedy that plays as tragedy. Yet when he finally suffers tragedy, it is mistaken for comedy.

Despite the subject matter, this was a very traditional structure. Our biopics always follow this master plan. We enjoy telling underground stories with strange obsessions. The catch is, we also enjoy working in Hollywood. We like the studio system. So we get away with bizarro material by marrying it to Hollywood form. An executive might say, "What the hell is this? Some freaky guy running around in a dress, puttin' on plays??! Oh—page ten— he just met Bela Lugosi! Hey—page thirty! He just got a job!" We feel this creates a comfort level for the studios, as well as the audience.

However, we chose one daring gambit: The film would have no interest in chronological "facts." Andy's life was about altering truth, and it was thematically appropriate to tell the story that way. We'd be completely upfront. Also, this worked as a defensive move for us: On our previous biopics, we had killed ourselves trying to make the films factually accurate, piling in tons of true details. And our reward? Endless criticism from groupies we call "splitters," fans who are so hardcore, who know so much, that they can't possibly be pleased. The people whose approval we craved the most were the ones guaranteed to slam us because Criswell's wife was omitted, or Larry Flynt's court date was changed.

So on the opening page we had Andy state, point blank, that everything is mixed up. There! We're Teflon. Now you can't bust us. Our goal was to make the movie that Andy would have made, and so history was liquid.

Blatantly apocryphal anecdotes became "real stories," and events were reshuffled in ways we'd never have dared on other films. Carnegie Hall was our gutsiest move. The real concert was in 1979, early in Andy's stardom, but the show he was proudest of. We moved it to 1984, weeks before his death. Structurally, this gave us a schmaltzy, emotional climax. Now Andy was ill, and fighting to prove himself physically and artistically. When Andy reached the top, it would be as a weakened, Camille-like last hurrah.

We were delighted with this lie. We thought it worked great. Of course, wouldn't you know it, at the very first public showing of the film, in Danbury, Connecticut, a fan proclaimed he loved the movie, then immediately started complaining that Carnegie Hall was set in the wrong year.

In the screenplay the biggest challenge was balancing Andy's light and dark sides. From the interviews, it was clear that Andy led an idiosyncratic life. He was almost childlike. He didn't spend his money on lavish perks—instead, he lived simply, spending his days at amusement parks, playing pranks, meditating, and rewarding himself with ice cream and chocolate cake. He had an id-like joy, and we needed that in the script. This sweetness would offset his onstage belligerence and nastiness.

Additionally, we had to figure out how to integrate Andy's routines. There were dozens of famous choices, as well as berserk guerrilla street performances we had heard about. We owed the fans a fair number, although we didn't want to turn into a K-Tel Greatest Hits collection. Our approach was similar to *Ed Wood*—use the man's art to illustrate his state of mind, and make it a plot point whenever possible. And because we were unconcerned with chronology, we had total freedom. Thus, Mighty Mouse became Andy applying TM philosophy to comedy. *Great Gatsby* was Andy punishing his audience for loving *Taxi*. The *Fridays* fight was the turning point where Andy's sanity became his act. "Touch my cyst" was a man spiraling into Third Act depression—and a foreshadowing of his sickness. Plus, we worked in tons of Andy true-life weirdness: Fake boogers . . . fake accents . . . fake neck brace. . . .

Another decision was dealing with *Taxi*. Andy is beloved from that show, and in all honesty it's the source of his fame. Some folks expected a Latka movie from us. However, we had no particular affection for the show, and as we learned in interviews, neither did Andy. Plus, we had the dilemma of Danny's plans to portray George, when by any logical analysis he should clearly have portrayed Danny. Our solution was to rush through *Taxi* as fast as possible. Use it as a plot point, whip past the *Taxi* cast with a handful of lines, then move on. We omitted the real Danny, and our producers grabbed whoever else was available to play themselves. This un-*Taxi* approach is strange in the sense that it was Andy's "biggest" achievement, but again, it's how Andy would have wanted it. Andy saw *Taxi* only as a jumping-off point, and so did we.

Once we were writing heavily, we started becoming obsessed with lies and manipulation. They felt like the point of the movie, and we kept going back again and again to George's tapes of Andy, listening to Andy expound on audience reactions. Suddenly, we were hit by a creepy thought: These tapes were a little *too* convenient. *Why* had George recorded them? What if they were actually *new?* What if Andy had faked his death and hidden all these years, and he and George had made these tapes recently? It was unsettling . . . we could be the biggest suckers of them all. This was Andy's ploy to get the movie made! We brooded over this idea for a day, then shrugged it off.

While writing, we encountered a novel problem: We knew everybody. *Ed Wood* and *Larry Flynt* had been unauthorized bios, meaning we only got to know people after there was a script. But on this one, we had met practically every single character who wasn't Andy Kaufman. It made it tough, because we write satirically. It's in our nature to make characters look a little selfish, or unsavory, or dumb. But now we were friendly with them. We ate lunch together. Some of them were even our producers, which meant we were writing about our bosses. So perhaps we compromised our instincts a bit, because we felt bad hitting below the belt.

As we reached the end of the script, we sensed things coalescing thematically and dramatically. The third act was what the movie was about. With biopics, it's important that the story end with resolution. Real events need shaping, just like fiction. We knew about Andy's trip to the Philippines, and we'd heard that it ended sadly, with Andy returning broken, knowing he was doomed. This was the climax to our Boy Who Cried Wolf story. But what we added . . . was Andy's laugh. His laugh gave it joy and catharsis. He *appreciated* the scam, and the moment became a bittersweet punch line. Andy saw Fate zapping him with his own medicine, and he *got* the joke.

When we printed out the script, it was 210 pages. We spent a few weeks whittling it down to showable length, then pulled out one last trick: We typed *Man on the Moon* on the cover page, without warning anybody this was the title. We didn't have permission, but it seemed perfect. *Man on the Moon* was an R.E.M. song from 1992, a tribute tune to Andy. It was beautiful and sad, and had intrinsic goodwill. We felt these qualities would help the project, so

we gambled that some lawyer would finagle it for us. Of course, Milos had the last laugh. He liked the title, but had no idea that there was a song. When it was played for him, he was so impressed that he simply called up R.E.M. and asked them to score the entire film.

Before our script was turned in, we had no clue what to make of it. The first draft had taken a year, and we'd lost all perspective. Wanting an outside opinion, we gave a 154-page version to our agent, Tom Strickler, with the caveat that "it might be really good, or maybe worthless. We're not sure. Let us know." He quickly read it, said it was great, then told us to turn it in and get back to work. The Jersey gang—Danny, Stacey Sher, and Michael Shamberg—loved it. Danny enthusiastically promised the movie would get made. Universal was happy. But Milos was tougher: He was pleased, but thought it ferociously overstayed its welcome. The movie shouldn't run over two hours. And the second act was much too convoluted, with too many manipulated moments. He wanted many of the middle set pieces reordered, and he preferred connected events to be combined into long continuous scenes. So, while pre-production commenced, we set about simplifying and stripping down the movie, a game of tug-of-war that continued until shooting.

At this point, the *Man on the Moon* circus began. From casting through the end of production, the process itself became Kaufmanesque, every step heightened and surreal. Word got out that the part of Andy was up for grabs, and the gold rush began. Milos has a history of casting whoever is best for the part, regardless of their relative stardom. So he said he'd consider anybody, as long as they submitted a videotape. He needed to see if they could "do" Andy's comedy act. A list of sterling actors applied: Jim Carrey, Edward Norton, Kevin Spacey, Hank Azaria, John Cusack. A number of unknowns auditioned, most startlingly an uncanny lookalike named Craig Anton.

Then, dark horse Gary Oldman surfaced, calling from London. He started pestering Danny, Milos, and Francine Maisler, our casting director. He insisted he was the best choice for the part—an odd claim for a brooding non-comic with a British accent. Out of respect, Francine sent him the script, only to have Gary call back a week later, livid that his American agents were idiots. He had never received it. So he had her resend it, directly to his home in London. Eventually, his audition tape showed up, a shadowy, hard-to-see thirty minutes of cockney babbling. He seemed to be in makeup, although he didn't look like Andy *or* Gary. Everybody watching the tape was bewildered. Was Gary Oldman this clueless? Was this even Gary Oldman? Finally, at the end the lights brightened, and "Gary" was revealed as an imposter. He was a struggling London actor, and this was his way of getting in. The real Gary Oldman didn't know anything about our project.

At the end of the day, Jim Carrey was the unanimous choice. His audition was terrific, and we knew he had the comedy chops for the performance scenes. Plus, he seemed destined for the part: He was incredibly passionate about the movie, he and Andy shared the same birthday, and most incredibly, years before his fame, he had gone up to George at an Andy tribute and boldly announced that one day he would play Andy Kaufman.

At this point, the team was presented with a casting dilemma: replicating well-known personalities. Milos loves re-creating reality, and so the production defaulted, when possible, to people playing themselves: David Letterman, the *Taxi* cast, Jerry Lawler, Budd Friedman, Andy's buddy Little Wendy, and Lorne Michaels. Then, Francine started rounding up actors (or nonactors) who had a connection to the world of the movie: Peter Bonerz, Norm MacDonald, Richard Belzer. . . . Finally, since Danny was a real-life character playing somebody *different,* why couldn't more folks do that? So George Shapiro played a club owner, his partner Howard West became a network executive, and Bob Zmuda morphed into Jack Burns. Danny's real-life assistant, Pam, became, his on-camera assistant. Even Andy's actual granddaughter played Andy's baby sister, Carol. The ultimate test was when Milos considered having Andy's brother, Michael, play their father, Stanley. It was intriguing, but probably would have created too many levels of psychodrama, so the idea was discarded.

The shoot itself was legendary. Primarily at Jim's prodding, *Man on the Moon* became life imitating art, with the production itself Kaufman-like. Jim was getting "into character," but what he really was doing was re-creating Andy's performance art. The set itself became tension-filled and unbalanced, as crew members struggled to figure out what was real and what was put on. It was one of the all-time great Hollywood experiences—and we missed it entirely. We were in Vancouver directing our first film, *Foolproof.* So we sadly report only a few production stories, as it all came to us third hand.

First of all, Jim appeared to lose his mind. He became possessed and could never be addressed as "Jim." Depending upon the scene being shot, he was either "Andy" or "Tony." The men had different cars and different dressing rooms. Andy was a spirited, happy goof. Tony was abusive and rude to the crew. One day Tony worked in the morning, and Andy in the afternoon. They passed at the studio gate, got in a fight, and Andy arrived on-set with a bloody nose. Paramedics had to be called.

Andy was quite childish, running around clutching Howdy Doody. The first day of shooting, he pulled up in an ice cream truck. He made the crew sing, then rewarded them with ice cream.

Tony was ruder. He often showed up drunk, in his red convertible. He didn't enjoy being stared at, so off-camera he wore a bag on his head. Unfortunately, he also drove this way, and he crashed his car into a sound-stage.

When the Universal executives visited, Tony locked himself in his trailer, refusing to see them. When they came back another day, he coated his body with Limburger cheese. After shaking hands with him, they stunk for hours. Tony also enraged the *Taxi* cast, arriving drunk with hookers, just like the real event twenty years earlier. When they escaped into their makeup trailer, he piped in the Chipmunks' "Christmas Time Is Here" on an endless loop.

During lunch breaks, Andy and Tony caused chaos on the Universal lot. Andy would dress as Mrs. Bates and hide behind the *Psycho* house. When trams drove by, he chased after them with an axe. Meanwhile, Tony broke into the Amblin compound, demanding to see Spielberg's shark.

Tony took a strong dislike to poor Danny DeVito. He tortured him daily, filling his trailer with crickets and smelly salami. One day Tony actually backed his car against Danny's dressing room door, trapping him inside. Tony then ran off and threw the keys in the trash. Danny was stuck for hours, until a tow truck hauled away Tony's convertible.

The Mama Rivoli's shoot (at Chasen's) was particularly strange. Tony amused himself spray-painting "Tony's Joint. Dames dine free, Hells Angels welcome" on the walls. Suddenly, motorcycles roared, and the real Hells Angels pulled up. Things became hopeless. Milos was told not to address Tony directly—he had to speak through the head Angel.

The grand upset was while shooting the Andy–Jerry Lawler brawl. Jim and the real Lawler "got in a fight," Jim spat at him, and Lawler threw Jim on his neck. Panic broke out. Extras were rushed away, the shoot shut down, and Jim was rushed to the hospital. The studio issued some quick "no comments." The event was astonishing—while re-creating Lawler breaking Andy's neck, Lawler had broken Jim's neck. It made the top of the news. Many shows reported Jim as possibly paralyzed. We never got the details.

Rumor was Lawler wouldn't finish the film. But then, months later, he was convinced to return for the Letterman shoot. Unfortunately, Andy staked out the fifth-floor window of the Ed Sullivan Theater. When Lawler walked into the building, Andy pelted him with eggs.

Once the movie wrapped, it was in post-production for almost a year. Milos had shot enough film for a four-hour opus, but he wanted it to be half that. Deciding what to keep was again reliving the old battle between sweet Andy and evil Andy. When he became unlikable, the film became unlikable, and so the question was, how much can an audience take? There was also the blend between Andy onstage and offstage. Milos gravitated toward the performance material, but the film's emotion was in the personal scenes.

The most interesting editorial argument was over the closing shot. In our script, Andy's sickness was played as not one-hundred-percent clear. The funeral felt open-ended. Then we threw in an Agatha Christie twisteroo ending: One year after Andy's death, Tony gives a concert. He sings "I Will Survive," the camera pans the audience . . . and Bob Zmuda applauds from the back. Fade out. The end. It was a cool, Kaufmanesque conclusion. We made up the Zmuda part, but it was absolutely ending things the way Andy would have. It made the reader go, "Huh? Who's that onstage? Andy??"

Readers of the script loved this ending. It was sophisticated and postmodern. However . . . it left our first test audience cold. After taking the journey, they wanted closure. So Milos experimented—and cut off the final shot. Through the wonders of editing, the ending now played as Bob Zmuda (or so we thought) giving his friend a tribute. This approach traded cleverness for emotion. Yet at the next test, the audience was *still* confused. But this was murky, unsatisfied confusion. And we all missed our joybuzzer, Andy-style ending. So the original version went back.

However, even if it changes *again,* you've got it in your hands! Because this published version is closest to our original draft. We feel that if you've purchased this book, you must be a big fan of Andy, or his comedy, or screenplays. If you simply wanted the film, you'd buy the video. So this version is absurdly encompassing, with micro-detailed tellings of Andy's life. This information would sadly never fit in a two-hour film, but we killed ourselves researching it, so we might as well publish it somewhere. In the scene notes, we explain how the film changed from original script to shooting script to dailies to final cut. Plus, there's even *more* extra scenes and goodies. Enjoy!

<u>MAN ON THE MOON</u>

Screenplay by
Scott Alexander and Larry Karaszewski

Jim Carrey and Courtney Love

FADE IN:

1   INT. VOID - DAY   1

    Sitting in a nonexistent set is ANDY KAUFMAN, looking a bit
    nervous. Wide-eyed, tentative, he stares at us with a needy,
    unsettling cuteness. His hair is slicked-down, and he wears
    his father's loud blazer.

    Finally, Andy speaks -- in a peculiar FOREIGN ACCENT.

                   ANDY (AS FOREIGN MAN)
         Hallo. I am Andy. Welcoom to my
         movie.
                (beat; he gets upset)
         It was very good of you to come...
         but now you should leave. Because
         this movie ees <u>terrible</u>! It is all
         LIES! Tings are out of order...
         people are mixed-up... what a MESS!
                (he composes himself)
         So, I broke into Universal and cut
         out all de baloney. Now, it's much
         shorter.
                (beat)
         In fact -- this is the end of the
         movie. So tanks for comink! Bye-bye!

    Andy drops the needle on a phonograph. Swelling CLOSING CREDITS
    MUSIC begins to play. FINAL CREDITS roll onscreen.

    Andy stands frozen, looking awkwardly at the audience. Every
    time the music ends, he picks up the needle, then restarts the
    music.

    Finally, CREDITS END. Beat -- and then a sly smile. Andy leans
    in, DROPS HIS ACCENT, and WHISPERS.

                   ANDY (IN REGULAR VOICE)
         Okay, good. Just my friends are left.
         I wanted to get rid of those other
         people... they would've laughed in
         the wrong places.
                (beat)
         I was only kidding about the movie...
         it's actually PRETTY GOOD! It shows
         everything... from me as a little boy
         until my death --
                (his eyes pop; he covers his mouth)
         Oops!! I wasn't supposed to talk
         about that! Oh. Eh, uh, we better
         just begin. It starts back in Great
         Neck, Long Island...

    Andy picks up a little <u>toy Super 8 movie viewer</u>. He peeks in,
    holds it to the light and hits a button. WHIR! Andy smiles.

                              ANDY
                Oh, yes. I remember it well...

                                            CUT TO:

2   EXT. KAUFMAN HOME - 1957 - DAY   2

    Great Neck, 1957. An upper-class Jewish neighborhood with large
    homes. In the street, a group of crewcut BOYS plays t-ball,
    laughing and shouting.

    A fat convertible drives up, pulling in front of the smallest
    house. STANLEY KAUFMAN, 40, gets out, still in his suit. He's
    a well-meaning slave to his job -- tired, responsible.

    Stanley goes over to admire the t-ball game. At bat is his son
    MICHAEL, 6, a natural charmer. Michael swings -- CRACK! -- and
    hits a solid single. Stanley smiles.

                              STANLEY
                That's my boy! Good swingin', kiddo.
                     (warm beat; then, a look)
                Hey -- Michael... where's your
                brother?

                              MICHAEL
                He's inside.

    Instantly -- Stanley's mood turns black. He frowns angrily,
    then snatches his briefcase and marches in.

3   INT. KAUFMAN HOUSE - SAME TIME   3

    Baby CAROL is crying. Mom JANICE, 35, quickly peels carrots,
    trying to get dinner made. Stanley marches past.

                              STANLEY
                Is he in his room?

                              JANICE
                Of course he's in his room.
                     (aggravated)
                All his "friends" are in there.

    Stanley glowers. He huffs upstairs.

4   OUTSIDE ANDY'S ROOM   4

    Stanley hurries up to Andy's shut door. We hear little Andy
    doing VOICES.

                              ANDY (o.s.)
                     (as WORRIED GIRL)
                But Professor, why are the monsters
                growing so big?
                     (now as BRITISH PROFESSOR)
                It's something in the jungle water.
                I need to crack the secret code.

Stanley rolls his eyes. He opens the door... revealing ANDY,
8, performing for the <u>wall</u>. Andy is happy and enthusiastic...
as long as he's acting.

                    ANDY
               (as BRITISH PROFESSOR)
          Maybe I should talk to the natives.
               (as dancing NATIVES)
          Shoom boom boo ba! Shoom boom boo
          ba --

                    STANLEY
          Andy!

                    ANDY
               (startled)
          Oh!
               (as ANNOUNCER)
          Um... we're experiencing technical
          difficulties. We'll return to the
          Million Dollar Movie after these
          messages.

Frustrated, Stanley stares at his son. Turned off, the boy now
seems introverted... and awkward.

                    STANLEY
          Andy, this has to stop. Our house
          isn't a television station. There
          is <u>not</u> a camera in that wall.

Andy glances over at the wall. Hmm.

                    STANLEY
               (trying to cope)
          Son... listen to me. It isn't
          healthy. You should be outside,
          playing sports.

                    ANDY
          But I've <u>got</u> a sports show.
          Championship wrestling, at five.

                    STANLEY
               (he blows his top)
          You <u>know</u> that's not what I meant!
          Look, I'm gonna put my foot down! <u>No</u>
          <u>more playing alone</u>. You wanna
          perform, you GOTTA have an audience!

                    ANDY
               (he points at the wall)
          B-but I have <u>them</u>.

                    STANLEY
          No! That is NOT an audience! That
          is PLASTER! An audience is people
          made of flesh! They live and breathe!
          And I won't have a son of mine playing
          under... er... any other conditions!

Frazzled, Stanley turns and storms out. The door SLAMS.

ANGLE - ANDY

Well! He looks sadly at his wall, then considers his options.
What to do...?

                                                    CUT TO:

5   INT. FAMILY ROOM - DAY   5

Baby Carol sits in her crib, sucking a pacifier. Andy's hands
suddenly YANK her out.

6   INT. ANDY'S ROOM - DAY   6

Andy hurries in and plops Carol down on the floor. She
dutifully sits there, deadpan, unable to crawl.

Andy returns to the center of the room. He resumes his show.

                          ANDY
                    (as KIDDIE SHOW HOST)
               And now, boys and girls! It's time
               for... TV Fun House!
                    (he makes an APPLAUSE SOUND)
               Hi, everybody! Are you ready for a
               singalong? I'll say the animal, and
               you make his sound! Okay? Okay!
                    (he starts to SING)
               "Oh, the cow goes......"

Carol stares, unblinking. Then --

                          CAROL
               Moo.

                          ANDY
                    (he smiles, pleased)
               "And the dog goes......"

                          CAROL
               WOOF!

                          ANDY
               "And the cat says......"

                                                    DISSOLVE TO:

7   CLOSEUP - ANDY   7

now GROWN UP. 26-years-old, still performing the song.

                          DRUNK AUDIENCE
               MEOW!!

WIDE

It's 1975. A small, hip New York nightclub.

                          ANDY
         "And the bird says..."

                    DRUNK AUDIENCE
         TWEET!!

                          ANDY
         "And the lion goes..."

                    DRUNK AUDIENCE
         ROAR!!

                          ANDY
         "And that's the way it goes!"
                  (he grins)
         Thank you. Goodbye, boys and girls!

Andy takes a bow. There's faint scattered applause.

Andy sighs. A burly TUXEDOED MANAGER steps onstage. He shoots
Andy a disgruntled look, then takes the mike.

                          MANAGER
         The comedy stylings of Andy Kaufman,
         ladies and gentlemen!

In the b.g., Andy starts packing up. Hand puppets, conga drums,
a phonograph, all his junk goes into the big bulky case from his
childhood.

                                        CUT TO:

8   NIGHTCLUB - LATER   8

The club is empty. At the bar, the Manager cleans up. Andy
eagerly comes over. Offstage, his presence is soft, placid --
his voice barely above a whisper.

                          ANDY
         So, Mr. Besserman, same slot
         tomorrow...?

                          MANAGER
                  (awkward)
         Eh, I dunno... Andy. I'm... thinkin'
         of letting you go...

                          ANDY
         You're firing me??
                  (beat)
         You don't even pay me!

                          MANAGER
         Look -- I don't wanna seem insulting.
         But... your act is like amateur hour:
         Singalongs... puppets... playing
         records...

A stunned beat. Andy is hurt.

>   ANDY
>   What do you want? "Take my wife,
>   please"??

>   MANAGER
>   Sure! <u>Comedy</u>! Make jokes about the
>   traffic. Do impressions. Maybe a
>   little blue material...

>   ANDY
>   <u>I don't swear</u>. I -- I don't do what
>   everyone else does!

>   MANAGER
>   Well, everyone else gets this place
>   <u>cookin'</u>! Pal, it's hard for me to
>   move booze when you're singin' "Pop
>   Goes The Weasel."

Andy stares, disheartened.

>   MANAGER
>   I'm sorry. You're finished here.

An uncomfortable beat -- and then Andy starts <u>crying</u>.

The Manager is dumbfounded. He doesn't know what to do.

Tears are rolling down Andy's cheeks. He's pitiful.

The Manager is confused -- totally disoriented.

Shamed, Andy covers his face, then runs out. Silence. The
Manager stares after him... having no idea what just happened.

>   CUT TO:

9   EXT. NIGHTCLUB - SAME TIME   9

Sobbing Andy bursts out the door. He steps onto the sidewalk --
and IMMEDIATELY STOPS CRYING. Just like that.

Andy lifts his big case and starts walking. Andy shakes his
head angrily.

He turns down a dark street -- and TWO MEN start following him.
Andy glances back and moves faster. He's alone in Hell's
Kitchen, a frightening neighborhood late at night. The men walk
faster. Andy wants to speed up, but is slowed by the case.

Their shadows close in. Andy is trapped. Resigned, he puts
down the case and slowly turns. The two thugs glare menacingly.

>   THUG #1
>   Give us your wallet.

The guy flashes a KNIFE.

Andy stares fearfully. An anxious moment. He thinks...
considering his options.

Then, he suddenly stammers in a thick FOREIGN ACCENT.

> ANDY (AS FOREIGN MAN)
> I -- doo not unterstand!!

> THUG #1
> Give us your money!

> ANDY (AS FOREIGN MAN)
> What?? What mooney? Abu daboo! I
> do not have mooney!

The thugs glance at each other.

> ANDY (AS FOREIGN MAN)
> Pleaze! I just move to America
> yezterday! I do not know!!

> THUG #1
> What's in the case?

> ANDY (AS FOREIGN MAN)
> NO! Eeet, eet is just perzonal
> trifles from my homeland --

> THUG #2
> Shut up! Gimme that thing!

The guy snatches the case. He impulsively BREAKS the lock.

The suitcase opens -- and clothes, congas and records fall out.

The thugs are dismayed.

> THUG #1
> Goddamn immigrants!

> THUG #2
> This guy's pathetic. Let's go.

Harsh glances. They angrily pocket the knife and leave.

Andy takes a nervous breath, then starts picking his things off
the street. He shouts after the guys:

> ANDY (AS FOREIGN MAN)
> Tank you veddy much...!

> CUT TO:

10 EXT. NEW YORK IMPROV - NIGHT   10

The Improv, the biggest comedy club around. People are lined
up, buying tickets.

A man walks up -- GEORGE SHAPIRO, 40s, a Hollywood talent
manager. George is old school: Bronx accent, shmooze and a
hug... but with a surprising sweetness that is quite disarming.

George gets in line. Inside, owner BUDD FRIEDMAN sees him and comes out.

> BUDD
> George! For Christ's sake, you don't
> have to wait in line.

Budd smiles and pulls George in.

11   INT. IMPROV - SAME TIME   11

The bar is packed with COMICS and SHOW BIZ TYPES. A few turn and wave -- "George!" "George!" George greets an OLDER MAN.

> GEORGE
> Hey, congrats. I heard your show got
> renewed.

> OLDER MAN
> Yeah, thank God. How 'bout Van Dyke
> as a guest star?

> GEORGE
> Sure. Pay his quote.

George smiles and drifts away. He turns and goes into the

SHOWROOM

Where the show's in progress. A WAITRESS sees George, runs over, and hugs him. She gives him a front row table.

George sits -- then gives the stage his undivided attention. Up there is a WISEASS COMIC.

> WISEASS COMIC
> So I'm getting my mother-in-law a
> special Christmas present: A pre-paid
> funeral! The mortician asked me if
> I wanted her buried, embalmed or
> cremated. I said, "Make it all three!
> I'm not takin' any chances!"
> > (the crowd LAUGHS)
> Thank you. Good night!

The comic waves and exits. APPLAUSE. George politely claps. A PIANO PLAYER jumps in with an unbeat show tune.

We think there's a break... when Andy suddenly, awkwardly steps on stage. He is in character as Foreign Man. Pink jacket, tie, hair slicked back, frightened like a deer in headlights. He puts down his big case, pulls out various junk, and arranges it on chairs.

The room hushes, uncertain as to who the hell this guy is. Andy tentatively grabs the mike. The stagefright is agony.

                    ANDY (AS FOREIGN MAN)
Now? Now...?
          (looking around)
Tank you veddy much. I am very happy
to be here. I tink -- this is a very
beautiful place. But one ting I do
not like is too much traffic. Tonight
I had to come from, eh, and the
freeway, it was so much traffic. It
took me an hour and a half to get
here!

Andy chuckles, as if this were a punchline.

Silence. The crowd is baffled.

                    ANDY (AS FOREIGN MAN)
But -- talking about the terrible
things: My wife. Take my wife, please
take her.

Yikes. A few NERVOUS LAUGHS.

Andy gestures, as if they got the joke.

                    ANDY (AS FOREIGN MAN)
No really, I am only foolink. I love
my wife very much. But she don't know
how to cook. You know, one time, she
make steak and mashed potato. Ehh,
and the night before, she make
spaghetti and meatballs. Her cooking
is so bad... is terrible.

People are embarrassed. Some avert their eyes. A couple
hipsters laugh mockingly.

George leans forward. Andy wipes sweat from his brow.

                    ANDY (AS FOREIGN MAN)
Right now, I would like to do for you
some imitations. So first, I would
like to imitate Archie Bunker.
          (no change in his voice)
"You stupid, everybody ees stupid!
Ehh, get, get out of my chair
Meathead... go in the, eh, Dingbat
get into the kitchen, making the food!
Ehh, everybody ees stupid! I don't
like nobody, ees so stupid!"
          (pleased, he proudly bows)
Now I would like to imitate Jimmy
Carter, the President of the United
States.
          (no change in his voice)
"Hello, I am Jimmy Carter, the
President of the United States."

Some people BOO and walk out. A few giggle, getting in the
groove.

George is intrigued.

>   ANDY (AS FOREIGN MAN)
>   And finally... I would like to imitate
>   the Elvis Presley.

A woman LAUGHS caustically. Andy grins stupidly, then turns
his back to us. He presses "Play" on a CASSETTE RECORDER...
and the THEME FROM 2001 starts playing.

House lights dim dramatically. With a flourish, Andy pulls tape
off his pants -- revealing rhinestones. He removes his pink
coat -- putting on a white jeweled jacket.

He combs his hair.

Then he brushes his hair.

Then he combs his hair some _more_.

Finally he picks up a guitar, strikes a pose -- and spins
around.

He is ELVIS. CONFIDENT. SEXY. LIP CURL. DEAD-ON PERFECT.

The crowd is blown away.

Vegas Elvis INTRO MUSIC suddenly blasts. Andy/Elvis swaggers
stage left and takes a bow. Then he goes stage right and takes
a bow. Then he _returns_ stage left for another bow.

Music STOPS.

>   ANDY (AS ELVIS)
>   Thank you very much.

Wow. Flabbergasted, people APPLAUD. This man _is_ Elvis.

Suddenly -- "BLUE SUEDE SHOES" guitar kicks in.

>   ANDY (AS ELVIS)
>   (SINGING)
>   "Well, it's one for the money!
>   Two for the show!
>   Three to get ready,
>   Now GO CATS GO!"

ANGLE - GEORGE

He is astonished. George cannot quite figure out what's going
on... but he wants in.

He waves Budd over. Budd leans down, and George WHISPERS.

>   GEORGE
>   Pst. What's the story with this guy?

>   BUDD
>   I think he's Lithuanian. None of us
>   can understand him.

George nods admiringly.

> GEORGE
> He does a hell of an Elvis.

                                        CUT TO:

12   BACKSTAGE - LATER   12

Andy is packing up his things. He very methodically folds each
item of clothing, then checks the creases.

George strolls up.

> GEORGE
> Hey, I really enjoyed your set.

> ANDY (AS FOREIGN MAN)
> Tank you veddy much.

> GEORGE
> So I understand you're from Lithuania?

> ANDY (AS FOREIGN MAN)
> No. Caspiar.

George is puzzled.

> GEORGE
> Caspiar? I haven't heard of that.

> ANDY (AS FOREIGN MAN)
> It's a veddy small island in de
> Caspian Sea.
>   (beat)
> It sunk.

> GEORGE
> Oh. Hm. I'm uh, sorry.
>   (beat)
> Well look, I just wanted to say I
> think you're very interesting. If
> you ever need representation, give
> me a call.

George hands him a BUSINESS CARD.

Andy reads it -- then his eyes pop. He <u>DROPS the accent</u>.

> ANDY
> Mr. Shapiro, <u>it's an honor</u>!!

George realizes it's all been an act. He laughs heartily.

> GEORGE
> Caspiar, huh?!

                                        CUT TO:

13   INT. SOHO HEALTH FOOD RESTAURANT - NIGHT   13

Andy and George sit in a bohemian health food restaurant.
Hippie waitresses in sandals mill around.

Andy and George are trying to get a sense of each other.

                    ANDY
          You see, I want to be the biggest star
          in the world.

George is surprised at this hubris.

                    GEORGE
          People love... comedians.

                    ANDY
          I'm not a comedian. I have no talent.
                    (he shrugs)
          I'm just a song-and-dance man.

George looks up at Andy -- and inexplicably there is a giant
MOIST BOOGER hanging from Andy's nostril.

George cringes. He doesn't know what to say.

A waitress brings over two plates of awful 70's HEALTH FOOD --
beans, sprouts, seaweed. George frowns. Andy beams.

                    ANDY
          Mmm! I particularly recommend the
          Lotus root.

Andy pulls out a little Handi-wipe and cleanses his hands. Then
he starts arranging the food in compulsive little piles: Beans
in pinwheel shapes. Sprouts in piles.

George peers at the bizarre food behavior.

                    GEORGE
          You show a lot of promise... but...
          my concern is I don't know where to
          book you. You're not a stand-up.
          Your act doesn't exactly translate
          to films. It's not a series...

                    ANDY
                    (bright)
          I've always wanted to play Carnegie
          Hall.

                    GEORGE
          Yeah, ha-ha. That's funny.

Andy dips his silverware in the water glass. Two dunks, then
he dries it with his napkin.

George stares, perplexed. He looks back up -- and Andy's booger
has suddenly switched nostrils.

Huh?

> ANDY
> See, I don't want easy laughs or
> polite applause! Any bozo can get
> those!

Andy's about to eat -- but first bows his head in silent prayer.

George raises an eyebrow.

Andy snaps his head back up.

> ANDY
> I want gut reactions! I want that
> audience to go through an experience.
> They love me! They hate me! They
> walk out -- it's all GREAT!

Andy triumphantly sticks a bean in his mouth. George smiles.

> GEORGE
> You're insane.
> (beat)
> But -- you also might be brilliant.
> (sincere)
> Alright, Andy... let's do it.

George warmly extends his hand.

Andy slowly smiles, then takes George's hand. The men shake.
A moment of supreme importance.

> CUT TO:

14   EST. BEVERLY HILLS - DAY   14

The glitz strip of Los Angeles. Money. Beauty.

15   INT. SHAPIRO/WEST - DAY   15

Real working showbiz offices. No glamour at all. It looks more
like an insurance company.

George sits in his office with a YOUNG COMIC. The guy is upset.

> YOUNG COMIC
> George, I don't wanna open for David
> Brenner!

> GEORGE
> Sammy, it's a good gig. You'll be
> on the road... get some exposure...

O.s., a SECRETARY shouts out.

> SECRETARY (o.s.)
> Tony Clifton on the phone!

                        GEORGE
          Who?

                        SECRETARY (o.s.)
          He says he's an associate of Andy
          Kaufman's.

                        GEORGE
          Oh.
                    (to his guest)
          Excuse me one sec'.
                    (he picks up the phone)
          Hello? George Shapiro here.

On the phone, a STACCATO, ABRASIVE NASAL VOICE blares.

                        TONY CLIFTON (v.o.)
          Uh, yeah. Is this GEORGE SHAPIRO?

                        GEORGE
                    (beat)
          Er, yes. Speaking.

                        TONY CLIFTON (v.o.)
          "Speaking"! Reeking, seeking,
          creaking. ...Freaking!

George is baffled.

                        GEORGE
          Can I help you with something?

                        TONY CLIFTON (v.o.)
          Yeah! You stay away from that Andy
          Kaufman, if you know what's good for
          you!

                        GEORGE
                    (stunned)
          Who is this?

                        TONY CLIFTON (v.o.)
          You -- you know damn straight who it
          is. Tony Clifton! A name to respect.
          A name to fear.
                    (beat)
          Beer. Gear. Deer. Ear.

                        GEORGE
                    (unsure what to say)
          Look... I don't know what your problem
          is. But Andy shows a lot of promise,
          and I want to work with him.

                        TONY CLIFTON (v.o.)
          Kaufman's a lying bastard! If you
          sign him, I'll RUIN YOU!

CLICK. Clifton hangs up.

George is bewildered.

                                              CUT TO:

16   EXT. MEDITATION INSTITUTE UNIVERSITY - DAY   16

      MIU -- the national headquarters for Transcendental Meditation.
      A quiet, simple retreat in rural Iowa.

17   INT. MIU CLASSROOM - DAY   17

      Fifteen barefoot STUDENTS sit on mats in a circle. Eyes shut,
      bodies in different yoga positions, they are all meditating.
      Andy is one of the students. The teacher is LITTLE WENDY, a
      teeny lady with an absurdly high-pitched voice.

                    LITTLE WENDY
            Alright. Now while continuing your
            deep breathing, slowly open your eyes.
            You should feel rested, relaxed, and
            alert.

      The students all open their eyes. Wendy smiles.

                    LITTLE WENDY
            Do any thoughts come...?

                    STUDENT #1
            My mind is clear. I feel great.

                    STUDENT #2
            All the tension is gone from my body.

                    ANDY
            Yeah. I've been so stressed since
            this show I did last Tuesday. I was
            playing a country-western bar, and
            the audience just didn't get my vibe.
            But now my manager's lined-up a TV
            gig for me -- it's some late night
            loser show, but I'm still excited.

      Oh. Everyone politely shrugs.

      A MAN IN A TURBAN silently enters. He discreetly WHISPERS in
      Andy's ear -- and Andy is startled.

                    ANDY
            Really?!

18   INT. HALLWAY - DAY   18

      Andy nervously walks down a long dim hall. Finally, he gets
      to a door -- "HIS HOLINESS, MAHARISHI MAHESH YOGI."

      Andy gulps.

19   INT. MAHARISHI'S OFFICE - DAY   19

      His Holiness the MAHARISHI sits in his spartan, humble office.

Maharishi smiles beatifically at Andy. He speaks in a melodic
Indian accent.

                    MAHARISHI
          I'm told that in your visits here,
          you've shown great progress and
          discipline. Is that true..?

                    ANDY
               (confessional)
          Yes. When I... started seven years
          ago, I was aimless. I was fighting
          with my family.

                    MAHARISHI
          Families are important.

                    ANDY
          Uh-huh. But TM got me <u>focused</u>. I
          stopped drinking. I gave up drugs.

                    MAHARISHI
               (he smiles)
          Transcendental Meditation opened your
          awareness to the reservoir of energy
          and creativity.

                    ANDY
          Now I meditate three hours a day.
          It's the center of my life...

                    MAHARISHI
          We're all impressed. And because of
          this dedication, we wish to make you
          a Governor of the program.

Andy is awed.

                    ANDY
          Wow. Thanks, Your Holiness!

                    MAHARISHI
          Do you have any questions?

                    ANDY
          No. Thank you.
               (he starts to rise; then)
          Oh -- wait. Yes!
               (beat; he works up his nerve)
          Is there... is there a secret to being
          funny?

TIGHT - MAHARISHI

Huh? He thinks hard... squinching up his face... then finally
nods and speaks.

                         MAHARISHI
           Yes. Silence.

                                              CUT TO:

20   INT. SATURDAY NIGHT LIVE - NIGHT   20

     It's the first "Saturday Night Live." Backstage, CAST MEMBERS
     in Killer Bees outfits goof off and push each other.

     On stage is Andy, alone. The THEME FROM "MIGHTY MOUSE" plays
     -- but Andy just blankly stands there. He's purposefully doing
     nothing.

                    MIGHTY MOUSE THEME (v.o.)
           "Although we are in danger,
           we never despair,
           Because we know where there is danger
           he is there!"

     IN THE BOOTH

     The SNL PRODUCER is panicked.

                         SNL PRODUCER
           Oh my God, he's doing nothing.
           It's dead air...!

     BACK ON ANDY

                    MIGHTY MOUSE THEME (v.o.)
           "We're not worrying at all.
           We're just listening for his call..."

     Then SUDDENLY -- Andy comes to life and triumphantly LIP SYNCS.

                    MIGHTY MOUSE (v.o.)
           "Here I come to save the day!"

     Shocked, the crowd HOWLS with LAUGHTER.

     Then instantly -- Andy resumes his blank expression.

                    MIGHTY MOUSE SINGERS
           "That means that Mighty Mouse is on the way!"

     The audience SCREAMS with glee. The tune ENDS, and the audience
     APPLAUDS CRAZILY.

     Delighted, Andy grins and bows.

                                              CUT TO:

21   EXT. CONEY ISLAND - DAY   21

     A crisp, sunny day. Cars plummet down the Cyclone's big hill.
     Andy and his family whip through the rollercoaster -- arms up,
     SCREAMING.

ANDY AND THE KAUFMANS
          Aaaaaahhhhh!!!

Andy is filled with terror and euphoria. Everyone seems too
old for this. The siblings are in their 20s. The parents,
their late 50s.

The cars race to the end and suddenly BRAKE. The passengers
slowly climb out. Exhilarated, Andy beams at his family.

                    ANDY
          Let's do it again!

                    STANLEY
          No, enough is enough. We've been on
          it three times.

                    CAROL
          If I go again, I'll puke.

                    ANDY
          But it's Mom's birthday. We gotta
          have <u>fun</u>!

                    MICHAEL
               (to his mother)
          <u>I</u> thought we should take you to a
          Broadway show.

Andy is a bit insulted.

                    ANDY
          Hey! She can still see a show..!

                                        CUT TO:

A garish SIGN. It says "FREAK SHOW."

22   INT. FREAK SHOW TENT - DAY   22

Strangeness everywhere. Andy exuberantly pulls his queasy
family through the exhibits.

                    ANDY
          Isn't this great...?
               (he sees a BANNER)
          Whoa! They've added a <u>lizard lady</u>!
          I wonder if she has a <u>tail and eats
          bugs</u>?!

Grinning, Andy excitedly runs around the corner...

And finds the LIZARD LADY. Sitting tiredly on a stool. She's
just an old woman with bad skin and scabs on her face.

Yow. Andy is caught off-guard. There is <u>nothing</u> fun about
this. She slowly looks up... and peers sadly at Andy.

The two of them stare uncomfortably at each other. Until --

                    LIZARD LADY
          Hey, weren't you on TV the other
          night?

ON THE FAMILY

They're waiting. Suddenly, Andy staggers up. He tightens his
face, holds his stomach... and VOMITS. He spits a hunk of yuck
onto the ground.

BYSTANDERS are appalled. People grimace and hurry away.

But the family's unimpressed. They stare at the vomit, bored.

                    JANICE
          That's cute. Now put it back in your
          pocket, so we can go home.

Andy frowns -- eyeballs her -- then <u>picks up</u> the vomit. It's
rubber.

                                        CUT TO:

23   INT. GEORGE'S OFFICE - DAY   23

George jumps up from his desk. Andy is walking in.

                    GEORGE
          Andy, c'mon IN! Thanks for flyin'
          out here!!

                    ANDY
          The stewardess let me keep my
          headphones.

                    GEORGE
          That's -- terrific. But I got
          something <u>better</u>. Something BIG...!
               (giddy; milking the moment)
          You are getting a once-in-a-lifetime,
          unbelievably lucrative, unheard of
          opportunity to star in a PRIMETIME
          NETWORK SITCOM!!!!

Andy freezes up.

                    ANDY
          <u>Sitcom</u>...?

                    GEORGE
          And this is a CLASS ACT! It's the
          guys who did the Mary Tyler Moore and
          Bob Newhart shows! It takes place
          in a taxi stand! And you're gonna
          be the Fonzie!

                    ANDY
               (confused)
          I'm -- Fonzie?

                              GEORGE
          NO! The Fonzie! The crazy breakout
          character! The guy that all the kids
          impersonate and put on their
          lunchboxes!

                              ANDY
                    (soft)
          George, I hate sitcoms.

                              GEORGE
          HANG ON, you ain't heard the best
          part! ABC has seen your foreign man
          character, and they want to turn him
          into --
                    (he checks his notes)
          "Latka," a lovable, goofy mechanic!!!

    Long pause. Then -- Andy responds.

                              ANDY
          No.

                              GEORGE
          "No"? "No" to which part??

                              ANDY
          No to the whole thing. None of it
          sounds good.

    George is flummoxed.

                              GEORGE
          Andy... this is every comedian's
          dream.

                              ANDY
          I told you, I'm not a comedian. And
          sitcoms are the lowest form of
          entertainment: Stupid jokes and canned
          laughter.

                              GEORGE
                    (shocked)
          B-but, this is classy... they did Bob
          Newha--

                              ANDY
          I'm not interested. I want to create
          my own material.

    Beat. George glares.

                              GEORGE
          You have to do it.

                              ANDY
          I refuse.

                    GEORGE
               (he explodes)
          LISTEN, you arrogant putz! I've been
          in this business for twenty years!
          I know! If you walk away from this
          opportunity, you will never, NEVER
          see another one like it again!!!!

Long pause. Andy stares at George, amazed at this passion.

Then Andy gets up and looks around the office. He stares at
the awards... the gold records... emblems of success and
experience.

Andy thinks -- then nods.

                    ANDY
          Okay. Fine, I'll do it.
               (beat)
          But I have a few terms.

                    GEORGE
               (relieved)
          Of course! That's what negotiations
          are for.

                    ANDY
          Okay. I'll write them out for you...

Andy sits and WRITES DOWN a few requests.

George watches patiently.

Andy clicks his pen, done. George smiles and takes the list.
He scans it... then his face gets totally befuddled.

                    GEORGE
          What the --? This is RIDICULOUS!

                    ANDY
               (blase)
          Those are my terms.

                    GEORGE
          They're IMPOSSIBLE!! Jesus!
               (he points at one item)
          I mean -- "two guaranteed guest shots
          for Tony Clifton"??! I don't even
          know who this is!!

                    ANDY
          He's a Vegas entertainer. I used to
          do impressions of him. We sorta...
          got in a fight over that.

George gets a look.

                    GEORGE
          Wait a second -- this Clifton called
          me up. He's a loon!

                              ANDY
                    Nah, he just talks tough. But I owe
                    him one.

Andy smiles ingenuously, then turns stern.

                              ANDY
                    If I'm the new Fonz... ABC's just
                    gonna have to give me what I want.
                              (a sarcastic FONZIE IMPRESSION)
                    Heyyyyyy!

George winces. He stares at the list.

                                        CUT TO:

24   INT. ABC OFFICES - DAY   24

George sits across a conference table from three NETWORK SUITS.

George stoically reads the men his demands.

                              GEORGE
                    Mr. Kaufman will only appear in half
                    the episodes.
                              (beat)
                    Mr. Kaufman requires an undisturbed
                    90 minutes of meditation prior to
                    filming.
                              (beat)
                    Mr. Kaufman won't rehearse.
                              (beat)
                    Mr. Kaufman gets his own network
                    special.

The execs are stupefied. Finally -- George delivers the
clincher.

                              GEORGE
                    And Taxi must guarantee two guest
                    appearances to... Tony Clifton.

                              NETWORK GUYS
                    WHO???

                              GEORGE
                    Tony Clifton.

                              NETWORK GUY #1
                    Who is he?!

                              GEORGE
                              (solemn)
                    I don't know.

Long pause. The execs stare at George like he's lost his mind.

                              GEORGE
                    But these are the terms.

The execs' leader, MAYNARD SMITH, shudders hopelessly.

> MAYNARD
> Couldn't Kaufman ask for more money,
> like everyone else?

Beat. George sadly shakes his head: No.

                                        CUT TO:

25   INT. ABC PARKING STRUCTURE - DAY   25

George shuffles back to his car. He's dazed. He starts to
unlock his Jaguar, when he notices a bright pink FLYER on the
windshield.

George reaches for it. He looks around, and notices the PINK
FLYERS on every car. Hm. Curious, George turns it over. It
says "TONY CLIFTON! At MAMA RIVOLI'S, ONE NIGHT ONLY!"

George is rattled.

                                        CUT TO:

26   INT. MAMA RIVOLI'S - NIGHT   26

Mama Rivoli's, a dark Italian restaurant with red booths, wise
guys, and cigarette smoke.

George enters, unsurely. He approaches the MAITRE'D.

> GEORGE
> Excuse me, is Tony Clifton appearing
> here?

> MAITRE'D
> Who?

> GEORGE
> He's an entertainer.

> MAITRE'D
> Oh -- the asshole.
>   (he checks his watch)
> Yeah, he's about to go on.

The Maitre'd guides George to a booth. The "stage" is a six-
foot space in the back of the room.

The lights dim. A BLARING ANNOUNCER speaks.

> ANNOUNCER (v.o.)
> And now, Mama Rivoli's is proud to
> present International Singing
> Sensation... a man who has sold more
> records than Elvis and the Beatles
> combined...

George exhales, reassured.

                         GEORGE
          Okay. He can _sing_.

                         ANNOUNCER (v.o.)
          Ladies and Gentlemen, Mr.
          Entertainment... TONY CLIFTON!

The PATRONS applaud half-heartedly.

                         ANNOUNCER (v.o.)
          Out of respect for Mr. Clifton's vocal
          demands, could everyone please
          extinguish your cigarettes and cigars.

The crowd GRUMBLES angrily -- then irritably complies. One
ANGRY GUY thrusts his cigar into a water glass.

                         ANGRY GUY
          Goddamn, I paid five dollars for this.

                         ANNOUNCER (v.o.)
          And now! A man who needs no
          introduction... TONY CLIFTON!

A small BAND starts playing lounge standard "VOLARE"... and then
obnoxious TONY CLIFTON swaggers out. Tony has a black wig and
moustache, sunglasses, a padded belly, and a peach tuxedo with
blue shirt and velvet piping.

He is also clearly Andy Kaufman.

ANGLE - GEORGE

His eyes pop. WHAT?! A moment of brain melt -- and then he
EXPLODES with laughter.

WIDE

Tony glances momentarily at George -- then smirks at the
audience and sucks on a _cigarette_. He blows smoke rings at
them.

                         TONY CLIFTON
          Heh-heh. How ya all doin'?

The crowd is furious.

                         OLDER DINER
          Fuck you!

People light back up.

George looks around gleefully, then CACKLES louder.

Tony ignores the ruckus. He starts SINGING pinched and off-key.

                         TONY CLIFTON
                          (singing)
                "Volare!
                Whoa, whoa.
                Cantare,
                Whoa whoa whoa whoa."

George grins -- in on the joke.

                         TONY CLIFTON
                          (singing)
                "I got the wings of your love,
                I got the wings of a dove.
                I got the... uh...
                          (forgetting the words)
                ...the chicken wings from
                eh, Kentucky Fried...

The band is lost.

                         TONY CLIFTON
                Oh. Whoop do doo,
                whoop de di,
                stick a needle in your eye...

The band gives up and stops.

                         TONY CLIFTON
                Eh, the hell with that song.

One person CLAPS. Most BOO.

                         TONY CLIFTON
                So how ya doin'!
                          (leering)
                How ya doin' over here? How ya doin'
                over there?
                          (he approaches a WOMAN)
                How's that pasta carbonara?

                         WOMAN
                Leave me alone.

                         TONY CLIFTON
                Okay!
                          (he spins around)
                So, you havin' a good time, sir?!

Tony approaches a LONELY SAD SACK sitting at the bar. Tony
thrusts his mike at the guy.

                         SAD SACK
                Sure...

                         TONY CLIFTON
                So what's your name?

                         SAD SACK
                Bob.

                    TONY CLIFTON
               (he reacts as if this is enormously
                funny)
          "Bob"? BOB! Bob bob bob.
               (beat)
          Bob what?

                    SAD SACK
          Bob Gorsky.

                    TONY CLIFTON
          "Gorsky"? What is that, Polish?

                    SAD SACK
               (meek)
          Yes.

Tony gets indignant.

                    TONY CLIFTON
          Are you tryin' to do some of that
          Polack humor? Well if that's so, you
          can just get the hell out of this
          restaurant!

                    SAD SACK
               (timid)
          It's my name.

                    TONY CLIFTON
          SHUT UP! I hate them Polish jokes!

People are embarrassed.

                    TONY CLIFTON
          I do a clean show! Like, I wouldn't
          do that one... oh, you know it...
          "What do you call a pretty girl in
          Poland"?

                    SAD SACK
               (he giggles stupidly)
          A -- a tourist.

                    TONY CLIFTON
          See, that's EXACTLY what I'm talkin'
          about!
               (enraged)
          Here! I'LL give you a little humor!

Tony snatches Bob's water glass and POURS IT over his head!

George is appalled.

The crowd is aghast.

Bob is wet.

People BOO AND HURL THINGS.

Bob starts weeping, then bolts up and runs from the building.

                          TONY CLIFTON
          And _stay_ out, Fatso!

The room erupts, outraged.

CLOSEUP - GEORGE

looks like he's ill. He slowly covers his face.

                                        CUT TO:

27 LATER   27

The restaurant is empty. Employees sweep up.

George sits with Andy, still in the Tony get-up. But Andy is
now himself.

                          GEORGE
          I just don't understand this act.
          Why is that entertainment?

                          ANDY
                  (in jolly spirits)
          I dunno. Everyone loves a villain.

                          GEORGE
          Yeah? Well tell that to the _poor
          schlub_ who you humiliated!

Beat -- then Bob strolls over. His real name is BOB ZMUDA.

                          ZMUDA
          Hey Andy, good show.
                  (pleased)
          Really hot house.

                          ANDY
                  (he grins)
          Did ya see how upset that lady in
          front was?

                          ZMUDA
          Oh yeah! I thought her boyfriend was
          gonna shoot you!

George gapes at these two madmen.

He is absolutely speechless -- and then, SHOUTS BACK.

                          GEORGE
          Is it too late to get a drink?

                    ANDY
                 (innocently)
          Oh gee, my manners. I'm sorry.
          George Shapiro, I'd like you to meet
          Bob Zmuda. Bob and I have been
          buddies for years.

On closer inspection, Bob is cocky, aloof, and conniving.
George reluctantly shakes hands.

                    GEORGE
          Your name's not Gorsky?

                    ZMUDA
          Don't believe everything you hear.

                    ANDY
          Bob's a genius. He once faked a lion
          escaping from the Chicago Zoo. They
          had to close it for two days.

George eyeballs Zmuda -- then turns to Andy. Andy now has a
booger hanging from his nose.

George moans weakly.

                    GEORGE
          Please. No more of that.

Andy sighs -- then nods and removes the booger. It is rubber.
Andy takes out a plastic case labeled "SNOT," packs up the
booger, and pockets it.

Zmuda mutters darkly.

                    ZMUDA
          You told me he was fun.

Andy looks downcast.

                    ANDY
          I dunno, George. Maybe this isn't
          such a good fit. All relationships
          do run their course...

                    GEORGE
          Oh no you don't! "Run their
          course"???
                 (outraged)
          I've known you for a month! I marched
          into ABC and broke their heads making
          demands I don't even understand!!

                    ANDY
          You gave it your best shot.

>   GEORGE
>   You idiot -- ABC said yes! They
>   thought the terms were a brilliant
>   example of your "irreverent wit" --
>   and precisely why they want you.
>   (beat)
>   You're getting EVERYTHING!!

ON ANDY

Wow. An unexpected curve. He is astonished, enjoying a moment
of total rapture. Then --

>   ZMUDA
>   Hey, can I write the special?

Andy thinks, then flips a QUARTER. It lands heads-up.

Beat.

>   ANDY
>   Sure.

>   CUT TO:

28 INT. PARAMOUNT STUDIOS - STAGE 25 - DAY   28

The first week of "TAXI." The CAST rehearses on the taxi set.
PRODUCERS watch from the bleachers.

Latka works under a car hood -- but we can't see his face. A
transistor radio plays.

>   JUDD HIRSCH (AS ALEX)
>   "What's Latka listening to?"

>   JEFF CONAWAY (AS BOBBY)
>   "It's a New York radio station that
>   broadcasts Latka's language every
>   afternoon."

>   MARILU HENNER (AS ELAINE)
>   "Oh, that's nice to keep in touch with
>   home. Hey Latka! What's the news?"

Latka turns around -- and he is a bored BLACK STAND-IN. He
reads half-heartedly from a script.

>   BLACK STAND-IN
>   (listless)
>   "Well, they devalued the bracnick.
>   And Ichi Dam just set our country's
>   pole-vaulting record. He jumped 12
>   feet."

The cast glances around. Jeff Conaway loses his temper.

>   JEFF CONAWAY
>   Man, this is bullshit!
>   (he marches to the PRODUCERS)
>   Where's Kaufman? Why isn't he here??

One producer stands. This is tightly-wound ED WEINBERGER.

> ED
> You'll see him on Friday when we
> shoot. Now run the lines with Rodney.

An angry beat. The actors resume...

                                                CUT TO:

29   TWO DAYS LATER   29

The AUDIENCE is filtering in. They fill the studio bleachers.

BACKSTAGE

Actors mingle outside the dressing rooms.

> JUDD HIRSCH
> I'm taking bets we do the show with
> the stand-in.

> MARILU HENNER
> No, I hear Andy arrived. He's locked
> inside his dressing room.

> JUDD HIRSCH
> (surprised)
> Really?

30   INT. ANDY'S DRESSING ROOM   30

Andy is meditating. He's tranquil, at total inner peace.

Silence -- until a little clock radio CHIRPS.

Andy snaps his eyes open. He exhales a few calm breaths, then
sits upright. Andy reaches for a sealed envelope, rips it open,
and removes a SCRIPT.

Andy sighs, opens the script and starts flipping through. He
quickly scans each page.

> ANDY
> Good, I'm not in this scene. Good,
> I'm not in this scene.
> (suddenly, he reacts)
> Oh, darn --

Andy glowers, then leans back and starts reading the page...

                                                CUT TO:

31   LATER   31

The filming. Cameras roll. Everyone's in costume. Andy is
Latka: Wide-eyed, endearing, in mechanic's overalls.

The crowd HOWLS with laughter. Andy waves the radio.

                    ANDY (AS FOREIGN MAN)
          "And on de lighter side, it seems that
          a farmer made a miztake in the dark
          and tried to milk a billy goat!"

The crowd SCREAMS with delight and APPLAUDS.

A FLOOR DIRECTOR with headphones steps up.

                    FLOOR DIRECTOR
          And that'll be a cut.

The cameras turn off. Actors relax.

Andy walks up to Judd Hirsch and extends a warm smile.

                    ANDY
          Oh, hi. I'm Andy Kaufman.

                    JUDD HIRSCH
                (he rolls his eyes)
          Hi, I'm Judd Hirsch. Pleased to meet
          you.

They shake.

                                        CUT TO:

32   MONTAGE - "TAXI"   32

In quick succession, a series of Andy's best Latka moments.
He's beloved. The APPLAUSE grows louder, louder, LOUDER...

33   INT. ALPHA BETA SUPERMARKET - LATE NIGHT   33

2:30 a.m. Andy and Zmuda are playing Space Invaders. Andy is
focused intensely on the video game -- his fingers pounding the
buttons. On SCREEN, little spaceships blast his base.

                    ANDY
          What a mistake. Each show is worse
          than the next!

                    ZMUDA
          I dunno, that little mean guy in the
          cage is funny.

                    ANDY
                (upset)
          I can't even breathe up there. I'm
          tellin' George I'm quitting.

Andy tears open an envelope of Pop Rocks and pours them in his
mouth. His tongue explodes with fizzing.

Across the store, a PUNK-ROCK COUPLE are staring at Andy.
They're dumbstruck by his presence. Nervous, but inextricably
drawn, they finally mosey over.

                         PUNK GUY
          Hey, Latka.

                         PUNK CHICK
          Yo, Latka! Aren't you Latka?

Andy slowly turns, shocked at being recognized. He is confused
emotionally -- still angry, but pleased to have fans.

                         ANDY
          Yeah... I am... sort of.

The punks grin, wowed. Pop Rocks burst between Andy's lips.

                         PUNK GUY
          I <u>knew</u> his accent was bogus!

                         PUNK CHICK
                    (to Andy)
          Hey, we watched you on "Taxi Driver"!

                         PUNK GUY
          You were great!

                         ANDY
                    (pause)
          But... didn't it bother you that
          Foreign Man is usually a naive standup
          comedian, and now instead he's a
          garage mechanic?

The punks scratch their heads.

                         PUNK CHICK
          Eh, I don't know. I just thought it
          was some funny shit.

                         PUNK GUY
          Yeah, keep it up! ABC Comedy Tuesday
          RULES!

They high-five Andy and take off.

A moment of silence. Andy and Zmuda are awed.

                         ZMUDA
          Fuck. You've got <u>fans</u>.

                         ANDY
          That was cool...

                         ZMUDA
          A week ago, they would've thought you
          were some freak playing video games
          at three in the morning. Now, you're
          their god.

Andy is taken aback. He chews on his last Pop Rocks.

                    ANDY
          I don't believe in the worship of
          idols.

                    ZMUDA
                (mind racing)
          No, think about it. A hit show gets
          seen by forty million people every
          week! That gives you credibility.

                    ANDY
          What good is that?

                    ZMUDA
          The more people that know and love
          you... the more people's minds you
          can fuck with later.

ANGLE - ANDY

Hmm. He is intrigued...

                                        CUT TO:

34   INT. ABC NETWORK OFFICES - DAY   34

We're in the power office of Maynard Smith, the powerful ABC
exec. He shouts into a phone.

                    MAYNARD
          I don't care! Travolta signed a
          contract -- he's a Sweathog for life!
                (beat)
          Yeah? Just try to sue us.

He HANGS up. His ASSISTANT peeks her head in.

                    ASSISTANT
          Sir, they're having a problem down
          on the Kaufman special.

                    MAYNARD
          What kind of problem?

                    ASSISTANT
          Well... it's sort of weird. They say
          he's not following the network
          technical requirements.

Maynard is baffled.

                    MAYNARD
          "Technical"???

35   INT. TV STUDIO - DAY   35

Maynard marches irritably down a hall. He reaches the "Stage
Door" -- and blocking the way is pixie TM teacher Little Wendy,
meditating within a ring of candles.

                    MAYNARD
        Excuse me honey, I gotta get through.

                    LITTLE WENDY
                 (she opens her eyes)
        I'm sorry, no looky-loos.

An astonished beat.

                    MAYNARD
        And who the hell are you?!

                    LITTLE WENDY
        I'm Andy's personal secretary.

                    MAYNARD
        YEAH? Well I own the goddamn
        building! Now get this crap out of
        my way -- I'm going through!!

He kicks over some candles and barges in.

36   INT. TV STAGE - SAME TIME   36

Andy is in a booth, arguing with a HEAVYSET TECHNICIAN. Zmuda
watches and eats a banana.

                    ANDY
        Make it roll!

                    TECHNICIAN
        I won't.

                    ANDY
        DO IT! It's my show, and I WANT IT.

Maynard strolls up, buttoning his suit jacket.

                    MAYNARD
        Andy, I hear fabulous things about
        the special...
                 (delicate pause)
        Eh, I understand we've hit a teeny
        speedbump?

                    TECHNICIAN
                 (harried)
        Yeah, Kid Genius told me to mess with
        the horizontal hold! He wants the
        picture to roll!

                    ANDY
                 (happy)
        It'll be great. The viewer will think
        their TV is broken. They'll get out
        of their chair, they'll twist the
        knobs, they'll hit the TV, but they
        won't be able to fix it!

Maynard stares at a MONITOR. The picture rolls, totally indecipherable. A glum pause.

                    MAYNARD
          Andy... we don't want the viewer to
          get out of their chair. They might
          change the channel.

                    ANDY
          But it's funny! It's a practical
          joke. They'll get frustrated!

Andy beams giddily. Maynard gazes dully, struggling to reason.

                    MAYNARD
          Andy... uhh... this network has a
          longstanding policy: The viewer must
          be able to see the program.

                    ANDY
          But it's only for thirty seconds!

Beat.

                    MAYNARD
          Five.

                    ANDY
          Twenty!

                    MAYNARD
          Ten.

                    ANDY
          Deal.

Both men quickly extend their hands. They shake.

Beat -- then Andy pulls out a Handi-wipe and cleans his palm.

                                        CUT TO:

37   INT. ANDY'S APARTMENT - DAY   37

Andy's crappy apartment, looking like a freshman dorm: Cheap furniture, stained carpet. The only notable items are a Howdy Doody doll next to a framed photo of the Maharishi.

Andy is eating Haagen Dazs chocolate ice cream. He scoops it, then vigorously stirs it. He stirs and stirs, totally focused, until the ice cream is liquified.

Suddenly, KNOCK-KNOCK! Andy goes to the front door. It's the MAILMAN.

                    MAILMAN
          Got your mail, Mr. Kaufman.

He gestures down -- and there's THREE ENTIRE CRATES.

Andy's eyes bulge. He's practically salivating.

                                                    CUT TO:

38   LATER   38

HUNDREDS OF LETTERS are all over the floor. Andy happily chats
on the PHONE.

                         ANDY
               ...so you liked the show? Your letter
               said I was silly. Did you think I
               was too silly? ...Oh good. I'm glad.

                                                    CUT TO:

Another phone call. Andy holds a different letter.

                         ANDY
               Yes, it's Andy Kaufman! Really! I
               got your fan letter!

                                                    CUT TO:

Another phone call. Andy holds another letter, which has a
GIRL'S SNAPSHOT stapled to it. He is very nervous.

                         ANDY
               So Mimi, I got your picture...
                    (tentative)
               It was real nice of you to send it.
               Cause you knew what I looked like...
               and now, I know what you look like!

Andy flips the letter over. He glances at the return address.

                         ANDY
               So, um... San Bernardino...
                    (beat)
               That's just a couple hours away, isn't
               it..?

39   EXT. SAN BERNARDINO DOWNTOWN - DUSK   39

The sun is setting. In an ugly shopping district, Andy walks
along with sexy, wholesome MIMI.

                         MIMI
               ...so after I finish junior college,
               I'll go work for my dad's accounting
               firm. Unless, I decide to live with
               my friend Valerie, but she wants to
               move to Anaheim, and I don't want to
               do that.

A disinterested beat.

                         ANDY
               Oh.

Another beat.

>   ANDY
>   So do you wanna wrestle?

>   MIMI
>   Excuse me--?

>   ANDY
>   Do you wanna wrestle? It's a good
>   way of breaking the ice.
>   (pause)
>   That instant physical intimacy really
>   brings two people together.

Mimi is bewildered, and offended.

>   MIMI
>   What are you talking about?! We just
>   met an hour ago.

>   ANDY
>   (calm)
>   No no no, it's not sex! I mean --
>   it can lead to sex... but really, it's
>   just wrestling.

>   MIMI
>   I don't wanna talk about it!

An awkward silence. They continue walking. She points up.

>   MIMI
>   The sunset is really beautiful.

>   ANDY
>   What do you mean?

>   MIMI
>   (a bit offput)
>   I mean -- uh -- the colors in the sky
>   are so vibrant. I love this time of
>   day.

>   ANDY
>   (he shrugs dully)
>   I've never understood that. It's
>   just... getting dark.

Another awkward pause. Mimi is not enjoying this date.

Andy looks about for cheap thrills. He sees a BUSINESSMAN
strolling towards them. Andy smiles and winks conspiratorially.

>   ANDY
>   (whispering)
>   Hey, this should be good...!

Andy pulls out his shirt, messes up his hair... and puts the fake booger in his nose. He takes the girl's hand and pathetically shuffles over to the Businessman.

The Businessman looks up -- and takes a nervous step back. Andy is NOW A TERRIFYING STREET PERSON.

> ANDY
> (mumbling)
> Excuse me... sir... I don't mean to
> bother you... but I'm a little down
> on my luck... I lost my job... my wife
> is pregnant...
> (he pats Mimi's stomach)
> ...and I was wondering if you could
> help me out with a little spare
> change... maybe a dollar, if you
> could...

> BUSINESSMAN
> (frightened)
> Don't hurt me.

The Businessman fumbles with his wallet, hands Andy a dollar, and quickly hurries off.

Beat.

Mimi is appalled. Andy grins victoriously.

> ANDY
> Hey, we got some money! Let's go have
> some fun!

> MIMI
> I... w-why... eh....

> ANDY
> (he thinks)
> Or how 'bout this?? <u>I like you</u>! Why
> don't we fill the car with gas, drive
> to Tijuana, and GET MARRIED???

ANGLE - MIMI

Fear. She shivers, then hoarsely speaks.

> MIMI
> I wanna go home.

CUT TO:

40   INT. ABC NETWORK - DAY   40

A conference room. George screens Andy's TV special for Maynard and his team.

The network execs look constipated.

ON THE TV - Andy speaks tenderly, lovingly to famed puppet Howdy Doody.

>   ANDY (on TV)
>   Howdy, I've been watching you ever
>   since I was a little boy...
>   (choked up, nervous)
>   You're the first friend from
>   television I ever had. I always
>   wanted to meet you... and now... I
>   finally am.

Andy touches him and starts weeping.

THE EXECS

are horrified.

>   EXEC #2
>   This is NOT funny.

>   EXEC #3
>   (ominous)
>   "Artsy fartsy shit"...

>   GEORGE
>   (worried at this response)
>   No -- eh, it's <u>sweet</u>.

At that moment, the picture turns to FUZZY SNOW.

>   EXEC #1
>   Christ! We're the Number One network
>   -- can't we afford decent TVs?!

The executive angrily jumps up and POUNDS on the TV. BANG, BANG! George winces -- then mutters awkwardly.

>   GEORGE
>   No, um... it's part of the show.

An awful beat.

The executive is embarrassed. Finally -- Maynard explodes.

>   MAYNARD
>   Tell Kaufman we will NEVER air this
>   program!

He hits EJECT. On the TV, Andy hugging Howdy disappears.

                                             CUT TO:

41   INT. JERRY'S DELI - NIGHT   41

A delicatessen. Andy wears an apron and angrily cleans tables.
He stacks dirty dishes and wipes up the food.

A nearby BALD DINER gestures.

                          BALD DINER
          Excuse me, could I please have more
          coffee?

                          ANDY
          Yeah yeah, in a sec'.
                    (he lugs the dishes to the kitchen,
                     then shouts back)
          That was decaf, right?

                          BALD DINER
          Yes.

Andy hurries over with the coffeepot. He starts pouring.

                          BALD DINER
          You know, you look just like Andy
          Kaufman.

                          ANDY
          Yeah, I get that all the time.

Andy hurries off.

The bald guy's WIFE leans in, whispering.

                          BALDIE'S WIFE
          I'm telling you, it's him.

                          BALD DINER
          Nah, you're crazy. If that was him,
          he wouldn't be workin' here, pouring
          my coffee!

NEAR THE KITCHEN

Andy dumps out wet coffee grounds. He is sweating.

Suddenly, George enters the restaurant. He looks around, spots
Andy, and strides over.

                          GEORGE
          Andy, this is ridiculous. Take off
          that apron.

                          ANDY
                    (infuriated)
          NO! I'd rather work here, than at
          ABC.

Andy grabs a water pitcher and hurries off. George chases after
him.

                          ANDY
          A restaurant is an honest job.
          There's no lying. They don't promise
          you a job as a cashier, then suddenly
          make you a frycook!

                    GEORGE
               (trying to calm him)
          Look... we work in a creative
          business. You can't predict what
          people are gonna like --

                    ANDY
          The ONLY reason I did Taxi was so I
          could have my own special!

Beat.

                    GEORGE
          Tell you what. We'll show it
          around... see if somebody wants to
          buy it --

                    ANDY
               (bitter)
          Yeah, we can have a garage sale. "Hey
          look, I got a floorlamp and a network
          TV special for only fifty cents!"

A glum moment.

                    GEORGE
          I'll book you on some concerts. Those
          are always fun.

Andy ignores this. He fills water glasses.

                    ANDY
          How long is left on my Taxi contract?

                    GEORGE
          You signed for five years --
               (awkward)
          so four years, seven months.

                                        CUT TO:

42   INT. "TAXI" BACKSTAGE - NIGHT   42

"Taxi" is filming. We HEAR actors performing on-set.

Backstage, Andy fumes. His eyes rage pure bile. He silently
listens for his cue -- then suddenly, steps through a set door.

ON SET

Andy instantly transforms into cheery, cute Latka. He grins
and hands CAROL KANE a wallet.

                    ANDY (AS LATKA)
          "Simka, I tink I found de wallet!"

The studio audience LAUGHS.

Beat, then the Floor Director steps out.

                              FLOOR DIRECTOR
                    And that's a cut.

The audience APPLAUDS.

The smile drops from Andy's face.

The Floor Director listens to something over his HEADPHONES.

                              FLOOR DIRECTOR
                    Uh, hang on. We're gonna do a pickup
                    -- the writers want to add a button
                    to the scene.
                              (to the actors)
                    Carol, after Andy does the wallet
                    line, say "Keep it." Then Andy, you
                    smile and say "Tank you veddy much."

                              ANDY
                              (he gets pissed-off)
                    But I've already said "Tank you veddy
                    much" twice this show!

The Floor Director shrugs indifferently.

                              FLOOR DIRECTOR
                    I dunno... three's the charm.

TIGHT - ANDY

He stares daggers.

                                                  CUT TO:

43   EXT. COLLEGE - NIGHT   43

     A marquee says "TEXAS A & M PRESENTS - ANDY KAUFMAN, 8 P.M."

44   INT. COLLEGE AUDITORIUM - NIGHT   44

     An impatient AUDIENCE claps and CHANTS:

                              AUDIENCE
                    Start the show! Start the show!!

BACKSTAGE

Behind the curtain, Andy is obsessively measuring out stage
props. He positions the conga, then methodically walks heel-
to-toe to a mike.

Six and a half paces.

Befuddled STAGEHANDS stare. Andy peers down cryptically, then
paces back and slides the conga three inches. He squints, then
adjusts it a quarter turn.

Suddenly, Zmuda storms over.

                    ZMUDA
     Jesus Christ, ENOUGH! Andy, you have
     to go on!!

                    ANDY
                 (ticked-off)
     Fine! Raise the curtain!

Zmuda shoots him a look, then nods to the crew...

WIDE

The house lights dim. Huge APPLAUSE. Curtain rises.

Andy slowly walks out. The excited clapping swells louder.
He is truly a gigantic presence to these people.

Andy forces a smile and bows.

                    ANDY
     Thank you, it's great to be here.
     We're going to have a very nice time.
     We'll sing some songs --

                    SORORITY GIRL
     DO LATKA!!

Andy reacts, perturbed. He struggles to stay composed.

                    ANDY
     Uh, we'll play with puppets --

                    DRUNKS IN UNISON
     LATKA, LATKA!!!!

                    ANDY
     I --

                    CROWD
     LATTTTKAAAA!!!

Suddenly, Andy SNAPS. He barks through gritted teeth.

                    ANDY
     Excuse me one moment --

Andy hurries offstage.

IN THE WINGS

Andy runs up to Zmuda.

                    ANDY
     Give me the book.

                    ZMUDA
                 (startled)
     No! Andy, don't do it --

                              ANDY
                    <u>They're asking for it</u>.

Andy fiercely GRABS a small book from Zmuda. Zmuda winces.

ON THE STAGE

Andy strides back out. He gazes at the crowd.

                              ANDY
                    Since you're such a <u>special</u>
                    <u>audience</u>... I'm going to reveal, for
                    the first time ever, the <u>real me</u>.
                              (he goes into a CLIPPED BRITISH
                              ACCENT)
                    I'm actually British. I was raised
                    in London and educated at Oxford.
                    And though I dabble in clowning, I
                    do find it so boorish. So...
                    American.
                              (beat)
                    I prefer the fine arts. Henceforth,
                    tonight I'd like to grace you with
                    a reading of the greatest novel ever
                    written!
                              (he holds up the book)
                    "The Great Gatsby," by F. Scott
                    Fitzgerald!!

BEAT.

Heh? The crowd isn't quite clear if this is good or bad. A
confused murmur.

                         ANDY (BRITISH)
                              (he cracks open the book)
                    Chapter One.
                              (he starts READING)
                    "In my younger and more vulnerable
                    years, my father gave me some advice
                    that I've been turning over in my mind
                    ever since. 'Whenever you feel like
                    criticizing any one,' he told me,
                    'just remember that all the people
                    in this world haven't had the
                    advantages that you've had.'"

There's a little NERVOUS LAUGHTER. Is he really gonna read
this?

                         ANDY (BRITISH)
                    "He didn't say any more, but we've
                    always been unusually communicative
                    in a reserved way, and I understood
                    that he meant a great deal more than
                    that..."

                                             DISSOLVE TO:

45   LATER   45

> ANDY (BRITISH)
> "When I came back from the East last
> autumn I felt that I wanted the world
> to be in uniform and at a sort of
> moral attention forever; I wanted no
> more riotous excursions with
> privileged glimpses into the human
> heart..."

People start BOOING. Andy looks up.

> ANDY (BRITISH)
> Please, let's keep it down. We have
> a long way to go.
>   (he resumes READING)
> "Only Gatsby, the man who gives his
> name to this book, was exempt from
> my reaction - Gatsby, who represented
> everything for which I have an
> unaffected scorn..."

The crowd is incredulous.

> DISSOLVE TO:

46   LATER   46

> ANDY (BRITISH)
> Chapter Two.

The crowd is horribly bored.

Andy glances up, and sees some people leave. He knows he's gone
too far -- but he's committed. Andy must continue.

> ANDY (BRITISH)
> "About half way between West Egg and
> New York the motor road hastily joins
> the railroad and runs beside it for
> a quarter of a mile, so as to shrink
> away..."

> DISSOLVE TO:

47   BACKSTAGE   47

A clock says 11:30. The PROMOTER glares at Zmuda.

> PROMOTER
> Is he ever gonna stop?

> ZMUDA
>   (dour)
> Sure. When he reaches "The End."

> DISSOLVE TO:

48   LATER   48

    People are streaming out. Maybe fifty are left. Andy is
    fatigued, but plows on:

                    ANDY (BRITISH)
           "Tom was evidently perturbed at
           Daisy's running around alone, for on
           the following Saturday night he came
           with her to Gatsby's party. Perhaps
           his presence gave the evening its
           peculiar quality of oppressiveness..."

    A weak VOICE feebly shouts.

                    WEAK VOICE
           Do Latka.

    Andy looks up, shocked. Insulted, he "blows his temper."

                    ANDY (BRITISH)
           Look! I don't have to tolerate this
           impoliteness! Forget it -- I'm gonna
           stop the show. GoodBYE!

    He slams shut the book. People cheer.

    Andy starts to storm off -- then turns.

                    ANDY (BRITISH)
           No no, I'm only fooling.

    Loud GROANS.

    Andy sits and resumes reading.

                    ANDY (BRITISH)
           "His presence gave the evening its
           peculiar quality of oppressiveness
           - it stands out in my memory from
           Gatsby's other parties that summer..."

                            DISSOLVE TO:

49   LATER   49

    There are six people left in the audience.

                    ANDY (BRITISH)
           "Tomorrow we will run faster, stretch
           out our arms farther.... And one fine
           morning - So we beat on, boats against
           the current, borne back ceaselessly
           into the past."

    Andy somberly shuts the book.

                    ANDY (BRITISH)
           The End.

A moment of quiet personal euphoria. Andy looks enraptured, the man who has just climbed Everest.

A pause -- but no applause. It's dead silence. Andy looks out... and sees the few audience members are asleep.

He shrugs, stands up, and shuffles off-stage.

IN THE WINGS

Exhausted Zmuda sighs.

                    ZMUDA
          Are you happy?

Andy nods.

Beat.

                    ZMUDA
          The audience left.

                    ANDY
               (defensive)
          Six or seven people stayed.

                    ZMUDA
          Six or seven people went to bed.

Zmuda hits a big metal switch.

WIDE

The house lights go on. The snoring people don't move.

Zmuda rubs his eyes.

                    ZMUDA
          Nobody likes anarchy more than me...
          but this is science fiction.

Pause. Andy smiles.

                    ANDY
          You always say, you can never go too
          far for a joke.

                    ZMUDA
          When it shows up -- tell me.
               (he lightens)
          C'mon, let's grab a bite.

Zmuda opens the metal stage door... and BLINDING SUNLIGHT blasts in. It's morning.

Both guys squint.

                    ANDY
          We'll make it breakfast.

                                        CUT TO:

50   INT. GEORGE'S OFFICE - DAY   50

      George is yelling at Andy and Zmuda. They are seated on his
      couch, heads bowed in shame.

                    GEORGE
          What kind of a show was this??!
                (angrily reading off a LIST)
          There were three-hundred walkouts!
          The promoter wants a refund!

      Andy mumbles in a pipsqueak whimper.

                    ANDY
          I'm sorry, George...

                    GEORGE
          You're DAMN RIGHT you're sorry!

                    ZMUDA
                (a guilty sigh)
          We might have lost our focus...

                    GEORGE
                (turning on Zmuda)
          And you -- you're the road manager!
          You should be watchin' out for him!

      George paces furiously.

                    GEORGE
          When you play the Midwest and South,
          you DON'T MINDFUCK THESE PEOPLE! It's
          not postmodern -- it's rude.
                (beat)
          If you wanna perform in Texas, you
          give 'em Mighty Mouse! You give 'em
          Elvis!!

                    ANDY
          But George, I like to push the
          boundaries...

                    GEORGE
          And that's great. But do it in L.A.
          and New York! The Improv is your
          playground. There you experiment!
          Show up with a sleeping bag and take
          a nap on the stage! I don't care!

      Hmm. Andy thinks.

                    ANDY
          How long would they let me sleep?

                         GEORGE
              I don't know!
                   (he composes himself and lowers
                    his voice to a hush)
              Andy... you have to ask yourself: Who
              are you trying to entertain? The
              audience... or yourself?

ANGLE - ANDY

He doesn't know the answer.

                                              CUT TO:

51   INT. HALLWAY OUTSIDE SHAPIRO/WEST - DAY   51

Zmuda waits in the hall, next to a bathroom. He's bored. Zmuda
checks his watch, then opens the bathroom door a crack.

INSIDE the bathroom, Andy is manically washing his hands.
Liquid soap from the dispenser, then rubbing under the water.
Then more liquid soap. More rubbing. Then more liquid soap...

Zmuda sighs and shuts the door. Beat -- and George comes
walking up. He speaks softly.

                         GEORGE
              Bob... I'm gonna cancel the next month
              of shows. Andy needs to rest before
              he goes back to Taxi.

                         ZMUDA
              He's meditating every day.

                         GEORGE
              It's not enough. His stress level
              is affecting his work.

                         ZMUDA
                   (he thinks)
              The Tony Clifton guest shot is coming
              up. Maybe that'll chill him out.

Beat.

                         GEORGE
              I highly doubt it. Bob... Andy needs
              to RELAX. See if you can get him away
              from all this. Find him something
              special. Something nice...

Zmuda mulls this over.

                                              CUT TO:

52   EXT. NEVADA DESERT - DAY   52

A tattered sign says "Welcome to the Mustang Ranch."

The world-famous whorehouse sits behind a barb-wire fence. Dusty connected trailers sit in the sand.

A cab idles out front. Andy and Zmuda sit inside. Andy is scared.

> ANDY
> I dunno about this...
> (worried)
> What will my mother think?

> ZMUDA
> She'll say, "Now my son is a man."

> ANDY
> It's so dirty.

> ZMUDA
> Nah. The girls sponge off between johns.

Andy nods.

> ANDY
> Okay.

53   INT. MUSTANG RANCH - DAY   53

The reception room -- wood paneling and black-lite posters. Twenty deadpan HOOKERS are lined-up, while Andy picks out who he wants. But he IS NOW GERMAN, with a monocle and a stiff walk.

> ANDY (GERMAN)
> I vill haf _dat_ fraulein...
> (looking around)
> unt... oh my, the vun vith the big strudels.

The two chosen girls take Andy's hands and lead him off. He reaches the door -- and turns. Andy gives Zmuda a nervous look. Zmuda smiles reassuringly. Andy gulps, and goes in...

Beat. Zmuda turns to the older, jaded MADAM.

> ZMUDA
> This is a big day. It's my friend's first time with a prostitute.

> MADAM
> (mocking)
> What're you talkin' about? Andy comes here almost every weekend.

Zmuda's jaw drops, stupefied.

> ZMUDA
> You're talking about... _Andy_?

                    MADAM
          Oh, he doesn't always call himself
          that. Sometimes he's <u>Tony</u>, and wears
          a tux.

Disbelief -- then Zmuda LAUGHS sharply. He's been conned.

54   INT. MUSTANG RANCH BEDROOM - DAY   54

Andy and the two hookers are WRESTLING. They grapple and roll
around, all three of them in their underwear.

Suddenly Andy flips the girls over and pins them with his arms.

Breathing hard, he stares down.

                    ANDY
          You <u>let</u> me win.

                    HOOKER
                (she giggles sexily)
          <u>What if we did</u>...?!

Andy grins and leans down...

                                              CUT TO:

55   INT. BURBANK BAR - NIGHT   55

George sits in a dark bar with Ed, the "Taxi" producer. Empty
glasses are piled up. George looks haggard.

                    GEORGE
          ...And you <u>cannot</u> tell anyone else!
          Christ, if Andy knew I was telling
          you, he'd never forgive me.

                    ED
          So Clifton is Kaufman... but Kaufman's
          <u>not Clifton</u>...

                    GEORGE
          Exactly! In the spirit of fair play,
          I thought you should be warned.

Ed stares at his drink. He empties the glass.

                    ED
          You know, George... maybe you're too
          close to this stuff. It's just a
          guest shot. We can have fun with this
          kooky character --

                    GEORGE
                (ominous)
          You've never met Clifton --

                        ED
Look, Andy made Latka one of the most
popular characters on television.
       (blase)
Who's saying lightning can't strike
twice???

                                  CUT TO:

56   INT. ANDY'S APARTMENT - NIGHT   56

Mission Control. Zmuda, Little Wendy, and a Mustang Ranch
Hooker sit on the couch, watching intently.

Andy is seated in a makeup chair. A long-haired MAKEUP MAN is
gluing elaborate prosthetics to his face.

                      ANDY
"Taxi" is a well-oiled machine -- a
triumph of Hollywood art, commerce,
and technological know-how.
       (beat)
Our goal... is to <u>destroy</u> it.

The group is shocked. The Makeup Man nods.

                MAKEUP MAN
Okay, Andy, you're ready.

Andy spins around... and is now RUBBER-FACED TONY CLIFTON. The
transformation is startling. He's unrecognizable -- his face,
gestures, even body language all different. He snaps.

                TONY CLIFTON
Who the hell is Andy??

                                  CUT TO:

57   INT. TAXI REHEARSAL ROOM - DAY   57

The Taxi cast sits irritably around a big table, holding
scripts.

                TONY DANZA
This guy is an hour late.

Beat -- then the door SLAMS open. Tony bounds in, filthy drunk,
clutching a bottle in a brown bag.

                TONY CLIFTON
Taxi! Laxy! Just the factsy, Maxie!
Them's all the words that rhyme with
taxi!

Wendy and the Hooker sashay in, dressed as tarts. Tony feels
them up, and they SQUEAL. The cast stares in horror.

                    TONY CLIFTON
          Eh, why the blue faces? You musta
          read the script!
                    (he chuckles)
          Well, don't worry! Your pal Tony
          stayed up all night, writin' some
          fixes on it.
                    (he pulls out SCRIBBLED PAGES)
          I added me a musical number, cut out
          Judd Hirsch, and changed the location
          to Mardi Gras!

Ed's expression goes ashen.

                                        CUT TO:

58 LATER   58

Tony is tap-dancing on top of the conference table. The cast
watches. Tony does a "fancy" move, and his booze bottle
suddenly flies away and CRASHES against the wall.

                                        CUT TO:

59 ON THE TAXI SET - LATER   59

A failed rehearsal. Tony is SINGING.

                    TONY CLIFTON
          And now, the new theme song!
                    (he starts SINGING)
          "Oh yes, we drive a taxi,
          And we're havin' fun.
          Yeah, we work together,
          And we get the freakin' job done."

UP IN THE TECH BOOTH

Beleaguered Ed sits with George.

                    ED
          George, we HAVE to let him go! We've
          lost two days. If I miss the Friday
          filming, the studio will eat a quarter
          of a million dollars.

                    GEORGE
                    (worried)
          I don't know how Andy's gonna take
          this...

                    ED
          So we'll go downstairs and tell him!

He points at Tony, swaggering around on the set. George shakes
his head.

                        GEORGE
            But that's <u>Tony</u> down there. That's
            not Andy. <u>Trust me</u>, it's like "Sybil"
            -- Andy's nowhere on the premises!

Ed glares.

                        ED
            Well whoever the fuck that is, I'm
            firing him!

                        GEORGE
                    (he sighs)
            Okay. But we'll have to warn Andy
            first. I think he's up in San
            Francisco, doing a concert.

Heh? Ed raises his eyebrows.

                                        CUT TO:

60   SECONDS LATER   60

George and Ed are both on the phone.

                        GEORGE (into phone)
            Hi, Diane, this is George. I'm trying
            to reach <u>Andy at that live show in</u>
            <u>San Francisco</u>.

A stilted pause.

                        SHAPIRO/WEST SECRETARY (v.o.)
            Oh yes. Andy is <u>up in San Francisco</u>
            <u>for that live show</u>. I'll see if I
            can reach him and patch him in.

Ed glances down at the stage... and suddenly <u>Tony is no longer</u>
<u>there</u>. He's magically vanished.

Beat.

Then CLICK! Andy's happy voice pops on the line.

                        ANDY (v.o.)
            Hi, George! Good to hear from you!

                        GEORGE
            Hi, Andy. How's the weather up there?

                        ANDY (v.o.)
            Oh, you know the Bay Area! Always
            chilly!

Ed looks totally off-balance. George winks at him.

                        GEORGE
            I'm here with Ed over at Taxi.
            There's been some trouble with Tony.

                        ANDY (v.o.)
            Oh no! Did he get hurt?

                        ED
            No no, Andy, nothing like that.
                    (nervous beat)
            But... Tony's not fitting in. His
            style of performance is too...
            burlesque.

                                        INTERCUT:

61   TONY'S DRESSING ROOM   61

     Tony is on the phone. He looks up, insulted.

                        TONY CLIFTON (AS ANDY)
            "Burlesque"?

                                        BACK TO:

62   INT. TECH BOOTH   62

                        ED
            Andy, I'm calling you up like this
            because I have the utmost respect for
            your artistry. But -- I need your
            permission to fire him.

                        ANDY (v.o.)
            Oh dear!
                    (upset)
            George, this is gonna <u>kill</u> Tony. He's
            waited his whole life <u>for</u> this break.

                        GEORGE
            There'll be other shots.

                        ED
            Andy, I <u>have</u> to do it. He's a
            <u>terrible</u> actor.

     Andy thinks about this.

                        ANDY (v.o.)
            I guess I understand. But Ed --
            please... let him down gentle.

     Ed nods, relieved.

                                        CUT TO:

63   INT. TAXI SOUNDSTAGE - NEXT DAY   63

     Tony SCREAMS insanely.

                        TONY CLIFTON
            FUCK YOU! I AIN'T GOIN'!!

WIDE

Ed is stupefied. The cast stands nervously behind him.

                    ED
          I said you're fired! Get off my
          stage!

                    TONY CLIFTON
          I GOT A CONTRACT!! I'm gonna take
          you to the DEPARTMENT OF LABOR!

Suddenly a FLASH! goes off. Ed squints and looks over. A
REPORTER has a camera.

                    ED
          Who're YOU?!

                    REPORTER
          I'm from the L.A. Times. We're doing
          a little puff piece on Mr. Clifton.
                    (beat)
          Mr. Kaufman arranged it.

Ed's temple pounds furiously. A bright vein pops.

TOP OF THE BLEACHERS

George enters. He looks down at the growing debacle -- and
winces. Uh-oh.

ONSTAGE

Ed is livid. He gazes harshly at Tony -- Tony's burning eyes
piercing through the rubber features.

                    ED
          We had a deal.

                    TONY CLIFTON
          I don't know what yer talkin' about.
          You musta talked to someone else.

Enraged, Ed blows up.

                    ED
          Security! Escort this man off the
          lot!!

IN THE BLEACHERS

George stares at this car crash... and starts to giggle.

ONSTAGE

Studio SECURITY GUARDS run over. They GRAB Tony.

                    TONY CLIFTON
          Stop! GETCHER HANDS OFF ME!

Tony scuffles.   The camera FLASHES.

>   TONY CLIFTON
>   LEMME GO!   I'M A BIG STAR!

IN THE BLEACHERS

George breaks into laughter.   Hysterical laughter.

ONSTAGE

Two Guards drag Tony to the door.

>   TONY CLIFTON
>   You'll be SORRY!   One day I'm gonna
>   OWN this town!!

Tony SCREAMS and gets removed.

Dead silence.   Then --

>   ED
>   I don't want those pictures getting
>   out.

>   SECURITY GUARD
>   (to the Reporter)
>   This is a closed set.   You'll have
>   to give me the film in that camera.

The Guard reaches for the Reporter's camera...

An uncertain moment -- until Zmuda authoritatively cuts in, from
out of nowhere.

>   ZMUDA
>   I'll take care of this.

Zmuda takes the camera.   He casually starts to make his way for
the exit... when Ed suddenly HOLLARS.

>   ED
>   Wait -- he's one of THEM!

Zmuda gasps.   Two guards go running for him.

Zmuda barrels away.   The guards chase him.   Zmuda tries to exit
-- but gets trapped.   He suddenly backs against the Taxi cage,
looking around helplessly, clutching the camera...

ON GEORGE

He stares sweatily at the situation... unclear about his
loyalties...

And then George leaps from his chair.

>   GEORGE
>   HEY!   I'M OPEN!!

WIDE

Zmuda grins, reaches back, and quarterbacks the camera across the soundstage.

It soars through the air... and lands in George's hands.

George hugs the camera to his chest and scampers feverishly across the bleachers. He disappears out the door.

64   EXT. PARAMOUNT SIDE GATES - SAME TIME   64

Tony Clifton gets dragged out, kicking and screaming.

                    TONY CLIFTON
          Stop! HELP! You wouldn't do this
          to Wayne Newton --

The Guards toss Tony out the gate, then slam it shut. He lands in a heap.

IN THE BACKGROUND

George sprints madly across the lot, more Guards chasing.

                    SECURITY GUARD #2
          Give us that camera!!

George serpentines between a few bystanders, ducks behind a bush -- then suddenly bolts for the exit.

The Guards race a step behind him, and he gets out.

OUTSIDE THE GATES

George collapses on the sidewalk, breathing heavily. He glances over... and Tony is lying next to him.

The men look at each other. There's a moment of understanding.

                    TONY CLIFTON
          Hey. Good hustlin'.

George slowly smiles.

65   INT. TAXI OFFICES - SAME TIME   65

Ed storms in, insanely angry.

                    ED
          That asshole! That FUCKING BASTARD!!
               (he SLAMS the door behind him)
          We had a fuckin' deal, and THAT
          COCKSUCKER SHAFTED ME!!

Ed is seething. His SECRETARY timidly speaks.

                    SECRETARY
          Um, Ed... you have a phone call --

                         ED
         I'M NOT IN!

                    SECRETARY·
         Well, um... it's Andy Kaufman...

Heh??! Shaking with fury, Ed stares at the telephone... then
slowly picks it up.

                         ED
         Yeah???

A long pause... then Andy's voice calmly speaks.

                    ANDY (v.o.)
         You were brilliant.

A flabbergasted beat.

                         ED
         Huh?

                    ANDY (v.o.)
         You were in the moment. You became
         a producer losing his mind.
                    (sincerely joyful)
         It was the best improv I've ever seen.

TIGHT - ED

He thinks intently about this. And then... amazingly, a
magnificent smile comes over his face.

                         ED
         Well -- thank you.

Pause.

                    ANDY (v.o.)
         Okay. See you next week.

Andy hangs up. Ed just sits there, astounded.

                                        CUT TO:

66 INT. HEALTH FOOD RESTAURANT - NIGHT   66

Andy, Zmuda, George and Wendy are squeezed in a booth, laughing
and celebrating. They eagerly read the L.A. Times.

INSERT - The headline says "WHO IS TONY CLIFTON?" Below is a
PHOTO of Tony being thrown off the Taxi set.

They all HOWL.

                    ANDY
         This is great! It makes Tony REAL
         -- three-dimensional! It's very good
         for his career.

Zmuda reads one paragraph.

> ZMUDA
> "Was this in actuality Andy Kaufman?
> And if it was Andy Kaufman, is Andy
> Kaufman crazy?"

> ANDY
> (he chortles)
> Boy, they totally fell for it! I'm
> only <u>acting</u> crazy!

Hmm. A few awkward glances.

Then -- Andy grins at his meal.

> ANDY
> Boy, this is tasty.
> (he shouts to a WAITER)
> Hey, can I please have some more
> seaweed?!!

CUT TO:

67 EXT. TENNIS COURT - DAY   67

Whack! George and Maynard are playing tennis. They bat the
ball back and forth, George making the points. Whack! He
smiles, then serves a hard SLAM. Ace! Maynard misses.

> GEORGE
> That's game, and set.

Exhausted, they both walk off. George towels himself.

> MAYNARD
> Good game.

> GEORGE
> Thanks.
> (beat)
> So why am I really here? And why'd
> you let me win?

They both sit. Maynard sighs.

> MAYNARD
> George, we have an ailing show, a
> cheap knockoff of Saturday Night
> Live...

> GEORGE
> "Fridays"? It stinks.

> MAYNARD
> No argument from me. Anyhow, we were
> thinking it could use a kick in the
> ass... some Andy Kaufman "nuttiness."
> (trying to be charming)
> Maybe get a little press...

George winces at this.

                    GEORGE
        There's <u>no way</u> he'd host "Fridays."
        It's a step down.

                    MAYNARD
        But we'd give him carte blanche! He
        can do ANYTHING he wants.

                    GEORGE
        That's what you said about his
        special. Then you didn't air it.

Beat. Maynard whispers mischievously.

                    MAYNARD
        George... I promise that this time
        we can't screw him. The show goes
        out <u>live</u>...!

Hmm?! George is intrigued.

                                CUT TO:

68 INT. FRIDAYS BACKSTAGE - DAY   68

The FRIDAYS CAST prepares. In a corner, Andy is arguing with
director JACK BURNS.

                    ANDY
        The monologue is okay, the newscast
        is sorta funny... but I'm not
        comfortable with the last sketch.
        I <u>told</u> you, I don't do drug humor!

                    JACK
        Andy, it'll be fine! It's what we're
        known for!
               (playing "stoned")
        "Maui? <u>Wowie</u>!"

                    ANDY
             (losing his temper)
        You're not listening to me --

                    JACK
        Don't worry. The kids love it --

                    ANDY
             (he BLOWS up)
        But <u>I</u> don't do drugs! And I don't
        enjoy making light of them!
             (YELLING)
        <u>I was promised creative control</u>!

Andy storms off. Eavesdropping cast shake their heads.

                    ACTOR
        What a prick!

69   INT. FRIDAYS AUDIENCE - LATER   69

The show is going, live. A SNIGGERING NARRATOR steps out front.

                    NARRATOR
          In this next sketch, two married
          couples are out to dinner. Now --
          everybody has secretly brought along
          a joint --
                    (crowd WHOOPS; he grins)
          So, when each person leaves the table,
          they sneak into the restroom to get
          a little high...

The crowd CHEERS rowdily.

In the front row, we reveal Michael sitting with a GIRL. He
whispers.

                    MICHAEL
          Afterwards, I'll take you backstage.
          You can meet my brother.

She smiles excitedly.

                                        CUT TO:

70   LATER - THE SKETCH IN PROGRESS   70

An overlit French restaurant set. Andy sits at a table with
actor RICHARDS and actress MELANIE. Another actress, MARY,
tiptoes back over, GIGGLING stupidly, playing stoned.

                    MARY
          "Gee, restaurants are amazing, aren't
          they? All these strangers sitting
          around... stuffing food in their
          faces! It's just incredible!"

She GIGGLES more. The other three play baffled.

                    MELANIE
          "If you say so."

                    ANDY
                    (he stands)
          "Excuse me, I'll be right back."

Andy walks out.

                                        INTERCUT:

71   INT. KAUFMAN FAMILY HOME - SAME TIME   71

Stanley, Janice, and GRANDMA watch the show.

                    GRANDMA
          Hmph! They sure didn't give Andy much
          to do.

> JANICE
> Mom! He said he's <u>coming back</u>!

72 INT. FRIDAYS - RESTAURANT SET   72

Actors read the menus. Suddenly Andy returns, a strange grin
on his face. He's swaying on his feet.

The audience WHOOPS: "Yeah! All right!"

Andy awkwardly sits. He has a strange hesitancy.

> ANDY
> "Gee, that bathroom is so colorf--"

Suddenly, he STOPS. The actors glance up.

Andy purses his lips, fretting.

An endless pause.

Uh-oh. Andy won't finish the line. The cast looks around
worriedly. Live TV is beaming out...

Finally, Melanie tries to cover.

> MELANIE
> You okay, honey? Something wrong,
> Carl?

> ANDY
> I can't, um...

Andy shakes his head.

The crowd laughs nervously.

> ANDY
> I can't play stoned.

UP IN THE BOOTH

The TECH DIRECTOR and his crew are bewildered. They flip
through script pages.

> TECH DIRECTOR
> Shit...! What's he doing??

ON THE SET

Silence. Andy is torn up inside.

> RICHARDS
> Just say it!

> ANDY
> (he shakes his head)
> I can't play stoned. I feel really
> stupid.

More silence. The actors are trapped.

> MELANIE
> <u>You</u> feel really stupid?
>   (upset)
> What about <u>us</u>?!

The tension is awful.

Unsure beat -- then fed-up Richards jumps up and storms off the set.

A CAMERAMAN unsurely starts to pan, not knowing whether to follow.

Mary continues giggling, playing stoned. She has no idea what else to do.

Richards returns... with the CUE CARDS. Irked, he dumps them over Andy's head.

The crowd CHEERS stupidly.

> ANDY
> You didn't have to do that!

Andy gets enraged, grabs his prop water glass and THROWS it in Richards' face.

> RICHARDS
> Hey! CUT IT OUT!

> MELANIE
> You JERK!

Melanie slaps her prop butter in Andy's hair.

WIDE

Jack runs up from the floor. He gestures at the booth.

> JACK
> Go to commercial, man!
>   (he turns to Andy)
> Get off the stage!

> ANDY
> I said I didn't want to do the sketch.

> JACK
>   (he JABS him)
> GET OFF!

> ANDY
> DON'T TOUCH ME!

Andy HITS Jack. Jack recoils and SLUGS him. They start FIGHTING.

Burly crewmen run in.

The crowd WHOOOOS.

Chaos. Andy swings wildly. The brawl goes wild. Actors duck.
Crewmen struggle to separate Andy and Jack. Everyone gets
dragged in.

IN THE AUDIENCE

Michael tries to run up and help. A SECURITY GUY blocks him.

IN THE BOOTH

The tech crew is freaking out.

> TECH DIRECTOR
> Go to three! Eh, go to four!

73   INT. KAUFMAN HOUSE - SAME TIME   73

Stanley, Janice, and Grandma are flabbergasted. Jaws to the
floor.

On their TV - fists are flying. Suddenly the BAND kicks in,
and the show abruptly cuts to COMMERCIAL.

They stare at the TV. Until, someone speaks.

> STANLEY
> I shoulda made him play outdoors.

                                                   CUT TO:

74   INT. FRIDAYS SOUNDSTAGE - LATER   74

The show is over. The disoriented audience shuffles out, a
shaky USHER waving them goodbye.

BACKSTAGE

Flabbergasted Michael leads his date backstage. Angry actors
hurry past.

> MELANIE
> He's a fuckin' psycho. I hope he
> never works again...

Michael gasps. He whispers to his date.

> MICHAEL
> This is terrible... all Andy <u>lives</u>
> for is his career! What's he gonna
> do??!

> GIRL
> (stepping away)
> Maybe it's a bad time for me to meet
> him.

> MICHAEL
> No, he needs my support.

Michael guides her to a door marked "GUEST HOST." A nervous gulp, then he opens it...

75   INT. DRESSING ROOM   75

And INSIDE is Andy, Jack, and Maynard, joyously LAUGHING and HIGH-FIVING EACH OTHER! Champagne bottles POP.

                    JACK
          Didja see Melanie's face when that
          grip punched you?!!

                    MAYNARD
          You guys were perfect! I never
          thought it would play so real!

Beat. Michael is stunned.

                    MICHAEL
          A-Andy...???

                    ANDY
              (surprised to see him)
          Michael...?!
              (beat; then)
          Get in here and close the door! The
          cast doesn't know!

They shut the door. The girl is totally confused.

                    GIRL
          I don't understand... what's
          happening?

                    MICHAEL
              (eyes widening in realization)
          They faked the whole thing...!

                    ANDY
          I was engaging a passive audience.

Beat -- then Michael runs at Andy and brotherly RABBIT-PUNCHES him.

                    MICHAEL
          You bastard! You gave me a heart
          attack!!

                    ANDY
              (he laughs)
          S-sorry...!

                    MICHAEL
              (laughing)
          I thought you'd ruined your career!

Everyone cracks up, laughing.

                                        CUT TO:

76   INT. ANDY'S APARTMENT - NIGHT   76

Andy is home, scanning through his ANSWERING MACHINE tape.

                    CONCERNED WOMAN (v.o.)
          Andy, are you okay? We saw the
          show... and uh, if you need someone
          to talk to --
                    (he FAST FORWARDS)
                    SOOTHING MAN (v.o.)
          ...everyone at TM supports you in your
          time of need. You seem out of balance --
                    (he FAST FORWARDS)
                    STANLEY (v.o.)
          I'm cashing out your long term
          investments! Cause you're
          unemployable! You'll need the money
          to LIVE on!

BEEP! Hmm. Andy thinks about this -- and slowly smiles.

77   INT. GEORGE'S OFFICE - DAY   77

Andy sits with George. A New York Times sits between them.
George is both amused and uncertain.

                    GEORGE
          We're in a very curious position.
          The good news, AND the bad news, is
          that you're on the front page of the
          New York Times. This is an
          unprecedented feat for a TV comedian.

                    ANDY
                    (correcting)
          Song-and-dance man.

                    GEORGE
          Right, song-and-dance man.
                    (he smiles and pulls the article)
          The gist of the article -- is that
          you're completely insane. One man
          even theorized that it was morally
          wrong of ABC to take advantage of such
          a clearly unstable individual.

Andy nods.

                    ANDY
          How can we capitalize on this?

                    GEORGE
                    (sarcastic)
          Hmm. Capitalizing on going berserk
          in front of 20 million people.
                    (beat)
          Well -- your schedule's wide open...
                    (more)

                              GEORGE (Cont'd)
                    Three concert promoters called today
                    to cancel -- they're worried you're
                    too unreliable.

                              ANDY
                    Leak that to the press.
                              (pleased; wheels spinning)
                    I think this could be big. People
                    will pay money to see me melt down.

Pause.

George leans back, contemplating the world he lives in. A gaze
crosses his face.

                              GEORGE
                    Andy... maybe I'm coming around.
                              (thoughtful)
                    You just might have been right about
                    everything.

Andy smiles.

The intercom BUZZES.

                              SECRETARY (v.o.)
                    Maynard Smith on line two.

                              GEORGE
                              (grinning at Andy)
                    He must be ecstatic! You singlehandly
                    got the world talkin' about a show
                    they couldn't give away.
                              (he PICKS up the phone)
                    Maynard! Hey lucky man! Did we
                    deliver??!

                                             INTERCUT:

78   MAYNARD SMITH ON THE PHONE   78

Maynard is sweaty and beleagured.

                              MAYNARD
                    George... it's a disaster. My bosses
                    have been chewing my ass out all
                    morning.

                              GEORGE
                              (startled)
                    Why?!

                              MAYNARD
                    They said the show was too radical.
                    It looked like anarchists taking over!
                    You know, when there's a coup in a
                    tiny country, the first thing they
                    do is grab the TV stations --

                              GEORGE
          Maynard, this wasn't a coup. You
          okayed it.

Maynard grimaces -- pained by what he has to say.

                              MAYNARD
          Regardless, they're demanding an
          on-air apology.

                              GEORGE
          That's ridiculous!

                              MAYNARD
          They're insisting. Andy has to inform
          the world that it was pre-scripted.
          We need to prove that the American
          Broadcasting Company is not out of
          control.

A heavy beat. George glances nervously at oblivious Andy.

                              GEORGE
          Oh boy...

                                        CUT TO:

79 EXT. FRIDAYS SOUNDSTAGE - NIGHT   79

A looming soundstage. A sign over the door says "FRIDAYS."

Beat -- then Andy tentatively walks up. Zmuda is backing him.
Andy glances anxiously at his friend, then enters.

80 INT. FRIDAYS BACKSTAGE - NIGHT   80

Andy crosses the stage... and actors angrily turn away. He's
a pariah. Nobody will look him in the eye.

81 INT. FRIDAYS DRESSING ROOM   81

Andy and Zmuda enter the empty room -- and there is an envelope
sitting there. It says "ANDY KAUFMAN APOLOGY - 2 Minutes."

Andy rips it open, removing one TYPED SHEET OF PAPER. He and
Zmuda crowd together, reading it... and their faces drop.

                              ZMUDA
          Are they kidding?? They want you to
          give away the trick!

                              ANDY
                    (upset)
          I never, NEVER wink at the audience!

                              ZMUDA
          Man, it's like one of those Viet Cong
          confessions -- with someone offscreen
          pointing a gun at the POW's head!

Beat.   Andy BECOMES a brainwashed POW.

                    ANDY (AS POW)
          "I confess I was a spy.   I denounce
          the imperialist United States of
          America"...

They both laugh.

Then -- Andy gets a dangerous gleam.   Bob gets worried.

                    ZMUDA
          Andy...!   You promised to behave --

                    ANDY
          But Bob, they're <u>daring</u> me to go
          further!   ...It's LIVE.

82   INT. SOUNDSTAGE - MINUTES LATER   82

Commercial break.   The audience waits for the show to resume.

A lone chair sits in a spotlight.   Suddenly, Andy staggers into
view... TRANSFORMED INTO A SHELL-SHOCKED P.O.W.   His face is
smudged, his eyes are glazed, and mucus runs from his nose.

Busy Jack Burns strides into view.

                    JACK
          Alright, Andy, you're gonna be
          sitting --
                    (his eyes pop)
          Oh SHIT!

Jack takes a horrified look at Andy.   He is speechless.

                    ASSISTANT DIRECTOR
          Coming out of commercial in fifteen
          seconds.

                    JACK
          Oh, Jesus... Andy, no...

                    ASSISTANT DIRECTOR
          Five seconds!

Andy glances derangedly at Jack, then sits in the chair.   The
camera LIGHT goes on.

Andy looks into the camera... hesitant, dazed, and emotionally
unstable.   He refers stiffly to the SCRIPT PAGE in his hand.

                    ANDY
          "I've agreed to appear on this program
          tonight, to make a statement.   Because
          ABC would like you to know the truth.
          The truth is -- last week was staged.
          We wanted to do something
          different..."
                    (more)

>   ANDY (Cont'd)
>   (choking up)
>   and... um...
>   (unable to speak)
>   I can't do this.

Andy breathes heavily. He throws the script down.

>   ANDY
>   I won't do it. I can't say it. I'm
>   sorry.
>   (struggling to continue)
>   I'm sorry. This has been a very hard
>   week for me.

The crowd LAUGHS nervously. Andy is shaken.

>   ANDY
>   Why are you laughing? I'm not trying
>   to be funny right now. Because of
>   this incident, my job at Taxi is in
>   jeopardy. My agent is finding it hard
>   to convince anyone in the show
>   business community to hire me.

A LAUGH. Andy gives the audience a strange look.

>   ANDY
>   You laughing at this... I think your
>   laughing at this is very tasteless.
>   (a long sigh)
>   My friends won't talk to me.
>   (trying not to cry)
>   And my wife... thanks to last week
>   my wife has left me. And she took
>   the kids, little Howard and Maria...

A few GIGGLES. Andy shakes his head in shock.

>   ANDY
>   I don't know where you people are
>   coming from.
>   (distraught)
>   Maybe I went too far... I don't know.

He starts weeping. He can't continue.

Andy sits there, shuddering. It's very uncomfortable.

UP IN THE BOOTH

The Tech Director stares at this sight. An endless pause...
until he realizes Andy has nothing else to say.

>   TECH DIRECTOR
>   (frazzled)
>   Cut to black. Cue commercial.

                                        CUT TO:

83   INT. MAYNARD SMITH'S HOME - EARLY MORNING   83

Maynard is passed-out on his couch. Empty liquor bottles are
everywhere. A gun sits on the coffee table. Last night was a
horror.

The doorbell RINGS. Maynard moans, rubs his head, and staggers
to the door. He opens it, and a fresh-scrubbed RUNNER holds a
packet.

                         MAYNARD
                What's that, my resignation...?

                         RUNNER
                No, Mr. Smith. It's the overnight
                ratings.

Maynard groans. Pained, he opens the packet, shielding his eyes
in fear. Finally... he looks -- and GASPS in SHOCK.

                         MAYNARD
                Oh my God!

84   INT. ALPHA BETA - DAY   84

Andy is in the supermarket, playing Space Invaders.

In the b.g., George appears in the window. He feverishly peers
around, then suddenly spots Andy. George grins and runs in.

Beat -- then he races up to Andy and grabs him.

                         GEORGE
                Andy! ANDY, I've been to every arcade
                in town, looking for you!!

                         ANDY
                      (staring at the screen)
                Oh, hello George. What's up?

                         GEORGE
                Oh, just THE BIGGEST RATINGS IN THE
                HISTORY OF FRIDAYS!!!

Andy jerks, startled. On the VIDEOGAME, his space station BLOWS
UP. Andy is off-balance. Discombobulated.

                         ANDY
                So I'm -- not in trouble...?

                         GEORGE
                They want you to guest host the first
                show of next season! They're gonna
                air your special, and pay you for it
                AGAIN! Time Magazine wants to profile
                you! Rolling Stone wants to profile
                Tony Clifton! And concert dates are
                pouring in like there's no tomorrow!!

TIGHT - ANDY

Whoa. He is momentarily speechless.

                    ANDY
          I should've cracked-up sooner.

                                        CUT TO:

85   EXT. BOSTON THEATER - NIGHT   85

A marquee says "ANDY KAUFMAN - SOLD OUT." A line of waiting
FANS goes around the block.

                    FAN #1
          I hear he's gonna sing "99 Bottles
          of Beer" all the way through.

                    FAN #2
          I hear he's gonna blow his brains out.

86   INT. THEATER - BACKSTAGE   86

Exuberant Andy huddles with sister Carol, her straightlaced
fiancee RICK, and striking blonde bombshell PRINCESS.

                    ANDY
          Here's the deal. I've reached the
          moment I've always dreamed of. I can
          get away with anything -- and people
          expect it. So I wanna go out there
          tonight and do stuff that's so
          disturbing, it's probably ILLEGAL!

Rick grimaces fearfully.

                    RICK
          I-I-I dunno about this, Andy. I'm
          really not much of a performer --

                    ANDY
          HEY. You wanna marry my sister, you
          have to join the family!

                    CAROL
          You make it sound like the Godfather.

An anxious pause. Andy smiles reassuringly.

                    ANDY
          Don't worry, it'll be fun. I'm gonna
          be a hypnotist, and I'll pick three
          people from the audience... which'll
          just happen to be you, you and you.
          Then I'll make you do incredibly
          humiliating things, while you pretend
          you're someone else.
                    (to Carol)
          So you're not my sister...
                    (more)

                              ANDY (Cont'd)
                         (to Rick)
                    You're not my maybe future
                    brother-in-law...
                         (to Princess)
                    And you're not a stripper from that
                    club on Fourth Street.
                         (Andy chuckles)
                    Just pretend you're regular folk.

                                             CUT TO:

87   INT. THEATER - LATER   87

     The show's in progress. The crowd is SCREAMING in shock.

     Onstage, Carol, Rick, and Princess are shaking like epileptic
     attacks.

     Carol is violently picking her nose.

     Rick's pants are soaked yellow from urine.

     Princess Cheyenne is nude.

     Andy wears a turban and waves his arms at the three.

                              ANDY
                    You're all under my spell! You'll
                    do anything I say!

     CLOSEUP - RICK'S HAND

     We see him squeeze a plastic bulb in his hand.

     WIDE

     The yellow stain grows across his pants.

     The crowd HOWLS LOUDER.

                              ANDY
                    And NOW, we take advantage of these
                    hypnotized subjects!!

     Andy opens a SUITCASE -- revealing assorted SEX TOYS.

     Jesus Christ.

     The crowd ROARS in horror.

     WIDE - AUDITORIUM

     Suddenly, BAM!! The HOUSE LIGHTS go on.

     Everyone spins in shock. WHISTLES blow -- and a DOZEN POLICEMEN
     barge in the back of the theater!!

                              POLICEMAN #1
                    STOP THE SHOW!

                    POLICEMAN #2
        You four are under arrest, for
        violating the morals laws of the city
        of Boston!!!

The cops race down the aisle.

Onstage, the four stop the "act." Princess frantically covers
herself. Everyone is terrified.

                    RICK
        Oh my God, we shouldn't have done
        this!

                    CAROL
                (panic-stricken)
        Andy, you said this would be okay!

Cops with nightsticks WHACK the theater seats.

                    POLICEMAN #1
        Clear the building! Fun's over!!

People bolt from their seats.

It's total mayhem.

Onstage, the four are frozen in fear.

                    POLICEMAN'S VOICE
        Move! OUTTA MY WAY! All four of you
        are goin' in the paddywagon!!

This last cop pushes through -- and he is Zmuda.

Disorientation -- then Carol's jaw drops.

Instant realization. She looks at Andy -- and he knowingly
winks back.

Carol dazedly grins.

Zmuda jumps onstage. He spins Andy around, and phony handcuffs
get SLAPPED onto Andy's wrists.

                                        CUT TO:

88 INT. PHOTO STUDIO - DAY   88

FLASH! Rubber-faced Tony Clifton is being photographed by a
FASHION PHOTOGRAPHER. Tony smirks and preens -- arms up, arms
out.

                    TONY CLIFTON
        I feel sexy! This looks good!
                (pelvis out)
        I know the ladies love this!

                              PHOTOGRAPHER
                    If you say so.
                              (beat)
                    Hang on, I gotta reload.

The photographer walks off.

We reveal George in back, watching the session. George comes
over and sits with Tony.

                              GEORGE
                    So, I heard you had quite a show in
                    Boston the other night.

                              TONY CLIFTON
                    I don't know what yer talkin' about.
                    I never been to Boston!

George smiles wryly. He leans in and corrects himself.

                              GEORGE
                    Sorry, I mean -- Andy had a good show.

                              TONY CLIFTON
                    Yeah, he did. I talked to Kaufman.
                    He told me it was one of the most
                    satisfying performances of his career.
                              (sincere)
                    Kaufman especially enjoyed trickin'
                    his sister.

                              GEORGE
                    She wasn't in on it?

Tony smiles. There's a feeling of genuine intimacy with George.

                              TONY CLIFTON
                    Oh, she thought she was -- but there
                    were circles within circles. That's
                    the thing with Kaufman's family...
                    they're complacent. They think they
                    know him, cause they grew up with
                    him... but they don't.

                              GEORGE
                              (agreeing)
                    They're not in the thick of it, like
                    we are...

Beat -- then Tony ominously shakes his head.

                              TONY CLIFTON
                    I disagree, George. Nobody knows
                    Kaufman.

A strange pause. Then, an ASSISTANT shouts.

                              ASSISTANT
                    Andy Kaufman's here!

                    PHOTOGRAPHER
          Okay, send him into makeup.

Huh?

Confusion. George slowly turns --

As ANDY strolls in the door. Andy waves cheerily.

                    ANDY
          Oh, hi, George.

CLOSEUP - GEORGE

A moment of staggering incomprehension.

Total brain melt. He looks at rubber-face Tony -- then he looks
at Andy -- then he looks back at Tony.

Finally he GRABS Tony and peers in his eyes.

                    GEORGE
          Who ARE you???!

                                        CUT TO:

89   LATER - SIDE ROOM   89

George is hyperventilating.

                    GEORGE
          What is the point of all this??

                    ANDY
          It's fun.

                    GEORGE
          It's NOT fun!

We pan over... revealing Tony with his makeup half-off. It's
Zmuda underneath.

                    ZMUDA
          I think it's fun. I like being Tony.
          Now I can dump a glass of water on
          someone else's head.

                    ANDY
          See, with all these articles coming
          out, people think they're insiders.
          They see Tony Clifton, and they say,
          "Ah, that's really Andy Kaufman." But
          that spoils it.

                    GEORGE
          No it doesn't. Tony always denies
          being Andy.

                         ANDY
          Ha-ha! But that's the beauty of it!
          Because NOW Tony will be telling the
          truth! The audience will be laughing
          because they think he's lying -- but
          actually, they're WRONG! He's not
          me!
                    (giddy)
          Then I can go on talk shows and deny
          being Tony! And the audience will
          be laughin' at me -- but actually,
          on the inside I'll be laughin' at
          them, because they're wrong and I'm
          right!!

George is dazed, and unimpressed.

                         GEORGE
          So you've got this big elaborate joke,
          which is really only funny to two
          people in the universe.
                    (dry)
          You, and you.

                         ZMUDA
          Yeah! But WE think it's hilarious!

Long beat. George turns serious.

                         GEORGE
          Andy... why is any of this necessary?

Pause. Andy sighs.

                         ANDY
          George... I'm at the point where the
          audience expects me to constantly
          shock them. But short of faking my
          death, or setting the theater on fire,
          I don't know what else to do.
                    (thoughtful)
          Cause I've always got to be one step
          ahead of them.

                         GEORGE
          But I feel like you're extending this
          philosophy to real life. It's
          obsessive. Nothing's ever on the
          level anymore.

A perplexed beat.

                         ANDY
          George, it never was.
                    (pause)
          Didn't you know that?

                                        CUT TO:

90   INT. THEATER BOOKER'S OFFICE - DAY   90

A slick BOOKER, sitting in a crowded office full of head shots.
He's on the phone.

                        BOOKER
            Mr. Shapiro, this is Gene Knight up
            at Harrah's Tahoe. We'd like to book
            Andy Kaufman for our showroom.

                                        INTERCUT:

91   George on the phone.   91

                        GEORGE
            Ehh -- Andy doesn't really like
            playing casinos. The audiences don't
            work well for him.

                        BOOKER
            Oh.

Disappointed beat. The Booker thinks.

                        BOOKER
            What about Tony Clifton?

                        GEORGE
                  (startled)
            Really?! You want Tony Clifton to
            headline Harrah's Tahoe??

                        BOOKER
                  (being tricky)
            Eh, sure. We're trying to expand our
            audience base -- and I know the
            college kids really love Andy Kaufman.

George winces.

                        GEORGE
            Look -- I gotta be clear with you.
            Tony Clifton is NOT Andy Kaufman.

                        BOOKER
                  (he LAUGHS merrily)
            Yeah yeah yeah! I know! I get it!

                        GEORGE
                  (frustrated)
            No, I'm serious. If you book Tony,
            you are NOT GETTING ANDY.

                        BOOKER
                  (LAUGHING harder)
            Wink wink! Nudge nudge! Of course!

George rolls his eyes in disbelief. Finally he shrugs.

                         GEORGE
              Fine, be my guest. Book him.

                                                    CUT TO:

92   INT. SPORTS ARENA - DAY   92

A crowded arena. Andy comes walking down the aisle with his
elderly Grandma.

                         GRANDMA
              You're such a good boy, Andy. I
              hardly ever get out anymore.

                         ANDY
              But I love you, Grandma. I like to
              do these special things for you.

A BRAWNY GUY jumps up from his seat.

                         BRAWNY GUY
              Kick him in the NUTS!

We GO WIDE - and reveal we're at a WRESTLING MATCH. Muscular
WRESTLERS throw each other around the ring. Their faces drip
blood.

Andy helps Grandma into her seat. He hands her a popcorn.

                         GRANDMA
              I can't tell you how many times I
              brought you here as a boy.

                         ANDY
              That's why grandmas are the best.
              They're just good to you. They never
              yell at you like parents. Grandmas
              are unconditional love.

He kisses her on the forehead.

In the ring, a melee breaks out. A MANAGER crawls in to help
-- and gets hurled. The crowd SCREAMS wildly.

                         GRANDMA
              Oh my Goodness! They just threw that
              poor man from the ring!

                         ANDY
                    (gently laughing)
              Grandma, it's not REAL! They're just
              pretending.

                         GRANDMA
              No, no, Andy. If it was fake, they
              couldn't call it sports.

The Good Guy Wrestler (in white) JABS the hooded Bad Guy. A
few CHEERS.

Andy smiles.

The Bad Guy retaliates by SMACKING the Good Guy. He topples
unconscious. The crowd BOOOOOOOOOS FURIOUSLY.

Andy looks around, amazed at this impassioned reaction.

The Bad Guy jumps on the Good Guy's head. The REF tries to stop
this -- and the crazed Bad Guy knocks out the Ref! The crowd
goes NUTS.

The Bad Guy grabs a chair and SMASHES it over his slayed
opponent. Then he does a smarmy victory dance. The crowd is
ENRAGED. They SHOUT, SCREAM, and HURL PROGRAMS at him.

CLOSEUP - ANDY

His eyes widen with glee.

                    ANDY
          Hey -- this is where the fun is...!

                                        CUT TO:

93   EXT. NEWSSTAND - DAY   93

Andy and Zmuda are thumbing through wrestling magazines. It's
page after page of SCOWLING BLOODY WRESTLERS.

                    ANDY
          Look at this! An evil Russian! Ooo,
          here's an evil Nazi -- he likes to
          fight dirty! Hey, here's an evil
          Japanese guy!

                    ZMUDA
          What is this, World War Two..?

                    ANDY
          These magazines are great! 68 pages
          of villains -- and no good guys!

                    ZMUDA
          Good guys suck.

                    ANDY
              ("fake insulted")
          Hey, Latka's a good guy...!

                    ZMUDA
          Latka sucks.

Andy laughs. He looks at Zmuda hopefully.

                    ANDY
          So, what do you think...?

                      ZMUDA
          No offense, man, but I just don't
          think you're built for it. These
          guys'll kick your ass. They're huge.

Andy's face drops. He realizes Zmuda's right.

Beat -- then Andy glances around. His gaze locks on an issue
of... "MS. MAGAZINE."

Hmm???! Andy's eyes light up. He reaches for the "MS."...

                                  CUT TO:

94   INT. MERV GRIFFIN SHOW - DAY   94

Andy and MERV GRIFFIN stand on an erected wrestling ring. Andy
wears a goofy wrestling outfit that resembles thermal underwear.
He is shouting like a wrestler.

                      ANDY
          ...and I vow to continue wrestling
          until I am BEATEN, in a three-minute
          match, with my shoulders pinned to
          the mat!!

                      MERV
            (nonplussed)
          By a _woman_.

                      ANDY
          Yes! BY A WOMAN!
            (emphatic)
          I'm doing this because I feel that
          a woman cannot beat a man in
          wrestling. Even if they train with
          weights... it requires a certain
          mental ability --
            (a clumsy pause)
          And, uh -- I just don't feel they have
          that...

The audience MURMURS uncomfortably. Andy laughs and backpedals.

                      ANDY
          No no! Women are superior in many
          ways. When it comes to cooking and
          cleaning, washing the potatoes,
          scrubbing the carrots, raising the
          babies, mopping the floors, they have
          it all over men. I believe that!

An appalled silence.

Merv winces. Some people start BOOING.

_We_ can tell Andy is pleased.

                              ANDY
             But when it comes to wrestling, forget
             it! If there's a woman that can prove
             me wrong, come up here. I'll shut
             my mouth and pay her 500 dollars.

Merv baitingly turns to the crowd.

                              MERV
             Any... volunteers...?

WIDE

All the WOMEN'S hands angrily shoot up!

We move through the crowd, finally picking out... a feisty
woman, LYNNE. She mutters, half hateful, half laughing --

                              LYNNE
             I wanna kill that jerk.

                                                CUT TO:

95   MINUTES LATER   95

Andy and Lynne stand in the ring. Zmuda is in a referee's
uniform.

                       ZMUDA (AS REFEREE)
             Will you please shake hands, go to
             your corners, and come out wrestling.

Lynne extends her hand. Andy fakes a shake -- then snidely
refuses and struts away. The crowd BOOS.

DING! It's the bell. The match begins. Lynne comes running
at Andy -- she's craving a victory, but terribly unprepared for
this experience. Andy immediately grabs her by the legs and
flips her over.

WHUMP! She's down. Andy has trained for this.

Zmuda gets on his knees, watching, trying to look official.
Lynne struggles and slithers away.

She grabs Andy's arm and forces him down. People CHEER. His
torso hits the mat. LOUDER CHEERS. But suddenly he rolls over
and pulls her hair! Her head snaps back. The crowd is
INCENSED. Zmuda hurries over and pantomimes a stern warning.

Andy nods, and they separate. They do a little dance around
the ring, Lynne looking for a hole. Suddenly, Andy spins her
into a Half-Nelson. Her arms are pinned. They struggle, then
he throws her down on her stomach. One! Two! Three!

And DING! It's all over.

Andy jumps up and sneers at the audience.

                              ANDY
          I'm the winner! I've got the BRAINS!
                    (he points at his head)
          Now baby, get back in the kitchen
          where you belong!!

Lynne glares.

Out of the blue, an old RECORDING OF BOUNCY PIANO MUSIC starts
playing. A chicken starts CLUCKING to the music, and Andy
lip-syncs along, doing an obnoxious cock o' the walk around the
ring.

                                             CUT TO:

96   INT. MERV GRIFFIN SHOW BACKSTAGE - LATER   96

Lynne is escorted by a GUEST COORDINATOR. Lynne is dazed. The
Coordinator hands her a bunch of crap.

                         GUEST COORDINATOR
          Here's your complimentary photo with
          Merv. Here's your Turtle Wax --

                              LYNNE
          I don't need Turtle Wax.

                         GUEST COORDINATOR
          Every guest of Merv gets it. And
          here's your dinner-for-two voucher
          at Red Lobster.

Lynne takes her junk and hobbles off. She passes Andy, who sees
her and grins.

                              ANDY
          Gosh, you scored! Look at all those
          goodies!

                              LYNNE
          Buzz off. Go patronize somebody else.

Lynne coldly hurries away. Andy chases after her.

                              ANDY
          Hey, I hope you didn't take that stuff
          I said seriously. It was just part
          of the show!
                    (eager to impress)
          It's like the old days, when a
          carnival barker would try to rile up
          the crowd.

                              LYNNE
          Oh. So you were just pretending to
          be an asshole.

Andy nods, pleased.

                              ANDY
               It's what I'm good at!

Lynne stares -- then begrudgingly cracks a smile.

                                              CUT TO:

97   INT. GOLD'S GYM - DAY   97

Jumbo-sized BEEFY MEN work out, sweating and groaning.

In a corner is Andy, lifting gigantic barbells. Sitting on a
bench, unhappily watching, is George.

                         GEORGE
               Merv Griffin has received 2000 pieces
               of hate mail. Andy, Merv Griffin
               doesn't GET hate mail.

                         ANDY
               That means it was a success. I woke
               up the audience.

                         GEORGE
               And now they detest you! And it's
               not that they detest a character that
               they sense you were portraying...
               they detest YOU, Andy Kaufman!

                         ANDY
               George, it's punk rock.
                    (he hands him a BARBELL)
               Here, take this.

                         GEORGE
               No, I'm not going to take it. If I
               take it I'll break my back. Put it
               down yourself.

George crosses his arms. Andy frowns and lowers the weight.

                         GEORGE
               Next time you make a live appearance,
               women are going to picket.

                         ANDY
               They're having a laugh...

                         GEORGE
               WRONG! You haven't given them any
               clues that it's a parody!

                         ANDY
               That's because they've only seen it
               once. But I'll do it again, and
               again, and AGAIN...
                    (a maniacal grin)
               They'll catch on!

George shudders. Suddenly a white-haired HARDASS marches over
-- bellicose BUDDY ROGERS, 70.

> BUDDY ROGERS
> Alright, QUIT THE YAPPIN'! Hit the
> ground and give me 50 pushups,
> Kaufman!

Andy dutifully follows orders and drops to the floor.

> ANDY
> George, I want you to meet my new
> manager, Buddy "Nature Boy" Rogers!

> GEORGE
> (baffled)
> "Manager"? I thought _I_ was your
> manager...

> BUDDY ROGERS
> (to George)
> You handle the song-and-dance crapola.
> _I_ handle the wrestling.
> (to Andy)
> UP DOWN! UP DOWN! UP DOWN...!

George stares in disbelief.

> CUT TO:

98 MONTAGE OF WRESTLING MATCHES: 98

MATCH 1 - Andy throws a FAT WOMAN to the ground.

MATCH 2 - Andy squeezes a SMALL WOMAN in a headlock.

MATCH 3 - Andy throws an ITALIAN LADY from the ring. He then
proudly waves a phony plastic belt over his head.

> ANDY
> I am the Intergender Wrestling
> Champion of the World!!!

> CUT TO:

99 INT. MOVIE THEATER LOBBY - DAY   99

At the boxoffice, Andy buys a ticket. He enters the theater,
hurries across the lobby, and goes up to the candy counter.

> ANDY
> Two large popcorns, extra butter.

Andy pays. He takes the popcorns... then WALKS OUT.

100 EXT. MOVIE THEATER - SAME TIME   100

Andy proudly leaves with the popcorns. He goes up to his parked
Cordova, which contains in the passenger seat... _Lynne_.

                         ANDY
          I love movie theater popcorn, but I'm
          NOT gonna sit through "On Golden
          Pond."

IN THE CAR

Andy hands Lynne her popcorn, then gets in. He starts driving.

                         LYNNE
          When my phone rang the other night,
          the last person I was expecting it
          to be was you.

                         ANDY
          Gosh. Gee... I was just so --
          impressed with your wrestling moves.

                         LYNNE
          You were impressed with something.
          It's pretty odd when a man sports a
          hard-on that large on national
          television.

Andy is shocked.

                         ANDY
          Oh! Uh, I hope I didn't offend you.

Beat.

                         LYNNE
          I'm here, ain't I?

A charged moment. Andy's eyes widen.

He is disconcerted -- and excited -- by her aggressiveness.

Lynne checks him out.

                         LYNNE
          Have you ever played Murder in the
          Car?

                         ANDY
               (unsure)
          No...

                         LYNNE
          Pull over next to that Buick.

Lynne points. At a red light, Andy pulls them over.

Suddenly, Lynne starts SCREAMING FURIOUSLY.

                         LYNNE
          YOU STUPID SON OF A BITCH! DID YOU
          THINK I WASN'T GOING TO FIND OUT ABOUT
          YOU AND MY SISTER??!

Beat -- then Andy realizes the game.

                    ANDY
          B-but, baby, it didn't mean
          anything...!

                    LYNNE
          I'LL KILL YOU!

                    ANDY
          I love you --

She lunges over and fakes CHOKING him. He flails helplessly and
SLAMS his head against the glass.

Lynne "throttles" harder. Popcorn flies. The HORN goes off.

IN THE BUICK

An ELDERLY COUPLE gapes in horror. Andy gestures desperately,
gasping through the glass.

                    ANDY
          Help...me....!!!

The old people are paralyzed. The man turns to his wife.

                    OLD MAN
          We're not getting involved.

Terrified, he HITS THE GAS and screeches away.

IN ANDY'S CAR

Andy and Lynne see their audience drive off. She stops choking.
Andy is sweaty... and exhilarated.

                    ANDY
          You were fantastic...!

He stares into Lynne's eyes.

                    ANDY
          Do you wanna go to Memphis and get
          married?

Beat.

                    LYNNE
          Why Memphis?

                    ANDY
               (he SPEAKS VERY FAST)
          Because Memphis is the wrestling
          capital of the world! I'll go in the
          ring, and I'll announce that I'll
          shave my head and marry any woman who
          beats me! Then you'll come up, we'll
          wrestle, and I'll let you win!
                    (more)

                              ANDY (Cont'd)
                    Then you'll scalp me, and we'll get
                    married on Letterman, just like Tiny
                    Tim did on Carson... right there on
                    the show! What do you say???

Whoa. Lynne stares into his eyes.

                              LYNNE
                    And all this will be for real?

                              ANDY
                         (a soft smile)
                    If you want...

                                                    CUT TO:

101   INT. MEMPHIS MID-SOUTH COLISEUM - NIGHT   101

A giant arena, filled with furious BOOING SOUTHERN WRESTLING
FANS. Ladies in hair nets. Men clutching beer cans. This is a
rougher crowd than we've seen before.

Andy stands in the ring, unshaven in a torn green robe. He's
screaming at them.

                              ANDY
                    SHUT UP!
                         (more BOOS)
                    SHUT UP! Show some respect! I want
                    SILENCE when I speak!!

Louder BOOOS. People throw debris.

Andy is pleased. In the corner, Buddy Rogers nods approvingly.

                              ANDY
                    If any woman can defeat me, I will
                    pay her 1000 dollars! Then I'll shave
                    my head BALD! And then as a bonus
                    -- that lucky lady will get to marry
                    me!!

Screeching JEERS and CATCALLS. Down front... Lynne jumps up.

                              LYNNE
                    Look here, Andy Kaufman! I'll take
                    you on -- SISSY!

The mob LAUGHS harshly.

                              ANDY
                    Ooo, the little lady's upset. Well
                    I say -- get back in the kitchen!

                              LYNNE
                         ("outraged")
                    No! YOU get in the kitchen. I'm
                    gonna make you dry my dishes!

The crowd APPLAUDS. Lynne grins and starts to climb in the ring. Andy's eyes are ablaze. But suddenly -- an oversized Southern MAN jumps in and snatches the mike away.

                    MAN
          STOP IT! This woman's a FAKE! She's
          nothing but Kaufman's <u>girlfriend</u>!

Andy and Lynne are startled.

                    ANDY
          T-that's not true --

                    MAN
          It's a set-up! And I <u>won't</u> allow our
          great sport to be degraded by a fix!!

The crowd angrily starts to HISS. Lynne whispers to Andy.

                    LYNNE
          Andy... who is that...?

                    JERRY LAWLER
          I'm <u>Jerry Lawler</u>, the KING of Memphis
          wrestling!!
               (this gets HUGE CHEERS)
          So if Kaufman wants to tangle, I've
          brought a <u>real</u> wrestler! She's
          trained and she's READY!! Kaufman,
          do you think you can handle... FOXY
          JACKSON???!!!

At that, a striking, muscular black woman stands -- FOXY.

The coliseum SCREAMS with excitement. People POUND their seats. The roar is deafening. Lynne looks worriedly at Andy -- he's concerned.

                                             CUT TO:

102 LATER   102

DING! The bell rings. Foxy comes out, ready to brawl. But Andy remains in his corner, running down the clock. He nonchalantly peels off his robe. Foxy dances around impatiently. Andy casually removes a towel from his neck. People BOO. Still stalling, Andy then takes off his <u>watch</u>.

People SCREAM so furiously they're red-faced. Andy is tormenting them. A TATTOOED GUY jumps up.

                    TATTOOED GUY
          Are you scared???

Andy sneers. He cracks his knuckles, finally walks over... and commences a WINDMILL. Absurdly, he spins his arms around and around, daring Foxy to get near him.

She rolls her eyes and waits. The REF jumps from the way. A minute has counted down. Finally Andy stops -- and the real wrestling begins. Foxy lunges at him and immediately goes for a chokehold. The crowd CHEERS, relieved. Jerry motions signals. Foxy yanks -- but Andy jerks away.

Andy is intrigued. She's coming to play! Andy gestures to the Ref and points UP. The Ref looks away -- and Andy SLAPS Foxy.

The crowd furiously JEERS. The Ref spins around, and Andy shrugs innocence. He then runs at Foxy and theatrically pushes her into the ropes. She bounces off, stumbles back -- and Andy drops to his knees. She trips over him and hits the mat.

Andy aggressively jumps onto Foxy's shoulders and pins her. The Ref counts, One! Two! Three! DING!!

It's over. But Andy stays on her, shaking his ass, leering rudely. Jerry Lawler yells from the corner.

> JERRY LAWLER
> Alright, you won. GET OFF HER!

Andy remains, flapping his arms like a chicken.

The BOOING grows. Louder. More emotional.

> ANGRY VOICES
> Jerry, help her! Get in there! Do
> something!!

Jerry hesitates -- then suddenly climbs in the ring and lifts Andy off! Jerry angrily PUSHES Andy down.

Andy is flabbergasted.

> ANDY
> W-what are you DOING?! I don't fight
> men!!

Lawler snickers and walks away. Completely overreacting, Andy grabs the mike.

> ANDY
> I'm gonna SUE YOU!

                                                    CUT TO:

103   INT. COLISEUM INTERVIEW ROOM - LATER   103

A supercilious TUXEDOED ANNOUNCER holds a microphone up to Andy. Disheveled Andy rants berserkly at the camera:

> ANDY
> Let me tell you something, Mr. Lawler!
> I am not a hick -- I'm a national TV
> star! And I DON'T like a dumb cracker
> pushing me around in the ring! I
> never agreed to wrestle you!
>   (more)

                         ANDY (Cont'd)
          So you know what I'm gonna do???
                         (seething)
          I've hired a lawyer to sue you for
          every cent you've got! This was
          assault and battery! In a court of
          law, I'm going to kick your Southern-
          fried rump!!!

104   LATER   104

Lawler stands on the same platform, bellowing at the camera.

                         JERRY LAWLER
          YEAH?! Well I got news for you, Andy
          Kaufman! Wrestling is a serious sport
          to me! I don't like anyone makin'
          fun of it, and I hate anyone insultin'
          the South! So we can settle this two
          ways: We can go to court... or you
          can get in the ring with a man, and
          wrestle for REAL!

Off to the side, Andy watches, fuming. He is INFURIATED.

                         ANDY
          He -- he can't get away with this.
          He's calling me chicken!

                         LYNNE
          Andy, no --

Andy pushes some TECHNICIANS aside and barges onto the camera
area. He sticks his face in shocked Lawler's.

                         ANDY
                         (sarcastic SOUTHERN ACCENT)
          You wanna "wraaastle" me?! You wanna
          "WRAAASTLE" ME?? Okay Lawler -- let's
          rumble! Yeah, I've only wrestled
          women, but they were bigger than you!
          In fact, they're probably smarter than
          you, cause you're from "Maaamphis,
          Taaanassee"!
                         (back to his regular voice, he
                          points at his head)
          I'm from Hollywood. I have the
          brains. That's how I win. And Mr.
          Lawler, I'm gonna make you cry "Mama"!

Andy bares his teeth. Enraged, Lawler tries to take a swing
at him. HANDLERS run in and separate the angry men.

105   EXT. MID-SOUTH COLISEUM - LATER THAT NIGHT   105

A nearly deserted parking lot. Andy and Lynne exit the back
VIP door, Andy swaggering arrogantly. Lynne is concerned.

                              LYNNE
          Is this an act -- or are you addicted
          to causing trouble??

                              ANDY
                    (he jokingly impersonates a drunk)
          I can shtop whenever I want...

She's unamused.

                              LYNNE
          Then stop treating me like a fucking
          prop.

                              ANDY
                    (he drops the act)
          I-I'm sorry. I got caught up in the
          action...!

She shoots him a stern look.

                              LYNNE
          I'm warning you, Kaufman: One morning
          you're gonna wake up... and your
          head's gonna be shaved.

Andy laughs.

                                        CUT TO:

106   INT. GEORGE'S OFFICE - DAY   106

George stares glumly at Andy. Andy is quite cheerful -- eating
a big piece of chocolate cake.

                              GEORGE
          Andy, do you realize you don't do
          comedy anymore?? Please, enough with
          the wrestling! You've lost touch with
          reality!

                              ANDY
                    (ingenuous)
          What, you don't think I can beat him?

                              GEORGE
          He is the Southern Heavyweight
          Champion. He'll kill you.
                    (very disapproving)
          First you piss-off women. Then you
          piss-off the South. Then you get
          killed!
                    (dry)
          And I did the bookings.

Andy shrugs, lacking a response. He eats more cake.
Aggravated, George hands him a packet.

GEORGE
Which brings me to your tickets for
Tahoe, for the Tony Clifton
engagement. Gosh, remember those
quaint old days, when <u>Tony</u> was your
most obnoxious character??

ANDY
Yeah.
                (trying to be reassuring)
Well, at least he's no longer really
me!

                                        CUT TO:

107   EXT. HARRAH'S TAHOE - DAY   107

Harrah's marquee brags "TONY CLIFTON"

Underneath, a CAB pulls up. Inside sit Andy and Zmuda. Zmuda
looks uneasy -- his usual bluster gone.

ZMUDA
Man, I hope I can pull this off...

ANDY
Doctor, you'll be fine. Nobody will
<u>ever</u> know it wasn't me.

108   INT. HARRAH'S CASINO - LATER   108

Andy spies into the crowded casino. Beat -- then he swings a
door open and parades through, broadly crossing the casino in an
exaggerated loop. A murmured hush follows.

WHISPERED VOICES
Hey, it's Andy Kaufman...! Look!
See, I <u>knew</u> Kaufman would be here!

Andy smiles mysteriously.

                                        CUT TO:

109   INT. HARRAH'S STATELINE CABARET - NIGHT   109

The big showroom is packed. Standing solo on the huge stage
is Zmuda in the Clifton makeup and peach tux. He's BELTING "I
Gotta Be Me."

TONY CLIFTON (ZMUDA)
"Whether I'm right,
 Or whether I'm wrong
 Whether I find a place in this world,
 Or never belong!
 I gotta be me! I gotta be me!
 What else can I be, but what I am?"

Zmuda is pulling it off. His voice is strong, his movements
jerky. He's just as bad as Andy.

IN THE AUDIENCE

Table after table of dressy people stare. Some grin, some are sickened.

                    PRIM LADY
      He's <u>awful</u>.

                    PRIM MAN
      Yeah, but it's <u>Andy Kaufman</u>.

ONSTAGE

The song FINISHES.

                    TONY CLIFTON (ZMUDA)
      Let's bring it on home --
             (he hits his off-key CLIMAX)
      "I GOTTA BE MEEEEEEE!"

The BAND ends with a brassy punch. The crowd begrudgingly applauds.

Then -- a HECKLING VOICE sotto voce, in back.

                    HECKLER (o.s.)
      You know who that is? That's that
      guy from Taxi!

                    ANNOYED WOMAN
      Shh --

                    HECKLER (o.s.)
      Don't you "shh" me!

We reveal the HECKLER. He has a big hat, long blonde hair, a droopy moustache, and glasses. Actually -- he's Andy.

                    HECKLER (ANDY)
      I'm tellin' you, he's a <u>fake</u>!

ONSTAGE

Tony bows.

                    TONY CLIFTON (ZMUDA)
      Thank you, thank you. That's one of
      my favorites. I wrote that tune for
      my friend Frank Sinatra. He had a
      nice little success with it... but
      forgot to thank me on the album.

                    HECKLER (ANDY)
      YOU'RE A LIAR! You didn't write
      nothing! You're not even <u>yourself</u>!

An awkward silence. Tony glares into the darkness.

                    TONY CLIFTON (ZMUDA)
          Q-quiet. I demand silence when I
          perform.

                    HECKLER (ANDY)
          You're Andy Kaufman!

The crowd MURMURS.

Tony looks around nervously.

                    TONY CLIFTON (ZMUDA)
          I -- I don't know nothin' about no
          Kaufman. He's been ridin' my
          coattails, smearing my reputation.
          Been usin' my good name, to get
          places.

IN THE CROWD

                    PRIM LADY
                 (to her husband)
          Why won't he just admit it?!

The Heckler stands.

                    HECKLER (ANDY)
          This show is a RIPOFF! People are
          payin' to see someone, and they're
          actually getting somebody else!

Suddenly two BOUNCERS IN SUITS glide over.

                    BOUNCER
          Sir, we're going to have to ask you
          to leave.

                    HECKLER (ANDY)
          It's FRAUD! That's why that man
          cannot admit he's Andy Kaufman!

                    TONY CLIFTON (ZMUDA)
                 (shouting from onstage)
          You're nuts. I'm as much Andy Kaufman
          as YOU are!

The Bouncers grab Heckler Andy.

                    HECKLER (ANDY)
                 (frantic)
          You're Andy Kaufman!

                    TONY CLIFTON (ZMUDA)
          No, YOU'RE Andy Kaufman!!

The Bouncers drag the Heckler out. He goes into a Clifton
voice.

               HECKLER (ANDY)
              (doing CLIFTON)
     GETCHER HANDS OFF ME! GETCHER HANDS
     OFF ME! AAAHHHH!

They haul him out. The crowd is beyond dumbfounded.

110   EXT. HARRAH'S TAHOE - SECONDS LATER   110

The lobby doors crash open. The bouncers carry out Heckler Andy
and dump him on the sidewalk. He sits there a second -- then
nonchalantly removes his hat, wig, and moustache. He throws
them in the trash and hails a taxi.

               ANDY
     Take me to the airport. My work here
     is done.

                          CUT TO:

111   SHOWROOM - LATER   111

Tony FINISHES "MY WAY."

           TONY CLIFTON (ZMUDA)
     "I DID IT MYYYYYYYY WAY!"

The band kicks in with brassy curtain call music. The crowd
APPLAUDS, and Tony takes his well-deserved bows.

TIGHT - TONY is dripping sweat. Underneath the rubber face, we
can see Zmuda's eyes -- overwhelmed, exhausted, and flying high.

112   INT. BACKSTAGE - MINUTES LATER   112

Tony walks backstage, toweling himself off. STAGEHANDS nod.

             STAGEHAND
     Great show, Tony.

           TONY CLIFTON (ZMUDA)
     Hey, thanks. Thanks a lot.

Smiling, Tony strides up to his DRESSING ROOM. It says "TONY
CLIFTON" in glitter on the door.

Tony opens the door... and inside is a NAKED BLONDE SHOWGIRL
with stunning breasts. Tony stumbles back, shocked.

           TONY CLIFTON (ZMUDA)
     W-who're <u>you</u>???

             NAKED GIRL
     I've always wanted to suck off Andy
     Kaufman.

Whoa.

Tony/Zmuda slowly glances in the <u>mirror</u> at himself.

A beat -- then he turns back to the girl.

>   TONY CLIFTON (ZMUDA)
>   (as ANDY)
>   Who am I to keep you from your dreams?

He walks toward her, as the door swings SHUT...

>   CUT TO:

113   INT. MID-SOUTH COLISEUM - NIGHT   113

Memphis wrestling. The Announcer stands center ring, booming
into the mike.

>   ANNOUNCER
>   And now, the MAIN EVENT of the
>   evening! The match you've been
>   waiting for! The King Jerry Lawler,
>   versus Hollywood Andy Kaufman!

The THEME FROM "ROCKY" plays -- and Lawler enters from the
tunnel, wearing a shimmery hero's cape! The crowd ROARS with
approval.

114   INT. COLISEUM DRESSING ROOM - SAME TIME   114

Andy is meditating, eyes shut, at rest in his private oasis.

Buddy Rogers shouts desperately.

>   BUDDY ROGERS
>   C'MON, KAUFMAN! Christ, you're ON!

Buddy violently SHAKES him. Andy awakens and smiles.

115   INT. COLISEUM   115

The THEME FROM "MIGHTY MOUSE" begins playing. Then, Andy
strides in, a sneer on his grungy face. The crowd SCREAMS and
BOOS pure pile. Andy is euphoric, loving the hatred.

Both men enter the ring. Andy takes the microphone.

>   ANDY
>   Before we begin this event, I just
>   wanna say a few things to you foul
>   people.
>   (beat)
>   This city is filthy! You Southerners
>   live like pigs! So I'm going to teach
>   you some lessons in hygiene... bring
>   you out of your squalor.

Holy cow. The crowd is flabbergasted.

Women in K-mart dresses gape. Ruddy men in trucker caps glare.

Down front are Lynne and George. He is ashen-faced.

                              GEORGE
               They're gonna lynch him.

In the ring, Andy reaches in his pocket and removes a bar of
SOAP.

                              ANDY
               People, this is a bar of soap. Does
               it look familiar to you? If you wet
               it, it'll clean your hands.

George's eyes bulge.

The crowd is enraged -- rumblings of imminent violence.

Andy smiles helpfully.

                              ANDY
               And now, for your next lesson: This --
               is toilet paper.

Andy holds up a ROLL OF TISSUE.

That's it. The crowd goes NUTS. Jerry Lawler races over and
snatches the mike, trying to maintain his dignity.

                              LAWLER
               Kaufman, we've had enough!! Let's
               you and me do what we came here for
               -- WRESTLING!

                                             CUT TO:

116 SECONDS LATER   116

And DING! That's the bell! Andy strikes a threatening pose.

Lawler takes a step forward -- and Andy instantly, cowardly runs
for the ropes and jumps out of the ring.

BOOOOO!!! Andy grins at the crowd and points at his brain: I'm
smarter.

                         ANNOUNCER (V.O.)
               And Kaufman's left the ring! Lawler's
               waiting for him to return.

                              LYNNE
                         (to George)
               It looks like Andy figured out a
               strategy.

Lawler disparagingly frowns. The REF checks his watch. Andy
crosses to the opposite end of the ring, gauging his rival...
then slowly climbs in --

Until the second Lawler moves. Then Andy quickly jumps back
out!

                     ANNOUNCER (V.O.)
         And Kaufman's left the ring <u>again</u>!
         He doesn't seem interested in actually
         making contact with his opponent.

Andy struts around the floor, pointing at his brain. He smirks
at various spectators... until suddenly finding himself
face-to-face -- with George.

An unexpected moment. Andy's finger frozen on his brain.
George shakes his head disapprovingly. A beat -- then Andy gets
HIT in the head with a cup.

People HOOT. Disoriented, Andy returns to the ringside. Lawler
is losing his patience.

                     LAWLER
         Hey! Did you come down here to
         wrestle, or to act like an ass?

Andy paces around, unsure of his next move.

                     LAWLER
         Look... if you get in here, I'll give
         ya a free headlock.

Lawler leans down and offers his neck.

Andy peers skeptically. People jeer. Andy looks at waiting
Lawler... then tentatively climbs in.

As promised, Lawler doesn't move. So Andy crosses over and
GRABS Lawler's head! Andy grins triumphantly. He squeezes his
arms tight, muscles flexing, riding high on this moment.

Until -- Lawler stands and flips him over. Andy SLAMS DOWN on
his back. CRUNCH!

                     ANNOUNCER (V.O.)
         It's a side suplex!!

Andy lies on the mat, unmoving. Lawler doesn't care. He picks
up Andy's prone body and grips it upside-down, against his
chest.

                     REFEREE
           (frantically gesturing)
        No! NO!

Lawler disregards the ref and slams Andy's head in a pile-
driver!!

A horrible THUD.

DING! The BELL immediately RINGS.

                     ANNOUNCER (V.O.)
         Lawler has committed a PILEDRIVER,
         which is an AUTOMATIC
         DISQUALIFICATION!

                    LYNNE
        Jesus Christ, he's not moving!

                    REFEREE
        Match goes to Kaufman by
        disqualification, after two minutes,
        twelve seconds!

Andy is splayed unconscious.

Raging Lawler promenades around the ring, arms over his head.
The crowd shouts, "AGAIN! AGAIN!" Goaded, Lawler picks up Andy,
raises him... and PILEDRIVES HIM AGAIN.

BAM!! Jesus -- Andy's floppy head SLAMS into the ground yet
again.

George runs to the ropes, SCREAMING for help.

                    GEORGE
        Andy! <u>Andy</u>!

Andy stares up, eyes glassy.

                    GEORGE
        Somebody GET A DOCTOR!!

                                        CUT TO:

117 EXT. MID-SOUTH COLISEUM - NIGHT   117

An AMBULANCE screeches up, SIREN wailing.

POLICE clear a path.

Andy is wheeled from the building on a gurney. He isn't moving.
Frantic Lynne and George run after him. PARAMEDICS quickly load
Andy into the ambulance.

118 INT. KAUFMAN FAMILY HOME - NIGHT   118

Stanley and Janice are asleep in bed.

Suddenly the phone RINGS. Janice groggily reaches for it.

                    JANICE
        Hello...
            (suddenly horrible news)
        OH MY GOD.

ANGLE - TV

Stanley and Janice run to their TV and click it on. A LOCAL
NEWSCAST is beginning.

                    LOCAL ANCHOR (ON TV)
        ...and in our top story tonight,
        comedian Andy Kaufman has been injured
        in a freak accident in a Memphis
        wrestling ring.

Stanley fearfully clutches Janice. We stay on their wan
faces...

> LOCAL ANCHOR (o.s.)
> Kaufman has been rushed to a nearby
> hospital, where doctors are checking
> him for possible paralysis. Fans will
> best remember him as lovable Latka
> on television's "Taxi"...

Overcome, Janice starts crying.

119   INT. MEMPHIS HOSPITAL - DARKENED ROOM - NIGHT   119

Andy is alone with a DOCTOR. They examine an X-RAY of Andy's
neck.

> DOCTOR
> I just don't see anything, Mr.
> Kaufman. Your neck has sustained no
> trauma whatsoever.

> ANDY
> (annoyed)
> You're SURE I didn't break it?

> DOCTOR
> Look at you -- you're sitting here
> fine! Perhaps it's sprained... but
> there's nothing on the X-ray.

Andy is irked.

In the b.g., a NURSE discreetly carries in the biggest flower
arrangement you've ever seen. Intrigued, Andy hurries over and
opens the CARD.

It says, "Andy, we're all praying for you. Your friends at
Taxi."

Andy chuckles. He turns to the Doctor.

> ANDY
> Maybe I need a neck brace.

> DOCTOR
> In my opinion, you don't. If it makes
> you feel better, you could try a
> little ice --

> ANDY
> I don't WANT any ice! I want a NECK
> BRACE!
> (he rubs his neck)
> C'mon, Doc. If you think it's
> sprained, a brace couldn't hurt...

The Doctor gives Andy a weird look.

                                                    CUT TO:

120   INT. MEMPHIS HOSPITAL - ANDY'S ROOM - LATER   120

Andy sits propped up in bed, happily wearing a NECK BRACE.

Lynne feeds him jello.

The phone RINGS. Andy answers it.

                         ANDY
              Hello?

                                              INTERCUT:

121   FRANTIC STANLEY AND JANICE   121

                         STANLEY
              God, ANDY! We found you!! Are you
              okay, son???!

                         ANDY
              Yeah, I'm fine.

                         JANICE
                    (crying)
              No matter what happens -- even if you
              can't ever walk again, we'll still
              love you --!!

                         ANDY
              Mom, Dad, calm down. Really, I'm
              fine. It's phony baloney -- I faked
              the whole thing.

A confused beat.

                         STANLEY
              B-but... we saw, on the TV -- you
              smashed your head...

                         ANDY
              No, it was just a yoga move. I tucked
              my head in -- it didn't hurt at all.

Silence.

Stanley considers all this... and then a FURY comes over him.

                         STANLEY
              Andrew -- HOW DARE YOU!!
                    (livid)
              For all we knew, you could have been
              DYING! Your mother and I were worried
              sick!

TIGHT - ANDY

He is genuinely shocked.

                         ANDY
              Geez... I'm sorry. I figured you
              realized it all by now.
                    (he slowly continues)
              Here's the rule of thumb: <u>Anything</u>
              <u>that happens to me</u>... IS NOT REAL.

                                                  CUT TO:

122   EXT. ZMUDA'S HOUSE - NEXT MORNING   122

Early morning. A door opens, and Zmuda shuffles out, wearing
a bathrobe. He picks up the morning newspaper -- and freezes.

The HEADLINE says "TAXI STAR ANDY KAUFMAN CRITICALLY INJURED."

A beat... then Zmuda LAUGHS heartily.

                         ZMUDA
              That's great...!

He giggles giddily and walks back in.

123   INT. MEMPHIS HOSPITAL - MORNING   123

George pushes Andy to the exit in a wheelchair. Andy proudly
wears his neckbrace. Lynne follows.

                         GEORGE
              Foreign Man was funny. Elvis was
              incredible... the best I ever saw.
              But <u>this</u> -- I don't understand...

                         ANDY
                    (whispering)
              George, people feel sorry for me.
              I'm America's hero.

                         GEORGE
              You're delusional. You're America's
              carnival freak.

The exit DOORS open...

124   EXT. HOSPITAL - SAME TIME   124

And outside is a wall of PHOTOGRAPHERS AND TV CREWS.

FLASH! FLASH! FLASH! A zillion cameras go off. Andy squints
into the light, trembling, jaw clenched over his brace.

                         ANDY
                    (very weak)
              I... feel... fine...

                                                  CUT TO:

125   EXT. ANDY'S APARTMENT BUILDING - L.A. - DAY   125

A cab pulls up. Andy gets out, still wearing the <u>neckbrace</u>.
He reaches for his luggage -- and the CABBIE quickly steps in.

                    CABBIE
          No, please -- let me carry it.

Andy raises an eyebrow.

126   EXT. PARAMOUNT STUDIOS - DAY   126

Andy drives up to the gate. He's wearing the neckbrace. The
studio GUARD sees him and hands Andy a BLUE HANDICAPPED plaque.

                    GUARD
          Here, Mr. Kaufman. The studio wants
          you to park right next to the stage
          door.

Andy smiles.

127   INT. TAXI SOUNDSTAGE - DAY   127

A dress rehearsal. On the set, Judd Hirsch motions to Andy.

                    JUDD HIRSCH (AS ALEX)
          "Hey Latka, can you figure out why
          my car's leaking oil?"

Andy nods. He starts to kneel and lie on a mechanic's
rollboard... but is constrained <u>by his neckbrace</u>. Like a piece
of absurd slapstick, he cannot seem to figure out how to lie
back and get under the car.

UP IN THE BOOTH

The show WRITERS stare at this mess.

                    WRITER 1
          This is ridiculous! <u>Latka doesn't
          wear a neckbrace</u>.

                    WRITER 2
          Do we have to explain it?

                    WRITER 3
          Maybe we can put him in a turtleneck.

At the CONSOLE sits Ed, glaring suspiciously at a small TV
screen. On it is <u>Andy's wrestling injury moment</u>. Like a man
possessed, Ed twirls an editing knob, going forward-back,
forward-back, analyzing the moment of impact like the Zapruder
film.

Ed growls. Frame by frame, Andy's head <u>bends under</u> as it hits
the mat. Suddenly -- Ed jumps up and rushes out.

128   ON SET - LATER   128

Andy is resting in a chair. Ed approaches.

                         ED
               Andy, can we talk?

                         ANDY
               Sure, Ed. Just gimme a moment.

Like an old man, Andy stiffly gets up, clenching his neck in the
brace. Ed waits irritably. Andy hobbles over...

                         ED
               Alright, you can cut the bullshit.
               I know you're not injured.

                         ANDY
                       (surprised)
               B-but... my neck --

                         ED
               No buts. I'm not playing your party
               games anymore. The ratings for Taxi
               aren't as good as they once were --
               and I can't afford to have Latka
               pulling some unexplained weirdness.

Oh. Andy considers this... truly comprehending the problem.

                         ANDY
               When is this episode gonna air?

                         ED
               The third week of October.

Beat.

                         ANDY
               Okay. My neck'll be better by then.

With a velcro RIP, Andy yanks off the brace.

                                                        CUT TO:

129   EXT. ROCKEFELLER CENTER - DAY   129

George sits with the "Saturday Night Live" Producer. They're
in an outdoor cafe.

                         GEORGE
               Thank you for seeing me.

                         SNL PRODUCER
               Thank you for flying 3000 miles to
               have lunch.

George takes a careful beat.

                    GEORGE
          I... I wanted to talk to you about
          booking Andy on "Saturday Night Live."

                    SNL PRODUCER
                    (uncomfortable)
          Gee... I don't know if Andy works for
          our show anymore. That wrestling
          stuff...
                    (choosing his words)
          is such a turnoff.

                    GEORGE
          We agree completely.
                    (tactfully begging)
          Andy has to reconnect with his core
          audience. So I got him on "Letterman"
          tonight. He's gonna apologize to
          Jerry Lawler, then repent for all his
          bad guy shenanigans.

The Producer mulls this over.

                    SNL PRODUCER
          That's smart.

                    GEORGE
          He's very sincere.
                    (quietly emphatic)
          He needs this.

Beat. The guy nods.

                    SNL PRODUCER
          Okay. It'd be good to have the old
          Andy back.

                                        CUT TO:

130 INT. DAVID LETTERMAN SHOW - NIGHT   130

Andy and Jerry Lawler are on DAVID LETTERMAN'S show. Andy is
pallid, hair shaggy, in a neckbrace and tweed jacket. Husky
Lawler wears loud red pants and gold chains.

Andy speaks timidly, in the style of his early-days sweetness.

                    ANDY
          I apologize for all the wrestling I've
          ever done. For all the abuse I've
          ever given...
                    (soft, regretful)
          I was just playing bad guy wrestler.
          That's not me... it's just a role.
          But Jerry took it personally.

Lawler and Letterman are unimpressed.

                         LETTERMAN
              You said some pretty inflammatory
              things.

                         JERRY LAWLER
              He thinks everything's a joke -- but
              it's not.
                         (to Andy)
              Did you laugh when you were layin'
              in the hospital??

The crowd WHOOOOS.

Angst flickers on Andy's sweaty face. He stammers.

                         ANDY
              T-there wasn't a reason to purposely
              hurt me --

                         JERRY LAWLER
              You're a wimp.

                         ANDY
                    (upset)
              My father said I should've gotten a
              lawyer --!

                         JERRY LAWLER
              Then your father's a wimp.

                         ANDY
                    (losing it)
              And, you're just poor white trash!

Lawler's had enough. Enraged, he wildly stands and SLAPS Andy.

BAM!

Andy crashes over and falls from his chair.

THUD. He's on the floor.

Dead silence. Everyone is astonished.

They're all slack-jawed. Even PAUL SHAFFER. Trying to cover,
Paul hurriedly kicks in with a ROCKABILLY TUNE.

Andy jumps up, crazed.

                         ANDY
              I'M SICK AND TIRED OF THIS SHIT!

Lawler freezes in his seat. Letterman hides behind his desk.

Andy storms over, out-of-control. From a safe distance, he
starts SCREAMING at Lawler.

                        ANDY
          YOU ARE FULL OF SHIT, LAWLER! I WILL
          SUE YOUR ASS! YOU'RE A FUCKING
          ASSHOLE!
                    (he POUNDS the desk)
          FUCK YOU! FUCK YOU! I WILL GET YOU
          FOR THIS!!!

Freaked, Andy leaps up and storms out.

The crowd CHEERS rowdily.

An unsure moment. Dave glances at Lawler.

Until, Andy stumbles back in. He tries to calm himself.

                        ANDY
          I am sorry. I am <u>sorry</u> to use those
          words on television. I apologize!
          I'm sorry!
                    (demented)
          But YOU -- you're a MOTHERFUCKING
          ASSHOLE!!!!

Andy SLAMS Dave's desk. Dave jerks nervously.

Crazed, Andy looks down at Dave's coffee cup. Uh-oh. Suddenly,
Andy <u>grabs the coffee and DUMPS it on Lawler</u>!

Lawler jumps, burned.

A SECURITY GUARD runs in.

Andy screams and hurtles away. He slams open the stage door
and barrels out of sight.

                                        INTERCUT:

131 THE SNL PRODUCER WATCHING THIS AT HOME   131

He gapes in disbelief.

                        SNL PRODUCER
          Jesus Christ.

                                        CUT TO:

132 INT. SATURDAY NIGHT LIVE - ONE WEEK LATER   132

The SNL Producer stands on stage, speaking into camera. The
show's going out live.

                        SNL PRODUCER
          Hi. Um, we were supposed to have Andy
          Kaufman on our show this week -- but
          now we aren't sure if it's such a good
          idea.
                    (more)

> SNL PRODUCER (Cont'd)
> (beat)
> Some of us at "Saturday Night Live"
> think Kaufman's a comic genius. But
> others disagree... they say he's just
> not funny anymore.
> (beat)
> So we're putting the decision up to
> <u>you</u>. Please call up and vote. To
> keep Andy, call 1-900-244-7618. To
> DUMP him, call...

133   INT. GEORGE'S OFFICE - DAY   133

Tight on Andy, staring at the L.A. Times. A small headline says
"JOKESTER ANDY KAUFMAN VOTED OFF 'SATURDAY NIGHT LIVE'"

He is bothered.

> ANDY
> This is bad. I only got 28 percent!
> I'm like McGovern in '72...

George sighs.

> GEORGE
> And this wasn't "Merv." This was the
> hippest audience on television.
> (grim)
> They've turned on you.

> ANDY
> (thinking)
> Maybe I can turn it into a bit. I
> can go back on the show, and say it
> was rigged. Demand a recount...

> GEORGE
> Andy! You don't get it!
> (somber)
> <u>They don't want you back</u>.

At that... we reveal that SOMEONE ELSE is sitting next to Andy.
But only the back of his head is visible.

George glares at him.

> GEORGE
> It's like you two guys <u>wanted</u> to
> destroy Andy's career! Upsetting all
> those people... putting out that toxic
> venom...
> (helpless)
> What did you THINK would happen??!

> ANDY
> (guilty)
> We were just trying to push the
> envelope.

                    GEORGE
          You're BLIND! There is no envelope
          anymore!!
                    (angry)
          It hurts me to say this... but there's
          only one solution --
                    (pained)
          I don't want you two to ever work
          together again.

WE WIDEN...

And the other person is JERRY LAWLER. He feels bad.

                    JERRY LAWLER
          I'm sorry. We thought it was funny...

                    ANDY
          Jer', it's not your fault. You were
          terrific.
                    (sad)
          But maybe George is right...

                    JERRY LAWLER
          That's fine. But I wouldn't have
          traded it for anything...
                    (poignant)
          Because for one brief, shining
          moment... the world thought that
          wrestling was real.

Andy gulps emotionally.

                    ANDY
          We'll stay in touch. Next time I'm
          in Memphis, I'll stop by the house,
          and Noreen can make me her double
          chocolate cake.

                    JERRY LAWLER
          Alright, buddy...
                    (choked up)
          Stay good.

Andy and Jerry hug.

                                        CUT TO:

134 EXT. MAGIC MOUNTAIN - DAY   134

Andy and Zmuda ride on a rollercoaster. They SCREAM happily
as the car drops down the hill.

                    ZMUDA
          It's good to have you back.

                    ANDY
          Were you jealous?

                        ZMUDA
          Oh, fuck you.

135 ANGLE - A CANDY CART   135

Andy goes up to a CANDY VENDOR.

                        ANDY
          Two cotton candies, please.

                        CANDY VENDOR
          Or what? You'll <u>hit</u> me?

Andy is taken aback.

He and Zmuda quickly pay, then hurry off.

                        ZMUDA
          God, you're on everyone's shit list.
          You gotta fix that.

                        ANDY
              (beat)
          If I died, they'd miss me. <u>Then</u>
          they'd be sorry.

                        ZMUDA
          It's working for Elvis.

                        ANDY
          Sure! He's layin' low, but when he
          comes back, he'll be bigger than ever!

                        ZMUDA
              (agreeing)
          How about this: Before your career
          went into freefall, "Fridays" said
          you could host. I could sneak a gun
          into the studio and shoot you!

                        ANDY
              (getting excited)
          Yeah! And I'll put fake brains inside
          a wig, so when I die my head <u>explodes</u>!

A giddy moment... until reality hits. The guys sigh.

                        ZMUDA
          This is <u>not</u> what George wants to hear.

                        ANDY
          He wants happy... nice. He wishes
          I were -- the Hudson Brothers.

Andy scratches his head.

                        ANDY
          What do really bad people do, when
          they need to clear their names?

                    ZMUDA
        The Watergate guys found God.

                    ANDY
                (his face lights up)
        Hey, that's good...

They grin naughtily at each other.

                                            CUT TO:

136 EST. BOOKSTORE - DAY   136

     A sign says "CHRISTIAN BOOKS AND MUSIC"

137 INT. CHRISTIAN BOOKSTORE   137

     Andy and Zmuda hunt through gospel records.

                    ZMUDA
              What about her?

     Zmuda holds up an album. The cover shows a backlit HEAVYSET
     BLACK WOMAN. It says "Touched By The Lord."

     Andy stifles a giggle.

                    ANDY
              That's funny -- but I wouldn't believe
              it. This could be my last shot...
              we've got to sell it.
                    (he goes through more records,
                     then grins)
              HEY, how about her??!

     He excitedly lifts an album: "Cathy Sullivan - Walking With
     Jesus." Gospel singer CATHY SULLIVAN has Osmond-size teeth and
     a Farrah Fawcett haircut. She reeks sincerity.

                    ZMUDA
              She's amazing. Look at those teeth!

                    ANDY
                (suddenly doubting)
              Oh, why would she go along with it?
              I've got nothing to offer her...

     Zmuda hits him.

                    ZMUDA
              You idiot, it's TV!
                (cocky)
              She'll get national exposure!!!

                                            CUT TO:

138   INT. FRIDAYS STAGE - NIGHT   138

Live television. Andy stands on stage, his appearance
completely changed: Gone is the unshaven sweaty face and the
messy hair. Andy is now CHRISTIAN ANDY: Freshly-washed face
with a rosy glow, neatly-trimmed haircut, and glistening, happy
eyes. He's dressed in a tidy, off-the-rack three-piece suit.

Andy smiles earnestly and empty-headedly. He has the grin of
a lobotomy victim.

                         ANDY
             I would like to thank "Fridays," for
             giving me the opportunity to come
             back, after what I did here.
                   (beat)
             That was a low point in my life.
             Since then, I've gone through a lot
             of changes. And I would like to bring
             out a person who has helped me a great
             deal through this period, and been
             very influential to me. Her name is
             Cathy Sullivan.

CATHY SULLIVAN strides out, a remarkably sincere Christian woman
in a long blue dress with a prim white collar.

Cathy crosses over to Andy. They look into each other's eyes,
then kiss sweetly.

                         ANDY
             I would like to announce that Cathy
             and I are engaged.

The audience is surprised, then APPLAUDS. Andy warmly hugs
Cathy. She holds his hand, smiling with anticipation.

                         CATHY
             During this past year... I've had a
             chance to share my faith with Andy.
             And there's been a big change.
                   (beat)
             Andy has recently become a Christian.
             And I just thank God that I was given
             the opportunity to not only turn
             around his life, but to be a part of
             it.

Andy hugs her tighter. Scattered applause. Andy fondly kisses
her forehead.

                         CATHY
             And we'll probably end up with a bunch
             of little kids running around the
             house, saying "Tank you veddy much!"
                   (she smiles)
             We'd like to sing a song for you, that
             really says just how Andy and I feel.
             It's called "Home Again."

They take handheld mikes. Cheesy CHRISTIAN MUSIC starts
playing. Andy drops his head reverently. Cathy stoically
begins SINGING.

> CATHY
> "Lord it's me... I'm home again."

> ANDY
> (he ardently JOINS IN SINGING)
> "Guess you've wondered where I've been."

Cathy beams proudly.

> ANDY AND CATHY
> "But I've been gone for quite awhile,
> And I've missed the mark a mile,
> And I'm finding I don't know where to begin."

IN THE WINGS

Lynne watches with Jack Burns.

> JACK
> Who woulda thought Andy would fall
> in love?

> LYNNE
> (nodding)
> I thought he only dated bimbos.

                                        CUT TO:

139   EXT. FAIRFIELD, IOWA - DAY   139

Andy and Little Wendy drive in a rental car, through Iowa. She
is confused.

> LITTLE WENDY
> So you're <u>not</u> marrying her?

> ANDY
> No! I barely know her.

> LITTLE WENDY
> It looked real to me.

> ANDY
> Wendy, it was just a goof! I'm not
> really born again.

Wendy frowns.

> LITTLE WENDY
> I dunno... Some things you shouldn't
> joke about.

They drive through some rustic gates. They're in Meditation
Institute University.

140   EXT. MIU FACILITY - PARKING LOT   140

Various TM FOLLOWERS get out of their cars, carrying suitcases
inside. Tranquil, benign, they greet each other.

                    TM LADY
          Hi! I didn't know you were coming!

                    TM GUY
          It's great to see you!

They happily hug.

Andy and Little Wendy walk up, carrying duffel bags. They
approach the building -- when a GENTLE MAN IN A ROBE steps up.

                    GENTLE MAN
          Hi, Andy...

                    ANDY
          Hi, Kevin!

                    GENTLE MAN
                (awkward)
          Could I... speak with you for a
          moment?

Anxious, he pulls Andy aside.

                    GENTLE MAN
          This is very difficult for me to
          say... but -- perhaps it would be
          best-if you didn't attend the retreat.

                    ANDY
                (surprised)
          What are you talking about? I attend
          every year.

                    GENTLE MAN
          Yes -- we do not doubt your devotion
          to TM. But we feel that perhaps...
          you and the program have grown apart
          philosophically.

Andy is stunned.

                    ANDY
          "Philosophically"?

                    GENTLE MAN
                (he sighs)
          The wrestling... the sexist remarks...
          that sarcastic Christian conversion...
          these things are not becoming of an
          enlightened individual.
                (beat)
          It seems you have no respect for
          <u>anything</u>.

Andy is stupefied. He doesn't know how to respond.

> ANDY
> Of course I do...

The guy shakes his head.

Andy can't believe it. He looks around, and notices FACES in an upstairs window. Ten MEN IN TURBANS stare down, watching.

Andy cracks.

> ANDY
> Please! You've GOT to let me take the classes! It's how I keep myself BALANCED!!

> GENTLE MAN
> It's obviously not working.

> ANDY
> So HELP ME! All I wanna do is MEDITATE!!

> GENTLE MAN
> (pained)
> Andy, don't raise your voice. We don't wish your presence here.

The man turns away and walks off.

Andy is broken.

He fights to bottle his rage -- then notices Little Wendy inside, peering through the glass doors. Beaten, Andy waves goodbye to her.

Wendy gulps and waves goodbye too.

> CUT TO:

141   INT. ANDY'S APARTMENT - DAY   141

Middle of the afternoon, Andy lies in bed. Covers pulled up to his face, expression glum, he's like a tragic still-life.

Suddenly DING-DONG! The doorbell rings.

No reaction. Andy ignores it.

Another DING-DONG! Then KNOCKING.

> ANDY
> Go away.

Then, odd SCRATCHING. He looks over, and a coat hanger creeps in under the door and struggles for the knob. Andy groans, resigned.

                    ANDY
          Oh, it's open.

The door opens. Lynne enters, holding a carton of ice cream.

                    LYNNE
          I brought you Haagen Dazs. Chocolate.

                    ANDY
                (mournful)
          I'm a horrible person. I don't
          deserve Haagen Dazs.

                    LYNNE
          Andy, you're not horrible. You're
          just... complicated.

                    ANDY
          I'm not enlightened.

                    LYNNE
          Forget what they said!
                (genuine)
          I like you.

He shakes his head.

                    ANDY
          You don't know the real me.

                    LYNNE
          Andy... there is no real you.

TIGHT - ANDY

An astonished silence.

And then... he slowly smiles.

                    ANDY
          Yeah, you're probably right.

They both giggle.

Andy studies her... looking at Lynne's face, body, eyes. Pause.

                    ANDY
          Do you wanna move in together?

Lynne smiles slyly. She leans down and kisses him.

                                        CUT TO:

142   EXT. LAUREL CANYON HOUSE - DAY   142

A moving van outside a funky 60's house. MOVERS carry boxes
in.

143   INT. LAUREL CANYON HOUSE - SAME TIME   143

Andy sits disoriented in the living room. Movers bustle around
him. Mirrors get leaned against opposing walls -- and he finds
himself looking into multiple reflections of himself.

In the b.g., Lynne arranges some vases, then hurries out. Andy
opens a box and pulls out his old Howdy Doody doll. He smiles,
then places Howdy on the shelf next to the vases.

Pause -- and he realizes how dumb Howdy looks in the grown-up
house. Andy frowns and quickly throws Howdy back in the box.

Suddenly a phone on the floor RINGS. He grins.

                    ANDY
          Hey! Our first phone call!
                    (he scrambles for the phone)
          Hello?

                    GEORGE (v.o., on phone)
          Andy... it's me. I've got some crummy
          news.
                    (long beat)
          Taxi's been canceled.

Silence.

Andy has no response.

                    GEORGE (v.o.)
          Do you want me to come over? Talk
          about it?

                    ANDY
          Um... no. Uh, I'm sorta busy right
          now. Thanks. We'll get together next
          week.

Andy hangs up. He just sits there... confused... unsure how
to react.

Andy scratches his head -- then feels something odd. He goes
over to the mirror. On the back of his neck... is an inflamed
red pimple. Andy grimaces.

                    ANDY
          Yuck!

                                        CUT TO:

144   INT. L.A. IMPROV - LATE NIGHT   144

Very late -- a clock says 1:15. A YOUNG COMIC is onstage,
performing to the DOZEN audience members left.

In back walks... Andy. Unshaven, morose, he quietly approaches
paternal owner Budd Friedman. Budd sees him, grins, and gives
him a hearty hug. Andy points at the stage and asks for
something -- Budd eagerly nods.

145   LATER   145

Budd is onstage.

                         BUDD
               And now we have a treat for you
               late-night diehards. The star of Taxi
               -- here in person, Andy Kaufman!

The sparse crowd applauds. Budd leaves, and Andy shuffles up.

                         ANDY
               Actually, Budd, you're wrong. I found
               out today that Taxi's been canceled.

The crowd AWWWWS sadly. Andy blinks.

                         ANDY
               Yeah, that's how I felt too... though
               I don't know why. Cause for years,
               all I wanted to do was get off that
               show.
                    (quiet, very confessional)
               But now that nobody will hire me, and
               nobody thinks I'm funny... I guess
               it was probably a pretty good job.

One guy LAUGHS sharply.

Andy gives him a look -- thinks -- then continues.

                         ANDY
               Not to mention that my wife and kids
               have left me.
                    (he sighs)
               I don't know what I'm gonna do with
               myself.   My options are sorta
               limited...
                    (beat)
               This morning, I noticed I've got a
               cyst, or some kind of boil, on the
               back of my neck. I'm gonna go see
               a doctor -- it's really disgusting.
               Look.

Andy turns. The red lump is bigger, grosser. The crowd GROANS,
revolted.

                         ANDY
               So I was thinking, since I'm sort of
               a quasi-celebrity, that I could charge
               people to touch it.
                    (candid)
               Does anybody want to pay a buck to
               touch my cyst?

A couple stoners GIGGLE and CLAP. Andy COUGHS, then frowns.

                         ANDY
               I'm serious.

Pause. Then... a few people stand and walk up to the stage.

The first taker is a GOOFY BLONDE WOMAN. She starts to reach for the cyst -- when Andy stops her.

> ANDY
> No no, you gotta pay first.

She nods, discomforted, and reaches for her purse...

                                                    CUT TO:

146   LATER - AT THE BAR   146

A BUSBOY sweeps up. Budd counts money in the cash register.

Andy shuffles out of the showroom. He waves some bills.

> ANDY
> I made six bucks. That's good money.

Budd stares sadly.

> BUDD
> This is a comedy club -- not a medical
> sideshow.
>   (trying to be kind)
> If you wanna perform here, take a
> shower, get some sleep, and pull
> yourself together. Come back and do
> the material that people love: Do the
> Mighty Mouse, the foreign guy! Andy,
> you gotta snap out of this funk! If
> you can -- I'll give you the headline
> spot tomorrow.

TIGHT - ANDY

He stares at Budd, wheels spinning.

                                                    CUT TO:

147   EXT. L.A. IMPROV - NEXT NIGHT   147

George is driving down Melrose, listening to the radio. He
glances at the passing marquee -- then does a doubletake.

It says "ANDY KAUFMAN - 9 P.M."

148   INT. IMPROV - MINUTES LATER   148

Puzzled George hurries inside. COMICS greet him: "Hey George!"
"George, you got a second?!" George distractedly waves and
moves toward the showroom...

At the door, he finds Budd.

> GEORGE
> Hey, what's going on here?

                              BUDD
              George, you won't believe it... I got
              Andy to do the <u>old material</u>!
                    (grinning)
              And he's <u>killin'</u> them!

Inside, there's HUGE LAUGHTER. George's eyes widen.

Piqued, he goes in...

149   SHOWROOM   149

And it's packed! Andy is onstage, playing <u>struggling, lovable</u>
<u>Foreign Man</u>.

                    ANDY (AS FOREIGN MAN)
              ...but one ting I do not like is too
              much traffic. Tonight I had to come
              on de freeway, and it was so much
              traffic...
                    (giggling)
              It took me <u>an hour and a half to get</u>
              <u>here</u>!

Foreign Man chuckles pathetically.

The crowd HOWLS. Andy's rockin'.

                    ANDY (AS FOREIGN MAN)
              But talking about the terrible things:
              My wife. Take my --

                    INTERRUPTING JERK
              "Take my wife, please take her."

                    ANDY (AS FOREIGN MAN)
              T-take my wife, please take her...

The rhythm is thrown. A couple laughs.

A flustered pause. Andy glances down, then continues.

                    ANDY (AS FOREIGN MAN)
              No really, I am only foolink. I love
              my wife very much. But she don't know
              how to cook --

                    INTERRUPTING JERK
              "Her cooking is so bad, is terrible."

                    ANDY (AS FOREIGN MAN)
              H-her cooking...
                    (Andy stumbles uncomfortably)
              Uh, cooking is so bad, is <u>terrible</u>.

The laughs are weaker. The act is getting wrecked.

IN BACK

George grimaces. Who the hell's doing this??

Angry, George hurries down front, looking for the loud jerk.
He scans the tables... and it's <u>Zmuda</u>.

> ANDY (AS FOREIGN MAN)
> But right now --

> ZMUDA (AS JERK)
> "But right now I would like to do for
> you some imitations. First, the
> Archie Bunker."

Andy freezes up.

The audience is embarrassed.

A frazzled confusion, then Andy <u>drops</u> the accent. He glares
at Zmuda.

> ANDY
> Sir, do you have a problem?

> ZMUDA (AS JERK)
> Yeah, my problem is you're <u>tired</u>.

Andy winces.

> ANDY
> I, I was <u>asked</u> to do this material --

> ZMUDA (AS JERK)
> Sure, because your new stuff's a bunch
> of <u>crap</u>. Kaufman, people are sick
> of <u>you</u>. The wrestling... the
> hoaxes...

> ANDY
> (defensive)
> Hey -- that stuff gets written-up in
> the papers --

> ZMUDA (AS JERK)
> Who gives a shit?! It's <u>not funny</u>!

ON GEORGE

He's dumbfounded.

> GEORGE
> Why...? Andy, <u>why</u>...?

ON ANDY AND ZMUDA

> ZMUDA
> I used to think you were original.

> ANDY
> I was <u>very</u> original!

                        ZMUDA
          Yeah, exactly -- "was"! But now,
          you're creatively bankrupt.
                    (he gleams cruelly)
          In fact, Ladies and Gentlemen,
          Kaufman's so desperate, he PAID me
          to do this tonight!! I'm a plant.
          It's just a fresh coat of paint on
          an old broken-down routine.
                    (back to Andy)
          Isn't that true???

Andy shudders.

The audience averts their eyes.

A painful silence.

"Andy Kaufman" has been destroyed.

                                           CUT TO:

150   EXT. L.A. IMPROV - LATE THAT NIGHT   150

Andy and George walk sadly down the street.

There is a horrible gloom over them.

                        ANDY
          I was just trying to keep in step with
          the times...
                    (sad)
          The world thinks Andy Kaufman sucks.
          So I was just giving 'em what they
          want...

George stops.

                        GEORGE
          Andy, they don't think you suck.
          They've just... lost a reason to love
          you.
                    (he gently takes Andy)
          You've gotta make the public embrace
          you again. You have to win back their
          sympathy...

No response. Andy knows he's right.

                                           CUT TO:

151   INT. LAUREL CANYON HOUSE - MORNING   151

Lynne wakes up in the new bedroom. She looks over -- and Andy's
not there.

Lynne's baffled.

                                           CUT TO:

152   INT. HOUSE - AFTERNOON   152

End of the day. Lynne's on the phone.

                         LYNNE
              Hey, Zmuda. Is Andy with you?
                    (concerned)
              It's weird... he's been gone all
              day...

153   INT. GEORGE SHAPIRO'S HOUSE - LATE NIGHT   153

George is asleep in bed. Suddenly the PHONE RINGS.

He jerks up, startled. The clock says 4 a.m. Groggy, he
fumbles for the phone.

                         GEORGE
              Hellllo...

                         ANDY (v.o.)
              George.

                         GEORGE
              Andy! Where have you been?! People
              have been worried sick!

                         ANDY (v.o.)
              There was some stuff I had to do.
                    (unsure pause)
              I've got something important to tell
              you. Can we get together for
              breakfast?

                         GEORGE
              Sure... what time tomorrow?

                         ANDY
                    (confused)
              Tomorrow? No -- NOW.

George tiredly looks at the clock. 4:01.

                                             CUT TO:

154   INT. DENNY'S - NIGHT   154

Late-night. Hollywood weirdos are scattered about.

In a booth, Andy sits with bleary Lynne, Zmuda, and George.
Zmuda admires the menu.

                         ZMUDA
              Look at that Grand Slam! Two eggs,
              two bacon, two sausage, two pancakes
              -- $2.99! How do they do it?

                         LYNNE
              They get you on the coffee.

                    GEORGE
                  (irritable)
          Excuse me -- but could Andy tell us
          why we're here???

All heads turn.

A long pause.

Andy stiffly speaks.

                    ANDY
          I have cancer.

Beat. Zmuda nods.

                    ZMUDA
          Hey, that's good! We can make that
          play.
                  (spitballing)
          And we'll really drag it out... You
          get better, you get worse --

                    GEORGE
          FORGET IT. It's in terrible taste!
          I want nothing to do with this.

Pause. Lynne is crestfallen.

                    LYNNE
          I think he's serious.

                    ZMUDA
                  (grinning)
          Serious like a heart attack! Maybe
          we can bring back Cathy Sullivan to
          tend to him!

Andy softly shakes his head.

                    ANDY
          No, it's true. I have lung cancer.

                    GEORGE
          That's ridiculous. You don't even
          smoke.

                    ANDY
                  (emphatic)
          I -- I got some freaky rare kind.
          It's called large-celled carcinoma.

Lynne's eyes tear up. She hugs onto Andy.

                    LYNNE
          Jesus, Andy! Can they cure it?

                    ANDY
          They don't know... they've gotta run
          more tests.

                    LYNNE
               (starting to cry)
          Have you told your family?

                    ANDY
          No, NO! I don't want them to know
          yet. It'll just weird 'em out!

George and Zmuda glance skeptically at each other. Hmm.

Confused, George leans in to Andy.

                    GEORGE
          Andy... you look me in the eye, and
          tell me this is real.

Andy gulps.

                    ANDY
          George -- it's real.

                                        CUT TO:

155 INT. DENNY'S BATHROOM - LATER   155

George confronts Zmuda.

                    GEORGE
          If I find out you're behind this,
          I'll kill you.

                    ZMUDA
          What are ya TALKIN' ABOUT?! I was
          the one saying I didn't believe it!

                    GEORGE
          Exactly. That's the sort of thing
          you guys would work out to fuck me
          up.

156 INT. LAUREL CANYON HOUSE - DAY   156

Andy is doing laundry. He empties the clean clothes, puts them
in a basket, and carries them to the rug. Then he sits down and
starts laying out pairs of socks in highly symmetrical patterns.
Focused, impassive, Andy pointlessly orders the socks like the
world depended on it.

Lynne enters, emotionally wrecked. She stares in frustration
at Andy's behavior.

                    LYNNE
          How can you be so casual??!

                    ANDY
               (he shrugs)
          Even if I'm dying -- I still need
          clean socks.

                        LYNNE
            You're NOT DYING!

                        ANDY
            Okay. You're probably right.

He keeps working. Lynne loses it.

                        LYNNE
            God, you're so <u>detached</u>!!

Lynne storms out.

Andy finishes his socks. Satisfied, he piles them up... then
turns on the TV.

ANGLE - TV

It's "Lassie." Little TIMMY is laid-up in bed, with a broken
leg in a cast. Suddenly LASSIE runs in, holding a book.

Lassie places the book on his lap. The boy smiles gratefully.

                        TIMMY
            Thank you, girl. You're my best
            friend.

Timmy warmly embraces the dog.

ON ANDY

He's terribly touched. Tears start rolling down his cheeks.

Genuine sobbing. Terrible grief, until he wipes his face. Andy
collects himself, then reaches for a phone. He dials a long
number.

                        ANDY
                     (on phone)
            Dad...?

                                                CUT TO:

157 INT. CEDARS-SINAI - DAY   157

Andy lies in a hospital bed. Wearied Stanley, Janice, Michael
and Carol surround the bed.

They all listen to a BLAND DOCTOR in a white coat.

                        DOCTOR
            The cancer started in Andy's left arm
            and spread to his lungs. We're going
            to initiate an aggressive radiation
            program... see if we can eradicate
            the affected cells.
                     (beat)
            Does anyone have any questions?

A somber silence.

                         DOCTOR
              Alright, then I'll leave you alone.

The family nods. The Doctor turns and walks away.

Carol glances down... and notices the Doctor is wearing old
tennis shoes. She raises an eyebrow. He leaves.

A stilted awkwardness. The family doesn't know what to say.

                         JANICE
              So... how long do you have to stay
              here?

                         ANDY
              Oh, they said I could probably go home
              Thursday.

                         JANICE
              That's good.

Pause. Andy mutely lies there.

                         STANLEY
              So how's the food?

                         ANDY
              Oh, okay... the vegetables are kinda
              overcooked.

Another pause. Andy coughs.

                         MICHAEL
              We should probably let you rest.

Everyone mumbles agreement.

158   INT. HOSPITAL CORRIDOR - SAME TIME   158

The family exits Andy's room. The door SHUTS -- and they all
turn on each other.

                         JANICE
              He looks good...

                         MICHAEL
              Of course he looks good. He's NOT
              SICK.

                         STANLEY
                    (angered)
              How dare you make light of this!

                         CAROL
              Dad, I cried when he broke his neck.
              He's not gettin' me again --

                         STANLEY
                    (impassioned)
              Jesus! He's got lung cancer!

A standoff moment. The siblings glare at the parents.

>   CAROL
>   See, that's exactly it! He picked
>   lung cancer, <u>because he doesn't smoke</u>.
>   That makes it weird! If he'd picked
>   leukemia, it'd be totally believable,
>   and we'd all be going, "Poor Andy,
>   he's really sick." So he chose lung
>   cancer, because he WANTS us to be
>   scratching our heads, saying, "Is this
>   real?"

>   JANICE
>   (trying to convince herself)
>   Of course it's real. We're in a
>   hospital...

>   MICHAEL
>   Mom, it's Cedars-Sinai! It's a
>   <u>showbiz</u> hospital! Andy's studio
>   friends probably run this place!

>   CAROL
>   I've seen how he does it. He plans
>   these things out, takes over the
>   facility, hires actors to play cops,
>   doctors...
>   (beat)
>   Personally, I didn't think that
>   "doctor" was very convincing.

>   MICHAEL
>   Did you notice his costume had the
>   wrong shoes?

>   CAROL
>   (excited)
>   Yeah! He didn't have <u>doctor shoes</u>!

Stanley shakes his head.

>   STANLEY
>   This conversation is disgusting.

>   MICHAEL
>   Dad... you <u>know</u> Andy's talked about
>   faking his own death.

>   STANLEY
>   Sure -- but what if he <u>isn't</u>?
>   (sad; poignant)
>   My son could be dying... and we're
>   actin' like we're on Candid Camera.

>   CUT TO:

159 EXT. LAUREL CANYON HOUSE - DAY   159

George pulls up in his car.

He gets out and walks to the door. He starts to knock -- when
suddenly it creeps open. It's Lynne. She puts her finger to
her lips: Shh!

160   INT. LAUREL CANYON HOUSE - SAME TIME   160

The house is dark. Lynne leads George... and they get to the
shrouded living room.

Andy sits in a lotus position, concentrating. In front of him
is a WILD-HAIRED GURU in a robe.

                    WILD-HAIRED GURU
          I want you to visualize. Visualize
          big, healthy white cells in your body.
          Now visualize little cancer cells.
          Now those big white cells are
          attacking the cancer cells...

                    ANDY
          I see them... I see the white cells...

IN THE CORNER

George stares at this. He's fighting his skepticism.

                                        CUT TO:

161   LATER   161

The drapes are open. Sunlight streams in. Andy hugs the guru
goodbye, and the man leaves.

George has been waiting in back.

                    GEORGE
          What was that all about?

                    ANDY
          It's visualization therapy. He's
          helping me turn inward and fight the
          disease.

Long beat.

                    GEORGE
          He's an actor. I remember him in "The
          In-Laws."

Ah.

Andy's eyes widen. His wheels are spinning fast.

                    ANDY
          Uh yes... that's true. But he's also
          ordained in holistic medicine.

ANGLE - GEORGE

He glares, stewing. He's fed up.

ANGLE - ANDY

An unspoken tension. Suddenly he breaks down.

> ANDY
> George, what am I supposed to do?!
> I'm sick, and I'm tryin' to get
> better... but everyone's lookin' at
> me funny! People visit me in the
> hospital, and I catch them sneaking
> peeks at the chart. You come to my
> home, and you act like I'm puttin'
> on a skit!

> GEORGE
> You must take a <u>little</u> pleasure in
> it.

> ANDY
> Of course!
> (beat)
> But that doesn't mean I don't need
> everyone's support! I can't be
> surrounded by negative energy.

George shakes his head.

> GEORGE
> Andy, you're surrounded by what you
> create. You are the KING of negative
> energy.

> ANDY
> (thrown)
> Y-yeah? Well, then it has to <u>stop</u>!
> Because if these bad vibes get out...
> then everyone will be talkin' about
> how sick I am, and it becomes a
> self-fulfilling prophecy, and then
> -- I'm dead.

Andy struggles to remain composed. George sighs.

> GEORGE
> So how can I help you...?

> ANDY
> I wanna go back to work and put on
> a happy show.
> (bright-eyed)
> The best show anybody's ever seen!

> GEORGE
> Do you wanna tour the clubs?

> ANDY
> No clubs. I wanna reach the TOP!
> (beat)
> <u>Carnegie Hall</u>...!

George gently smiles.

                                              CUT TO:

162   INT. NATIONAL ENQUIRER OFFICES - DAY   162

A STAFF meeting at the National Enquirer.

                        REPORTER 1
              I've heard one of the Brady kids is
              in rehab.

                        EDITOR
              Good... but not exactly cover
              material.

                        REPORTER 2
                    (puffing himself up)
              Okay, how's this: I've got a guy in
              the lab at Cedars. He says Andy
              Kaufman is dying of lung cancer.

Beat. The room GROANS.

                        EDITOR
              What bullshit! No. No more Kaufman
              stories! We got burned on that
              Christian wedding.

                        REPORTER 1
              Yeah, he's definitely not dying. He's
              playing Carnegie Hall next month!

The Editor frowns.

                        EDITOR
              Jesus. Only Kaufman would use cancer
              as a publicity stunt.

163   INT. LAUREL CANYON HOUSE - NIGHT   163

A 16mm PROJECTOR runs a scratchy 1930's movie short on the wall.
Smiling fake COWBOYS and COWGIRLS dance, the Cowgirls straddling
hobby horses. They all SING.

                    COWBOYS AND COWGIRLS
              "I've got spurs,
               That jingle-jangle jingle..."

WE WIDEN

Andy and Zmuda watch. Andy's face is enthralled like a kid.

                        ANDY
              This is great. The crowd's gonna love
              this!
                    (giddy; thinking)
              Hey... do you think any of those
              cowgirls are still alive?

                         ZMUDA
          I dunno. If they were, they'd be
          pushin' 80.

                         ANDY
          Well, call SAG. It'd be cool to get
          one on the show.
                    (excited)
          I want the evening to build and build.
          It's gonna have the most incredible
          ending: Singers, dancers, the
          "Hallelujah Chorus" -- then the sky
          opens, and Santa Claus comes flying
          down!

                         ZMUDA
          And you say, "Santa, what am I gettin'
          for Christmas?" and he says, "Cancer!"

                         ANDY
          No! NO NO NO! None of that! I want
          this show to be positive!

                                        CUT TO:

164   INT. CEDARS-SINAI DOCTOR'S OFFICE - DAY   164

       Andy sits glumly with his Doctor. X-RAYS of Andy's insides
       litter the walls.

                         DOCTOR
          The radiation didn't get the cancer.
          It has metastasized and spread.

       Andy looks down. He coughs.

                         ANDY
          What can you do?

                         DOCTOR
                    (grim)
          We'll progress to chemotherapy. But
          I've got to warn you -- it's going
          to really knock you out. You'll lose
          your hair... and you won't have as
          much energy.

       Andy nods tiredly. Okay.

165   INT. HOSPITAL - DAY   165

       Andy silently sits. The Doctor and two NURSES administer a
       chemo drip into Andy's body.

       He stares at the needle in his arm.

       The chemo begins.

                                        CUT TO:

135.

166   EXT. CARNEGIE HALL - NIGHT   166

A dressy NEW YORK CROWD pushes into Carnegie Hall. The marquee
says "ANDY KAUFMAN"

167   INT. CARNEGIE HALL - BACKSTAGE   167

Andy gets ready, moving a bit slowly. CHOIR MEMBERS get in
their robes. George and Zmuda run in.

                    GEORGE
          The place is sold-out!
               (beat)
          That means you're only gonna lose
          eighty grand.

                    ANDY
          I don't care about the money. I just
          want the show to deliver.

                    ZMUDA
          Good. Because thirty-five school
          buses with loading-zone permits don't
          come cheap.

Suddenly -- Andy starts COUGHING harshly.

The guys are taken aback. Andy heaves and holds his chest.

                    GEORGE AND ZMUDA
          Hey! Are you okay???

Still coughing, Andy gestures: I'm okay.

                    ZMUDA
               (worried)
          If you're not feeling good, I could
          go on in your place, as Tony Clifton.

                    ANDY
               (he shoots him a dirty look)
          No, Zmuda. I'll be fine.

                                        CUT TO:

168   INT. CARNEGIE HALL - LATER   168

The show's on. The audience is rapt. Andy effusively PLAYS
his conga drum and SINGS nonsense words to "Allouette, Gentille
Allouette."

                    ANDY
          Abbu daba, abi abbu daba! Abbu daba,
          abu dabu do!
               (to the crowd)
          Abbu dabbu da ba do...!

Everyone repeats. In the audience, George sings along too.

                        AUDIENCE
          ABBU DABBU DA BA DO!!

                        ANDY
          A ba du ba ti la ma na go!

                        AUDIENCE
          A BA DU BA TI... LA... MA NA GO...

                        ANDY
                    (grinning)
          Abbu da ba du ba ti lama na la gobo
          abi tabu la!

                        AUDIENCE
          ABBU DA BA DU...

The crowd hopelessly breaks out LAUGHING.

Andy laughs along. They're all having a good time.

                                        CUT TO:

169   LATER   169

The corny "Jingle Jangle Cowboy" MOVIE is playing on a big
screen. It finishes. Beaming Andy grabs the mike.

                        ANDY
          Ladies and Gentlemen! I'm pleased
          to announce that we have with us the
          one surviving cowgirl from that 1931
          film, Eleanor "Cody" Gould!!

Crazed APPLAUSE. Frail ELEANOR GOULD, 75, comes onstage.

                        ANDY
          It's such an honor to have you here.

                        ELEANOR
                    (squinting into the lights)
          Andy... this is so overwhelming...

                        ANDY
          Well, it's gettin' even better! Cause
          we found one of the original hobby
          horses! Do you -- do you think you
          could treat us to a few steps from
          "Jingle Jangle Jingle"?

Eleanor starts to protest -- but Andy hands her the HOBBY HORSE.
She blushes. Andy turns away, goes to the band, and starts
conducting.

They begin PLAYING "JINGLE JANGLE JINGLE." Eleanor awkwardly
starts dancing in circles.

Andy gets excited and starts conducting FASTER. Eleanor is
sweating. She dances faster.

Andy impatiently SPEEDS UP the MUSIC MORE. Eleanor desperately skips in circles, trying to keep up... when suddenly she grabs her heart.

Eleanor stops -- and collapses. She's down.

A horrified GASP from the crowd. The band stops playing. CREW MEMBERS run on from backstage. One checks her heart. She's not moving. Zmuda runs out, horrified.

>   ZMUDA
>   Is there a doctor in the house??!

The crowd is stunned silent. Pause -- then one man stands.

It's Michael.

Straight-faced, he hurries out of his seat, sprints down the aisle, and goes on stage. Michael checks her pulse and loosens her blouse. He presses on Eleanor's chest, trying to restart her heart. But then -- he shakes his head sadly. She's dead.

The crowd MOANS in horror. Michael takes off his jacket and covers Eleanor.

BACKSTAGE

Andy watches, pleased. He COUGHS. Andy drinks some water, puts on a goofy Indian headdress, and runs back out.

ONSTAGE

Eleanor lies dead centerstage. Andy skips over and starts doing an Indian war dance around her prone body. The crowd is baffled. Andy WHOOPS, he CHANTS... and then Eleanor starts to rise!

He WHOOPS triumphantly. She lives, like Frankenstein reborn!

The crowd CHEERS, surprised and giggling.

>   ANDY
>   Ladies and Gentlemen, she's alive!

Huge APPLAUSE.

>   CHOIR (o.s.)
>   HALLELUJAH! HALLELUJAH!

>   ANDY
>   Ladies and Gentlemen, the Mormon
>   Tabernacle Choir!!!

Rear curtains part, and the MORMON TABERNACLE CHOIR belts out the "Hallulujah Chorus"!

It's spectacular. The crowd goes nuts.

>   ANDY
>   Oh my gosh, it's the Rockettes!!

Yes indeed, TWO DOZEN ROCKETTES rush in from the sides, legs kicking high.

The crowd WHOOS.

> ANDY
> Girls and boys, it's <u>Santa Claus</u>!!

Snow starts falling, and SANTA ON HIS SLEIGH drops from above.

The crowd screams with excitement. It's unbelievable. They leap to a standing ovation.

In front are Stanley and Janice. They start crying.

Andy beams and takes the mike.

> ANDY
> And it's not over yet!! 'Cause I'm taking you all out to Milk and Cookies!!

The crowd laughs.

> ANDY
> I'm <u>serious</u>!!!!!!!

CUT TO:

170   EXT. CARNEGIE HALL - MINUTES LATER   170

A thousand people file out -- and THIRTY-FIVE SCHOOLBUSES are parked up and down Fifth Avenue!!!!

The crowd is awed.

Andy euphorically marches out, pushing his endurance. He's the Pied Piper.

> ANDY
> Single file! Don't rush!! There's enough cookies for everyone!!

171   EXT. ELEMENTARY SCHOOL - LATER THAT NIGHT   171

The schoolbuses pull up to a school. The disoriented passengers step out, not sure what to expect...

172   INT. ELEMENTARY SCHOOL CAFETERIA - NIGHT   172

The audience crowds inside... and LADY CAFETERIA WORKERS in hairnets are dispensing milk and cookies. It's remarkable.

At a little kids table sits Andy and Lynne. Andy's face is pure joy. He watches all the adults munching on their cookies, everyone giddy at the silliness of it all.

Andy smiles beatifically. He whispers to Lynne.

                    ANDY
          I don't want this to ever end...

Lynne squeezes his hand. Andy stands.

                    ANDY
          Hey EVERYBODY! The show's <u>not done</u>!
          Let's meet tomorrow morning at eight,
          at the Staten Island Ferry! We'll
          have MORE FUN!!

Everyone giggles -- what a nut.

Andy gingerly sits back down.

                                        CUT TO:

173 INT. WALDORF-ASTORIA - NEXT MORNING   173

Zmuda is asleep, wearing an eyemask.

Suddenly -- the phone RINGS LOUDLY. Zmuda jerks up, startled.
Bleary, he fumbles for the phone.

                    ZMUDA
          H-h-helllllllllo?

                    ANDY (v.o.)
               (chipper, on phone)
          Dr. Zmudie, wake up! It's 7:30! We
          gotta catch the ferry!

                    ZMUDA
               (groggy)
          Andy... weren't you jokin'? C'mon,
          no one's gonna be there.

                    ANDY (v.o.)
          Hmm. Well, even if there's just one
          guy -- we better show.

Zmuda moans.

                                        CUT TO:

174 EXT. STATEN ISLAND FERRY TERMINAL - EARLY MORNING   174

The waterfront is desolate. One lone CAB comes screeching up.

Andy and Zmuda come tumbling out of the cab. They look up --
and their jaws drop.

THEIR POV

At the dock are THREE-HUNDRED PEOPLE! Seeing Andy, they cheer
and wave.

TIGHT - ANDY AND ZMUDA

Zmuda's astonished.

Andy is radiant.

                    ZMUDA
          Wow.

                    ANDY
                 (wondrous)
          And a year from now we'll have a
          reunion. It'll all start over...!

Zmuda looks at his friend. In the morning light, Andy looks
fatigued... wispy...

Zmuda's face falls.

175 EXT. STATEN ISLAND FERRY - DAY   175

The boat whizzes across the water. Andy's gang fills it up.
A cool breeze blows, everyone energized by this experience.

Andy is smiling. But then -- his expression turns odd. He
holds his stomach, hurries to the railing, and vomits.

Zmuda rushes over to him. They whisper.

                    ZMUDA
          Are you okay?

                    ANDY
          I'm feelin' really weak.

Beat. Zmuda shouts to the crowd and points at Andy.

                    ZMUDA
          Seasick!

                                        CUT TO:

176 INT. LAUREL CANYON HOUSE - DAY   176

Andy lies in bed, a shadow of himself. His face is paler. His
hair has thinned.

George sits on the bed, reading newspaper reviews to him.

                    GEORGE
          The Times says, "Funnyman Kaufman is
          back. A triumph of Pirandelloesque
          nonsense." Variety says, "Subversive,
          yet captivatingly innocent."
                 (beat)
          Pretty good...!

Andy has a blank look.

                    ANDY
          I can't move my arm.

                         GEORGE
                 (he pauses awkwardly; this is hard)
            You got good days and bad days...

Andy winces. He softly sighs.

                         ANDY
            My hair's comin' out.

                         GEORGE
                 (whispered)
            Yeah...

They look at each other. George silently pats him.

177   INT. KITCHEN - LATER   177

Lynne and Little Wendy are cooking Andy lunch. Lynne mashes up
strange unidentifiable plant products.

                         LITTLE WENDY
            What is this stuff?

                         LYNNE
            It's all macrobiotic. Millet, burdock
            root, kelp... Andy says it'll purify
            him.

Suddenly -- a SHARP VOICE.

                         TONY CLIFTON (o.s.)
            What is that crap?! Looks like
            somethin' my dog would puke up!!

The women turn. It's Andy -- dressed as Tony Clifton.

A spooked moment.

Tony's wig, peach tux, and sunglasses are there... but Andy is
barely strong enough to bark out the attitude.

                         TONY CLIFTON
            How 'bout me and you dolls go get some
            REAL food: French fries and a
            Porterhouse steak!

                         LYNNE
                 (not sure what to say)
            ...Andy...?

Wendy's eyes pop: Oh no, she broke the rule!

Tony gets indignant.

                              TONY CLIFTON
          I ain't Andy! I'm TONY! Andy's sick
          -- pick, chick, kick, lick! The
          doctor says he's a goner.
                    (rousing himself)
          But Tony's built like a mule! Here,
          watch this!

Tony picks up a CHAIR and starts lifting it: Up, down, up, down.

Worried, the women rush to stop him. They take the chair.

                              LYNNE
          Stop it! C'mon, put that down.

                              TONY CLIFTON
          Yeah, you're right. We better get
          movin'. We don't wanna miss Happy
          Hour at Kelbos -- all the MaiTai's
          you can drink for $4.99.

Tony jauntily turns to exit. He gestures to the ladies.

                              TONY CLIFTON
          Let's go!
                    (he starts SINGING "New York, New
                     York")
          "These vagabond blues,
           Are washin' away,
           I'll make a brand new start of it..."

Tony reaches the doorway -- and collapses.

He clutches himself in pain.

                         LYNNE AND WENDY
          Andy!!

Shocked, they run over.

Tony lies huddled on the ground. He mutters sadly, defeatedly.

                              TONY CLIFTON
          Dammit...

                                                  CUT TO:

178   INT. LAX AIRPORT - DAY   178

A crowded terminal. Zmuda pushes Andy in a wheelchair. Andy
looks gaunt and very depressed. He wears a hat.

A few PASSERSBY notice Andy. They whisper.

                              DUDE #1
          Hey, look. It's Andy Kaufman!

                              DUDE #2
               Whoa, what's he doin'?! He's
               pretending to be sick!
                         (he snickers)
               That guy's a crack-up.

Excited, they approach Andy. The dudes grin and wave.

                              DUDE #1
               Andy Kaufman! Yo! What's happening?

                              ANDY
                         (frail)
               I'm going off to meet a crystal
               healer.

The guys LAUGH uproariously.

                              DUDE #2
               That's funny SHIT! It's even better
               than the time you broke your neck!

                              ANDY
               I'm serious.

                              DUDE #2
               Yeah RIGHT!

                              DUDE #1
                         (he leans in to Andy)
               Hey, you know what would be funnier?!
               Get an I.V. bag to hang on the chair!

A long beat. Then -- Andy smiles wryly.

                              ANDY
               That's good. I'll use it on
               Letterman.

The dudes grin and stride away. Andy absorbs this absurdity...
and chuckles. Zmuda pushes him on.

Suddenly -- a PAPARAZZO PHOTOGRAPHER jumps out.

                              PAPARAZZO
               ANDY!

Andy looks over. FLASH! The man snaps a picture. Andy is
dazed. The paparazzo turns and runs.

Instantly he's gone.

                              ANDY
               Now everybody's gonna know.

                              ZMUDA
                         (beat)
               It's not like they're gonna believe
               it.

Andy peers up.

                    ANDY
          Do you believe it?

                    ZMUDA
               (he smiles)
          Fuck no. You're just lying, as
          always.

Andy laughs faintly.

                                        CUT TO:

179 EXT. NEW MEXICO DESERT - DAY   179

     A stucco SPA RESORT sits in the middle of the rocky desert.

180 INT. SPA - SAME TIME   180

     A room with soft lighting and billowing curtains. A New Agey
     HEALER is laying crystals upon Andy's body.

     Andy COUGHS. His hat is off, revealing he's bald.

                    HEALER
          Now we'll place a blue crystal. Very
          high vibrations. It's wonderful for
          its healing powers.

                    ANDY
               (spellbound)
          Okay. Let's try two of those... and
          one of the pink ones.

181 OUTSIDE   181

     Zmuda stands with a smarmy ADMINISTRATOR.

                    ADMINISTRATOR
          Your friend is doing four crystal
          sessions a day, but it's just not
          helping.

                    ZMUDA
          I know...
               (beat)
          The cancer's terminal.

                    ADMINISTRATOR
          Yes. That wasn't made particularly
          clear to us when he checked in...

                    ZMUDA
               (irked)
          Look, personally, I think rubbing
          rocks on people is a load of
          horseshit. But if it makes Andy
          happy, that's all that matters.

The man purses his lips.

> ADMINISTRATOR
> I'm sorry to sound crass -- but we
> don't want to be "that health resort
> in New Mexico where Andy Kaufman
> died."
>> (beat)
> I'm going to have to ask you to leave.

Zmuda is speechless.

182   INT. SPA - ANDY'S ROOM - LATER   182

Zmuda angrily packs Andy's bags. Zmuda is seething.

But Andy is strangely calm and unaffected.

> ANDY
> It's okay, Bob. It wasn't really
> working.
>> (a gentle smile)
> We'll find something better.

>   CUT TO:

183   EXT. LAUREL CANYON HOUSE - DUSK   183

The sun is setting, purple and orange over the hills. Andy and
George lie on chaise lounges, serenely staring out. Andy has
lost more weight.

> ANDY
> Boy, look at the colors in the sky...

> GEORGE
> Yeah. It's really beautiful.

Andy's energy is sapped, but he forces himself to be upbeat.

> ANDY
> I've got an idea for a new TV show
> for me to star in. It's called "Uncle
> Andy's Fun House" -- it'll be a
> Saturday morning thing where I can
> goof off with the kids.

George is choked up. He goes along with it.

> GEORGE
> That sounds nice. Children have
> always loved your act.

> ANDY
> Yeah... it's kind of a throwback to
> shows I used to do in Great Neck.
> We'll have an audience of little kids,
> and I can do puppets, magic tricks,
> stuff like that...

                    GEORGE
               (he nods awkwardly; long pause)
          I think we can sell that.

Silence.

George struggles not to shatter Andy's enthusiasm.

Andy smiles gratefully.

                    ANDY
          Hey... thanks for always backin' me.

George clenches Andy's hand.

                    GEORGE
          Did your -- doctor say it's okay for
          you to go back to work?

                    ANDY
          Ehhh, you know those guys. If he had
          his way, I'd be stuck in the hospital,
          running tests all day.
               (beat)
          And anyway, I've found a new guy who's
          gonna be able to instantly remove the
          cancer.

                    GEORGE
               (startled)
          Really? Is he at a different
          hospital?

Andy laughs.

                    ANDY
          No! He's in the Philippines! His
          name is Jun Roxas. He's a psychic
          surgeon! I've read about him, and
          he's amazing! He rubs you and sucks
          the disease right out!

Andy beams. George stares sadly.

                    GEORGE
          The Philippines? I dunno... Andy...
          he sounds like one of your characters.

TIGHT - ANDY

His voice gets hushed.

                    ANDY
          No... this guy's special.
               (very sincere)
          He performs miracles.

George doesn't know how to respond.

Andy looks up pleadingly.

                              ANDY
                    He's my last chance.

                                             CUT TO:

184   EXT. BAGUIO CITY - PHILIPPINES - DAY   184

      Baguio, a tiny scratched-in-the-dirt Philippine city.

      Suddenly, a rattletrap COMMUTER PLANE lurches out of the sky.
      It hits a dirt runway.

      Dust flies. Chickens squawk and scatter.

185   INT. BEAT-UP TAXI - DAY   185

      Andy, Lynne, and Zmuda ride through the impoverished city.

      Andy stares in amazement.

      They reach a brick building. A sign says "CLINIC," with an eye
      over a triangle.

186   EXT. CLINIC   186

      Zmuda helps Andy into his wheelchair. Andy grimaces in pain.
      Suddenly -- a MOTORCADE OF ARMY JEEPS screeches up. SOLDIERS
      carry M-16s and red banners, "JUN ROXAS FOR MAYOR." Jun's stern
      face peers out.

      Then, JUN ROXAS himself jumps from a jeep. WELLWISHERS on the
      sidewalk cheer. Jun shakes hands and gives out ballpoint pens.

      Lynne and Zmuda glance at each other.

187   INT. CLINIC   187

      A NURSE hurriedly helps weakened Andy sign a bunch of forms.
      Money is handed over.

      Andy's clothes are stripped off. They're thrown in a locker.

188   INT. OPERATION ROOM   188

      A large white tiled room. Lynne and Zmuda roll in pallid Andy,
      his limp body unmoving.

      Andy looks up... and there's a LONG LINE OF SICKLY PEOPLE.
      Primarily Japanese, emaciated, all stripped to their underwear
      and barely able to stand.

      They have a look of desperation and reverence.

      At the head of the line is Jun at his workstation: A bench, a
      sink, and ATTENDANTS with clean towels.

      A SICKLY WOMAN crawls onto the bench. Jun impassively presses
      his hand into the fatty flesh of her stomach, kneading,
      searching. Pause, then he removes some BLOODY GUTS.

He flings them into a bucket.

The woman cries out.

Andy gasps.

The woman is helped away.

Jun turns and washes his hands. An attendant gives him a towel to dry with. Then a SICKLY MAN crawls up...

Andy rolls closer. He stares at all this with fear. Nervousness. Hope.

Jun impassively presses his hand against the man's head. He concentrates, searching... then pulls out some BLOODY GUTS.

He flings them into a bucket.

The man shakes. He is helped away.

Andy is wide-eyed. He gets closer... closer...

More patients. More bloody guts. More sobbing.

Andy's excitement builds.

Then -- he reaches the front.

A moment.

Lynne and Zmuda stare into Andy's eyes, drawn in by his total belief. They are overcome. It feels like they're saying goodbye. Lynne gives Andy a tender kiss. Zmuda starts to shake his hand -- then instead hugs him tightly.

Andy smiles, then the attendants lift him from the wheelchair. They help him up to the bench.

Andy lies down. Fluorescent lights buzz overhead.

He looks over, and Jun Roxas is washing his hands from the previous patient.

Andy shivers, anticipating the miracle.

Jun turns. An attendant gives him a towel to dry off.

Andy relaxes, readying for it all...

He glances at Jun's hands. Jun hands back the towel -- and under it the attendant quickly slips Jun a sack of animal intestines.

Jun discreetly palms it. He's a fake.

CLOSEUP - ANDY

A moment of stunned disbelief.

He is shocked. Outraged. Disappointed. Flabbergasted.

The faith is meaningless. The joke is cosmic. The con man has been conned.

Andy's overpowering emotions coalesce... and he starts to LAUGH.

It's sidesplittingly funny. Andy LAUGHS, and LAUGHS, and LAUGHS, like a crazy man with no salvation, the joy releasing him, the tears rolling down his cheeks.

His face flushes with color. Life sparkles in his eyes. Andy laughs and guffaws until he's hoarse. This is the best gag of them all.

                                        SLOW DISSOLVE TO:

189   INT. FUNERAL HOME - DAY   189

Andy lies at peace in a casket. He has died.

His expression is pleasantly bland. Almost Latka-like.

WIDE

Andy's funeral. The chapel is filled with flowers. Grieving MOURNERS in black slowly enter. It's very quiet.

Andy's family stands huddled together. They're all in a state of shock.

Lynne sits alone in a pew, crying.

Across the room, George gives Zmuda a hug. Little Wendy comes over... and they all comfort each other.

Everyone who ever knew Andy is there: Taxi cast, Fridays cast, TM followers, hookers, Buddy Rogers, Jerry Lawler, Ed Weinberger, Cathy Sullivan, Maynard Smith, Budd Friedman, it goes on and on...

But -- the people have odd discombobulated expressions.

There's lots of whispering.

                    MAYNARD SMITH
          So when's Andy gonna jump out?

                    ED WEINBERGER
          I say the body's made of wax.

Buddy Rogers ambles up to a curtain. He suspiciously peers behind it.

Grandma is weeping.

                    GRANDMA
          He was so young...

Two hookers discreetly whisper.

                    HOOKER #1
          You know, he used to play dead in bed.

                    HOOKER #2
                    (surprised)
          You too?

Tear-streaked Cathy Sullivan approaches Jack Burns.

                    CATHY
          Now he's with God...

                    JACK BURNS
          I refuse to cry. I don't wanna get
          scammed.

Janice slowly turns to Stanley.

                    JANICE
          It's his funeral. He's gone...
                    (very drained)
          So how come I don't believe it?

She starts sobbing. Stanley holds her.

ON ZMUDA AND GEORGE

They stare out.

                    ZMUDA
          It's a perfect Kaufman audience. They
          don't know whether to be sad or angry.

                    GEORGE
                    (beat)
          Too bad he's not here to see it.

                    ZMUDA
                    (longer beat)
          Who says he isn't?

TIGHT - ANDY IN THE CASKET

Andy lies in state. He's ostensibly dead... but seems unreal.
His face is caked with so much funeral-home makeup, it almost
looks like a mask.

We tilt up... and standing there are Judd Hirsch, Carol Kane,
and Marilu Henner. They stare morosely at the body, their faces
depressed and somber.

Beat. Nervous glances around -- then all three of them quickly
poke the body. POKE! POKE! POKE!

Freaked out, they compose themselves. They WHISPER.

                    JUDD HIRSCH
          What do you think?

                    CAROL KANE
         I dunno. He could be doin' some Yogi
         deep-breathing technique.

A frustrated sigh.

                    MARILU HENNER
         We'll never know.

EXTREME CLOSEUP - ANDY

He enigmatically lies there.

                                        FADE OUT.

FADE IN:

190 EXT. NEWSSTAND - DAY   190

A SUPER slowly appears: "EXACTLY ONE YEAR LATER"

The two Dudes from the airport are reading magazines. Dude #1
reads a comic book, Dude #2 flips through the L.A. Weekly.

Suddenly -- Dude #2's eyes pop.

                    DUDE #2
         No WAY!
              (stupefied)
         This is the freakiest thing I've ever
         seen! Look.

He shows his friend a FULL PAGE AD.

It says: "ONE NIGHT ONLY. TONY CLIFTON - LIVE!" Underneath
is a photo of cocky Tony.

Their jaws drop in amazement.

                    DUDE #1
         Man, we were right! He's not dead!

                    DUDE #2
         He's just been layin' low for a year!
              (hysterical)
         WE GOTTA GO!

                                        CUT TO:

191 EXT. COMEDY STORE - NIGHT   191

The marquee says "TONY CLIFTON."

The two dudes come riding up on skateboards. They look up --
and it's INSANITY. Traffic on Sunset is jammed. Police have
barricades. HONKING limousines jockey to pull in.

The guys desperately push their way through the pulsing mob.
People are screaming. Everybody wants in. The two reach the
front -- and a COP suddenly stops them.

                    COP
Uh-uh! If you don't have a ticket,
you can't go through.

                 DUDE #1
           (begging)
But you gotta let us in! We're huge
fans!! We wanna see Andy!!

                    COP
           (puzzled)
Andy? ...Who's Andy?
           (he points)
The sign says "Tony Clifton."

192   INT. COMEDY STORE - SAME TIME   192

It's packed. The place is filled with glittery Hollywood VIPs.
People make chit-chat... but there is a squeamish excitement
in the air. A brooding unease. Nobody knows what to expect.

Suddenly -- the lights go black. A BOOMING ANNOUNCER.

               ANNOUNCER (v.o.)
Ladies and Gentlemen! Please put your
hands together for... Tony Clifton!!

The THEME FROM 2001 starts playing. "DAAAAA, DAAAAA, DAAAAAA!
DA-DAAAA"!

A small SPOT appears -- on a peach tuxedo. The light grows
bigger, bigger... the tension magnifying... people gasping...
our view widening... until Tony Clifton is revealed onstage!

It's an extraordinary theatrical moment -- without response.

The crowd has no idea what to do.

Tony smirks.

               TONY CLIFTON
How ya doin'?!

Dead silence.

Tony struts downstage. He waves to the crowd.

               TONY CLIFTON
How you doin' back there!
         (to the front rows)
How you doin' up here?!

Still no response. Until -- a lone reckless VOICE.

                 VOICE
Andy!

Whoa. The crowd rustles nervously.

Tony grimaces.

TONY CLIFTON
Don't know nothin' about no Andy.
Just some dead guy tryin' to ride my
coattails.
        (to the BAND)
Let's HIT IT, boys! One, two, anda
one two three four!

The BAND kicks in with disco anthem "I WILL SURVIVE."

Tony starts SINGING the schmaltzy opening:

TONY CLIFTON
"First I was afraid,
I was petrified.
Kept thinkin' I could never live
Without you at my side."
        (he wipes away a pretend tear)
"Were you the one that tried to
hurt me with goodbye?
Did you think I'd crumble?
Did you think I'd lay down and die..?"

We PAN the room of enthralled spectators. At a front table
are George and Lynne.

Tony attacks the chorus.

TONY CLIFTON
"Oh no not I!
I WILL SURVIVE!
As long as I know how to love,
I know I'll simply stay alive!"

In the crowd, we pass face after face -- smiling... frowning...
intrigued... confused... until we settle on a man in the very
last row.

Bob Zmuda.

Enjoying the show more than anyone.

TONY CLIFTON
"I've got all my life to live,
I've got all my life to give.
I will survive..."
        (he hits his big finish)
"I -- WILL -- SURVIVE!!!"

The music CRESCENDOS, and the song ENDS.

Zmuda grins and APPLAUDS proudly.

                                        FADE OUT.

        THE END

Above: Tony Clifton, circa 1980. *Below:* Tony Clifton today.

SCENE NOTES

BY SCOTT ALEXANDER & LARRY KARASZEWSKI

Here we detail the impetus behind many of the scenes, and show how they became transformed in their transition from script to movie. We wrote seven official drafts. We hear about movies with ninety drafts, but we'd lose our minds if we were on one of those. Most changes were due to creative issues; only at the end did things change for budget or schedule: "We're running behind! Can you turn Tuesday and Wednesday into one day?!" The painful losses were often grace notes, small moments lost in the commotion of production.

In the script, we tried to be Kaufmanesque in two ways: One, tonally, by keeping the reader off balance; and two, creatively, by referencing as much of Andy's work as possible. Showbiz biopics have a weird obligation: They're expected to re-create famous performances. Some of our choices were obvious, but many others were bizarrely obscure. We'll highlight as many of these as we can remember.

Sc. 1: Andy's opening monologue. This is an homage to his ABC special. On that show, Andy claimed he'd blown his budget, said that the entire show was just him in a chair, and he advised viewers to change the channel.

Ed Wood has a similar opening, where Criswell addresses the camera and describes the film you're about to see. These scenes are playful reworkings of their protagonist's art—a fun way to set the mood and get the fans on board.

Sc. 2: Dad greets Little Michael. This little exchange was cut, indicative of the entire direction of the movie: Focus on Andy.

Sc. 4–6: Andy as a boy. In our final script, there's only one childhood scene. However, we originally had ten pages of this stuff. From our interviews with Andy's family, we were inundated with interesting, magical stories. It was clearly a way to round out Andy's character: magic, Judaism, eccentric childhood, love of family. . . . But ultimately, we had to conserve our running time for the main character. He's the one the audience is identifying with. So almost everything was cut, including these goofy boyhood scenes from our original 210-page printout:

INT. KAUFMAN DINING ROOM - 1957 - NIGHT

It is Passover. The Kaufmans, their two GRANDMOTHERS, and
assorted RELATIVES are seated around the dining table. Everybody
is dressed up.

The table is set with good china and assorted Passover para-
phernalia: parsley, shank bone, hard-boiled eggs, etc. The
group reads aloud from Haggadah prayer books.

                    JANICE
                  (reading)
     "Long before the exodus, the Passover was celebrated by
     the Israelites as a festival of spring. After the Jews
     were released from slavery in Egypt, the holiday assumed
     greater meaning."

She turns to portly Grandma PEARL. The old lady fumbles with
her glasses, then continues reading.

                    GRANDMA PEARL
                  (reading)
     "Elijah is the prophet who will announce the coming of the
     Messiah. In his honor, a special goblet of wine is placed
     on the table, to symbolize his coming."

Stanley lifts a glass of wine.

                    STANLEY
     "Behold this cup of wine. It is—"

                    ANDY
     Excuse me.
                  (beat)
     I have to go to the bathroom.

Andy meekly stands and shuffles out.

Stanley shoots him a look — then sighs. He turns to Michael.

                    STANLEY
     Michael, please continue.

Michael grimaces, not quite old enough to read. He struggles to
figure out the words.
                    MICHAEL
                  (reading)
     "It is...a symbol...of our...joy. Tonight."

                    SWEATY FAT UNCLE
                        (reading)
      "Let us now open the door, that the prophet Elijah, herald
      of tomorrow, may be honored in traditional fashion. He
      bears the tidings of hope—"

DING-DONG! It's the DOORBELL.

Odd glances.

                         STANLEY
      Who the hell is interrupting?

Suddenly — CLICK. The o.s. front door CREAKS open.

Everyone turns to look...and then a STRANGE FIGURE enters. A short
little person with black beard, hat, and a robe. It's Andy, playing
Elijah.

Elijah bows silently. The crowd stares back, mystified.

Elijah wiggles his bushy eyebrows. He goes to his chair, climbs
up, and grabs his glass of wine. Unsure pause — then he quickly
chugs it down.

Stanley's eyes pop. Elijah then quickly retreats. He jumps off
his seat, bows again, and hurries out. The door SHUTS.

Silence. The adults are speechless. Little Michael and Carol
grin at each other.

Unsure beat — then flustered Janice grabs her prayer book and
tries restarting the show. She flips to a random page.

                         JANICE
                        (reading)
      "And, eh...this is roasted lamb shank. It represents the
      lamb sacrificed during Pesach in ancient times."

O.s., a toilet FLUSH. Footsteps, then Andy casually strolls
back in from the rear. He sits down at the table.

All eyes stare. He innocently looks up.

                         ANDY
      Did I miss anything?
                                                   CUT TO:

INT. PSYCHIATRIST'S OFFICE - 1957 - DAY

A PSYCHIATRIST with owlish glasses stares across his desk.

                         PSYCHIATRIST
          Andy...do you know why you're here?

Little Andy lies stiffly on a couch.

                              ANDY
          No.

                         PSYCHIATRIST
          Your parents tell me you like to be alone.

                              ANDY
                         (taken aback)
          That's not true.

Pause. The shrink is confused.

                         PSYCHIATRIST
          It's — not...?

                              ANDY
          No! I love to play outside with my friends.

The shrink is baffled. He thumbs through his papers.

                         PSYCHIATRIST
          But...your father said—

                              ANDY
          My father says a lot of things. He likes to hit the sauce.

                         PSYCHIATRIST
                         (horrified)
          You mean...drink?

                              ANDY
          Day and night. Me and my sister and brother take care of
          ourselves.

                         PSYCHIATRIST
          But...isn't your mother around?

                              ANDY
          Nah. She's too busy selling her body to pay for Dad's
          booze.

The psychiatrist is dumbfounded.

                         PSYCHIATRIST
          This can't be true.

```
                    ANDY
                (mournful)
        I wish it weren't....

Dramatic pause. The shrink is totally disoriented.

He gathers his thoughts.

                    PSYCHIATRIST
        Look, Andy...either you've got an overactive imagina-
        tion... or your parents should be arrested.

Andy shrugs.


                    PSYCHIATRIST
        But in either case, you need to get out of the house.
        You're a bright kid. Try to channel your energies....

ANGLE - ANDY

He perks up. Hmm...
```

Of course, this dialogue is blatantly fabricated. All we knew from the family was that Andy and the shrink had "a lot of problems." It "just didn't work out."

Sc. 7: Andy becomes an adult. We originally planned on dissolving from young Andy to grown Andy with "Old MacDonald Had a Farm." Andy had a hilarious audience-participation routine, and it worked well in the nightclub. The problem is, that song is endless. It's impossible to shorten. So we went with a quicker tune.

Sc. 8: Mr. Besserman fires Andy. In the movie, the real George Shapiro plays Mr. Besserman, the manager. He's very good, adding a bizarre poignancy to the scene. On-set, George added his own Siamese twin joke.

Sc. 9: The mugging scene. Andy always claimed this was how he invented Foreign Man. We loved the event, because it felt like a "movie moment." It was cranked-up and explained things. For the exact same reasons, Milos hated it. He said it was clearly apocryphal and never happened. We argued that was beside the point. He relented and left it in the final shooting script . . . but it didn't get shot.

Sc. 12: Backstage at the Improv. Andy's "Caspiar" routine was from an early *Tonight Show*. Andy was a guest, but he refused to break out of his Foreign Man character. Johnny had to do the whole interview that way.

Sc. 13: Andy and George out to dinner. This scene has a ludicrous amount of real Andy quirks packed in: weird health food, cleaning his hands, fake boogers, claiming to be a song-and-dance man . . . it's a mini–Greatest Hits.

Sc. 15: George gets a call from Tony. Originally, we opened this scene with George watching Andy on *The Dating Game*. Struggling actors are often game-show contestants—but Andy had done it as Foreign Man. We were amused by this absurdity being Andy's demo reel.

Sc. 17–19: Andy and the Maharishi. We tend to like scenes to have little pre-scenes. We joke that if our character has a scene in an office, first we'll have him park his car, then enter the lobby, then wait in the reception room. In this case, we showed Andy and his TM friends, then took him down a hall and ushered him into a private moment with the Maharishi. It made things intimate, as they talked about Andy's life (and back story). However, Milos prefers scenes to play out continuously, so he compressed everything into one location.

Sc 21: Coney Island. This scene never made the shooting script, but we liked it. Even as adults, the Kaufmans always went on roller coasters together, which was eccentrically charming. It was a fun way to reintroduce the characters as grown-ups. But during revisions, Milos wanted the plot jump-started as soon as possible. The downside is that the first act is now extremely performance heavy.

In our first draft, Andy went to Coney Island with his girlfriend, Elayne Boosler. She was with him throughout his New York years, and we used her in his early struggling scenes. However, in later drafts, this section became so short that there was no way to keep her.

Also, for reasons unknown, Ms. Boosler was the only person from Andy's circle who didn't want to speak with us. When it came time to trim characters, we naturally sided with people whom we actually knew. The moral of the story: If you wanna be in the movie, talk to the writers.

Sc. 25–26: George discovers Tony. We loved the idea of George being manipulated in real life. The flyers are luring George into a trap. To keep Andy likable, it was important to sometimes make his pranks *inclusive*—meaning George gets suckered into the club, then laughs at the reveal *with* Andy. Andy is sharing the joke.

For Milos, this was too much game playing. He changed it to George simply calling Andy and learning about the club. Then, in the editing, this transition was eliminated.

Discovering a weird headliner in an Italian restaurant is taken from life—it happened to Andy and Zmuda. They stumbled upon an astonishing middle-aged lounge singer named Jim Brandy. This poor man was reviled by the club managers, but Andy and Bob became enamored with him. Brandy even shows up on Andy's *Soundstage* special.

Tony's routines are a composite of numerous television appearances. Tony had a thriving talk-show career—singin' a tune and telling inane stories. The giant joke is that sometimes he was Andy, and sometimes he was Zmuda. Dinah Shore and David Letterman didn't know the difference.

Andy and Zmuda did the Bob Gorsky routine many times. It seemed like an appropriate way to introduce the audience to Zmuda—by tricking them.

Sc. 27: George goes backstage. In the movie, this scene is much shorter, ending with "Don't believe everything you hear." The second half becomes two additional scenes—a rare instance when Milos had us break out and expand the beats. Now, George goes back to ABC and explains the scam, then he returns to Andy and tells him he got the job.

That final scene takes place around a video game—an example of our compulsively working in "real-life details." We make up lists of character traits that we shovel into our scripts. Andy used to spend hours a day in supermarkets, playing Centipede and Space Invaders. This habit made him seem down-to-earth. So in every draft, no matter which scenes were in or out, we made sure one of them took place at a video game.

Sc. 28-29: *Taxi* rehearsals. These were shot but cut. With *Taxi,* we tried to be elliptical enough so that Louie DePalma wouldn't be missed.

Sc. 32: The *Taxi* montage. We had no patience for figuring this one out. There were five years of tapes to wade through, so we let the production team deal with it.

Incidentally, *we* know that Christopher Lloyd and Carol Kane weren't in the first season. They're not in our pages. But Tony Danza wasn't available during the shoot, so the cast got surreptitiously fleshed out.

Sc. 33: Zmuda reassures Andy. This scene got moved to *Taxi* backstage. The fans got eliminated—now, Andy takes a swelling curtain call, then says he's quitting.

Andy's sentiment came to us from numerous interviews. Although the show was acclaimed and popular, he constantly bitched about it and tried to quit. In later seasons, he even negotiated *down* the number of episodes he'd appear in.

Sc. 37-38: Andy gets fan mail. This was shot but cut.

Sc. 39: Andy's date. We used this scene to showcase Andy's wrestling and street-theater obsessions. He actually conducted dates this way. However, only the first half was shot. It got moved to the wrestling section of the story—and then it got cut. In the film, Andy's wrestling is a self-contained block, whereas in our early drafts, it was an ongoing theme throughout his life.

Sc. 40: ABC dumps the special. The full scoop is that Fred Silverman couldn't stand the show, so ABC refused to air it. Later, George and Howard West were able to sell it to NBC. But before it aired, Fred Silverman moved to NBC, then blocked it again. Amazingly, George and Howard were able to sell it a third time . . . back to ABC. Free of Fred Silverman, the show finally aired.

Sc. 41: Jerry's deli. This is one of the great true stories. Andy really did work as a busboy, though purely for whimsical reasons. He just wanted to goof off and confuse customers. For dramatic purposes, we invented him taking the job as an incensed rebuttal to the network.

Sc. 42: Andy unhappy on *Taxi*. This was not in the final shooting script. We thought it helped motivate *Gatsby*, but it was probably beating a dead horse.

Sc. 43–49: "Great Gatsby." This scene's inclusion is astonishing to everybody who worked on the film. The movie had too many routines, so Milos yanked it from his first editorial assembly, just weeks after shooting. "Gatsby" remained cut for seven months. But then . . . days before locking the picture, Milos felt remorseful. So he slipped a shortened version back in.

Overall, our page count on performance pieces was way off—it should have been a minute a page, but everything doubled. The laughs and pauses ate time, and Jim Carrey went all out milking the jokes.

Andy was fond of *Gatsby,* reading excerpts from it at many of his concerts. Whether he ever really got to the end is unknown, although we like to believe it's true. We made up his angry motivation—again, as a way of justifying the scene's inclusion.

During our interviews, Zmuda and George told us tons of funny live-concert stories. Andy lived much of his life on the road, and we wrote many unused scenes. Only a few were shot, and none are in the finished film. Here is one of our favorites, rescued from the shredder. In it, Andy, as always, is running late:

```
EXT. LAX AIRPORT - DAY

Andy pulls up in his Chrysler Cordoba. Zmuda leaps from the car
before it's parked.

                    ZMUDA
        C'MON!! We're gonna miss the fuckin' plane!!

Zmuda grabs Andy's case and starts running. But Andy is deli-
cately walking around his car.

                    ANDY
        Goodbye, car. I'll see you in three days.
                    (he waves)
        Goodbye, front seat.
```

                              ZMUDA
        C'MON!

                              ANDY
                        (he waves)
        Goodbye, back seat.

                              ZMUDA
        MOVE IT!!

                              ANDY
        Goodbye, fender—

                              ZMUDA
        JESUS CHRIST! If we miss the flight to Chicago, we won't
        make the connection to the Mishawaka commuter plane! Let's
        fuckin' GO!

Zmuda frantically grabs Andy and runs for his life.

                                                    CUT TO:

INT. LAX TERMINAL - DAY

Plane ATTENDANTS are slowly shutting the gate door. Zmuda
SHOUTS manically down the corridor.

                              ZMUDA
        Please!! HUUURRY!!

IN THE TERMINAL

Andy calmly speaks to two LITTLE OLD LADIES.

                              ANDY
        Oh, thank you. I'm so glad you like Latka.

In the b.g., the gate shuts. Zmuda COLLAPSES screaming.

                                                    CUT TO:

EXT. MISHAWAKA SKY - NIGHT

It's pouring RAIN. A tiny two-engine plane banks through the gale.

INT. PLANE

Andy is obliviously meditating. Frazzled, Zmuda screams at the poor
PILOT.

                              ZMUDA
        LAND IT! Just land it ANYWHERE!!
                        (he points)
        Go DOWN!

EXT. MISHAWAKA LANDING FIELD - NIGHT

More rain. Andy and Zmuda burst out and run to a white rental car.
Andy casually reaches for the driver's door — and Zmuda knocks him
away.

>   ZMUDA
>   NO! I'M driving!!

>   CUT TO:

EXT. MISHAWAKA CIVIC AUDITORIUM - NIGHT

The marquee says "ANDY KAUFMAN - 8 p.m."

INT. MISHAWAKA CIVIC AUDITORIUM - SAME TIME

The AUDIENCE is losing their patience. They BEAT their hands in
rhythm. Clapping along is the SEXY GIRL who sent her picture.

BACKSTAGE

The poor PROMOTER looks suicidal. He pulls his hair.

>   PROMOTER
>   I'm gonna KILL that Kaufman. He's an hour late!!

>   ASSISTANT
>   Why hasn't the opening act gone on?

>   PROMOTER
>   Cause Clifton isn't here either!!

>   CUT TO:

INT. RENTAL CAR - NIGHT

Windshield wipers squeak. Zmuda crazily drives through the
drench. Andy sits next to him, eyes shut, chanting.

Zmuda squints into the distance — and smiles.

>   ZMUDA
>   Hey, we made it! There it is!

No reaction whatsoever from meditating Andy. Zmuda glares.

>   ZMUDA
>   This is fuckin' ridiculous.

EXT. MISHAWAKA CIVIC AUDITORIUM - NIGHT

The despondent Promoter paces in the rain. Suddenly — the
rental car SCREECHES up and parks on the curb.

Zmuda hops out. He and the Promoter SHOUT through the wind.

                    ZMUDA
          Hi! Sorry we're late!

                    PROMOTER
          Who're YOU? Where's Kaufman??

                    ZMUDA
          He's inside the car.

The guy runs for the passenger door. But Zmuda physically blocks
him.

                    ZMUDA
          Uh-uh! He can't come out for another —
                    (he checks his watch)
          eighteen minutes.

                    PROMOTER
          Are you INSANE??!

                    ZMUDA
          He needs to meditate ninety minutes before performing.

                    PROMOTER
                    (mortified)
          Christ on a stick!

A hopeless moment. The Promoter thinks.

                    PROMOTER
          Hey, what about Clifton?

                    ZMUDA
          Ehh...the crowd has to be prepped for him.

INT. AUDITORIUM - MINUTES LATER

The audience CLAPS louder, more violently. It's almost a riot.
Suddenly the back door opens — and Zmuda enters, in a pink-and-
white striped VENDOR'S OUTFIT. He carries a basket around his neck.

                    ZMUDA
          Refreshments!

MAN

    Hey, I'll have a popcorn.

ZMUDA

    I don't have popcorn. I have tomatoes.

Beat.

MAN

    "Tomatoes"??
               (discombobulated)
    Uh, how 'bout a Coke?

ZMUDA

        (he shrugs)
    Tomatoes are all I've got.

MAN

    I don't WANT tomatoes!

An angry pause. Finally —

MAN

    Ahh, _fine_. I'll have three.

He reaches for his wallet. His GIRLFRIEND pokes him.

GIRLFRIEND

    Why're you buying tomatoes?

MAN

        (frustrated)
    I dunno! It's all he's got.

                        CUT TO:

LATER

Tony Clifton is onstage, screaming furiously.

TONY CLIFTON

    STOP IT! Calm down, all of youse!!

Tomatoes PELT him in the head.

WIDE

Hundreds of people are HURLING TOMATOES at Tony. The crowd has
gone ballistic.

                    TONY CLIFTON
     HEY! Show me a little respect! I'm an <u>entertainer</u>!
                    (more tomatoes hit him)
          Here, I'll dance for you. Lookit me — I'm dancin', I'm
     <u>dancin</u>'!

Tony does a little soft shoe. A BOTTLE HITS him in the head.

IN THE WINGS

Zmuda laughs. But the Promoter is freaking.

                    PROMOTER
          This is a nightmare.

                    ZMUDA
          What are ya talkin' about?! It's working like a charm.

ONSTAGE

Tony staggers, then reaches offstage and defiantly pulls a pro-
tective <u>welding</u> <u>mask</u> over his head.

MUSIC starts playing. It's disco anthem "I WILL SURVIVE."

                    TONY CLIFTON
                    (singing)
          "Once I was alone,
          I was petrified..."

An avalanche of DEBRIS flies at him.

Suddenly a DANGEROUS MAN leaps from his seat.

                    DANGEROUS MAN
          I can't TAKE IT anymore!!

The dangerous man jumps <u>on</u> <u>stage</u> and pulls a KNIFE.

                    DANGEROUS MAN
          You get off this stage!!

Tony jerks away, trying to protect himself.

IN THE WINGS
                    PROMOTER
          You guys think this is entertaining...?

                    ZMUDA
          Actually — the biker's not with the act. He really wants to
          kill him.

ONSTAGE

The dangerous man jabs the knife at Tony. Tony pleads.

                    TONY CLIFTON
        H-hey buddy, can't we just be friends?

The guy responds by THRUSTING the knife <u>into</u> <u>Tony's gut</u>.

Beat — and then feathers fly out.

A disoriented moment...and then COPS barrel on stage and grab
the man. He gets dragged away.

TIGHT - TONY

He stares off, blinks, then pivots back to the crowd.

                    TONY CLIFTON
        If I have made just one person happy, it's all been worth it.
                        (beat)
        Thank you, and <u>good</u> <u>night</u>!

This sequence was an example of us taking lots of random anecdotes and combining them into a jumbo set piece. Andy saying goodbye to cars, Andy always missing his flights, the crazy two-engine plane, Andy meditating before curtain time, Tony getting knifed . . . these are all different stories.

Sc. 51: George and Zmuda discuss Andy. When "Gatsby" got cut, this scene, oddly enough, still remained. As shot, George was discussing Andy's *Gatsby* stunt. With the editorial lift, he now magically appeared to be referring to *Taxi* and the deli job. Editing is an amazingly fluid process.

Sc. 52: Driving up to the Mustang Ranch. This was shot but cut for pacing.

Sc. 53: The Mustang Ranch. This whorehouse was an integral part of Andy's life. We heard about this place from so many people, we felt obligated to include it. Even Andy's Mom used to say Andy was "going to camp."

As research, we went. No, just kidding. As research, we watched an obscure documentary about the facility, *The House That Joe Built.*

Sc. 55: George warns Ed. This was cut from the script. Now, George tips off ABC immediately.

Sc. 56: Andy becomes Tony. This was also cut from the script. We were drawing a distinction between early- and late-period Tony: At first his makeup was just a wig and mustache, but after Andy became more famous and ambitious, he hired a makeup artist to create a rubber face. Only then was he unrecognizable. Milos thought this overcomplicated, so in the film, Tony is always under latex.

Sc. 57: Tony destroys *Taxi*. Unbelievably, our first version of this was twelve pages long. All the participants brainwashed us with their lovingly detailed anecdotes, and we spun out of control. Eventually, we realized this wasn't life—this was a film—and it could only support a few pages. What's amusing is that all contemporary accounts indicate that the cast had no idea who Tony really was. But now they all wink and say they knew all along.

Incidentally, we realize that *ED WEINBERGER* should be spelled *ED. WEINBERGER*. But the extra period wreaked havoc on our word-processing program.

Sc. 64: Tony gets thrown off the lot. Jim ad-libbed the funny ending at the gate. Jim always looked out for Tony, beefing up his scenes with extra insults.

Sc. 65: Ed gets a call. This was shot but cut for time. The real Ed told us the story, and it truly impressed us. Andy was being inclusive. Initially he forced people into his psycho reality . . . but then afterward, he essentially hugged and thanked them. He made Ed feel good about the experience.

Sc. 67: The tennis game (and more). This scene was deleted. More essentially, the following 38 pages (through Sc. 112) are where the movie's structure radically changed. The script was too long, and this section took the heat. Working with Milos, we had to heavily reorder, and ten pages were cut. Many ideas were combined. Zmuda as Clifton was radically shortened. Three *Fridays* set pieces became one. The Boston police bust was cut.

What was lost of importance was cause and effect . . . the repercussions of Andy's actions. (Andy's down! Andy's up! Andy's up and down!) In the final script, *Fridays* just leads back to wrestling. And on a character level, we lost Andy choosing to market his insanity—his turning point.

This is the problem with a script that's too long to shoot. Different parties (director, producer, star) respond to different ideas. They like and dislike different things. Yet somehow, we have to keep everyone happy while getting the pages down.

Sc. 68–75: Andy on *Fridays*. This moved to the middle of the wrestling section. Michael was taken out—we tried to keep family in the movie, but he was expendable. Initially, we saved Maynard's reveal for the end, the moment when we realize he's in on it. Now, in the film, actor Vincent Schiavelli has a crazy, pleased smile for the entire scene.

Sc. 77–78: Fallout from *Fridays*. These were deleted, and the first and second "Fridays" were combined. We liked the absurdity of it all: Andy's sanity truly made the front page of the *New York Times*.

The Maynard scene is interesting because it takes Andy's stunt seriously. The Establishment is quite threatened by him.

Sc. 79–81: Andy preps for *Fridays*, Part 2. These transitions were eliminated. Again, we're using Andy's fury and unwillingness to compromise as motivation.

Sc. 83–84: *Fridays* hits the jackpot. These were also eliminated.

Sc. 86–87: The Boston show. This extravaganza was an early script cut. It was hard to defend—we just liked it as a fun bauble. It's sort of a true story, and then we exaggerated everything. Also, it was a nice way to keep sister Carol in the story. Our original script had lots of family—but in the movie, they barely register. It's a drag, but only so many facets of Andy's life could fit into the final film.

Sc. 88: Tony confides in George. This is our favorite lost scene. For a brief moment Andy seems to get genuine, and he shares a rare intimacy with George. It's a relaxed, special moment between friends. And then it turns out it's not Andy. This was the most painful loss when the script was restructured.

Sc. 89: George yells at Andy and Zmuda. This scene migrated to the end of the Tahoe sequence. Yet strangely . . .

Sc. 90: Tony gets booked. This *following* scene became the *beginning* of the Tahoe sequence.
A side note: In real life, George was forced to set up fictitious management for Tony Clifton. There was even a secret phone number that used code words and fake staff.

Sc. 92–93: Andy decides to become a wrestler. Initially, we had this beat take two pages. In the final script, we shortened it to one quick scene with Andy and Zmuda.

Sc. 95: Andy wrestles Lynne on *Merv*. This is completely made up. We knew Andy was going to wrestle women in the movie, so it seemed a logical place to introduce Lynne. Andy often dated his opponents. When casting, everyone cracked up at the idea of Courtney Love: We all agreed we'd enjoy seeing her wrestle.
In real life, Andy and Lynne met on a different, more obscure production: She appeared in the film *My Breakfast with Blassie,* which was directed by her brother, wrestling promoter Johnny Legend.

Sc. 97: Gold's Gym. In the final script, we cut out Buddy Rogers. He was written as a composite of himself and Freddie Blassie, two guys meaningful to Andy. We tried to include everybody, but there were just too many characters.

Sc. 99: Andy buys popcorn. This is the sort of small moment that comes out of interviews. Somebody told us that they once saw Andy walk into a theater on Ventura Boulevard, buy a container of popcorn, and walk out. We turned it into Andy's version of a date, but during editing, this joke got cut.

Sc. 100: Andy dates Lynne. The middle of the scene got cut from the script—Andy and Lynne doing street theater. These sorts of shenanigans were constant with Andy . . . and his way of testing whether people could be his friends. It was a way for Andy and Lynne to bond. In the movie, it just plays like he's instantly obsessed with her.

Sc. 101: Memphis. Lawler was the only major character we hadn't interviewed. Because we were giving away his secret, we were honestly afraid to talk with him. We didn't know what he'd make of us revealing he was "in on it." Pro wrestling has a weird secret-society code of honor. Until this film, people thought Andy and Lawler were huge enemies, particularly as Andy had worked things out: Brawls, threats, neck injury, and finally the Letterman fight. Therefore, we were quite relieved when Lawler agreed to play himself in the film—as written. His character is shown from only one POV . . . until his last scene, when we learn the truth. We wanted to make the audience gasp.

Sc. 106: George begs Andy. In this scene, George sends Andy to Tahoe. In the final draft, he sends him to *Fridays*.

Sc. 107–111: Tony in Tahoe. This is the most radically changed sequence that's still in the movie. It reflects a philosophical shift. In our initial draft (this version), we were loyal to a rather abstruse, esoteric concept that was important to Andy. He wanted Tony's public identity to be murky. They denied being each other, yet there was clear evidence for both arguments. On TV, it was almost arbitrary whether Andy or Zmuda played Tony. In Tahoe, it was Zmuda—yet Andy visibly paraded around the hotel to confuse people. On *The Midnight Special,* Andy conversed with Tony, but he was playing both parts. The one time Andy unilaterally tipped his hand, bringing Tony onstage with him at Carnegie Hall, it was actually his brother Michael!

This last event is the prototype for the shooting script version. Tony abuses the audience, which endures him because they believe him to be Andy. But then Andy makes a short appearance onstage. Tony chases him away, and the crowd realizes they've been screwed over. It's funny, in a totally different way. This version leaves the audience angry. Our initial version left them bewildered.

Sc. 112: Tony and the showgirl. Pretty silly, huh? Well, believe it or not, we actually had an even more ridiculous follow-up scene:

```
INT. TAXI DRESSING ROOMS - DAY

Andy strides up to his dressing room, opens the door...and
inside is the Tahoe Showgirl, NAKED AGAIN.

Andy gasps. The girl smiles sexily.

                         NAKED GIRL
        Hi, Andy. Did you miss me?

Andy is speechless.

Wow. His mind is racing, desperately trying to figure out just
who exactly this bombshell is.


                         ANDY
        Uh, uh...


                         NAKED GIRL
        Those nights in Tahoe were the sexual highlight of my life.

ON ANDY

His face is wracked with confusion — struggling to understand —
until, BING! — he suddenly figures it out.

Andy smiles slyly.

                         ANDY
        I'm even better when I'm not Clifton.

He walks towards her, as the door swings SHUT.

Beat.

Then, she squeals o.s.

                    NAKED GIRL (o.s.)
        Weird! I don't remember you being circumcised.
```

Yikes! How'd *that* get in the book? Well, we'll send it back to the British
sex comedy it fell out of.

P.S. Zmuda claims it's a true story.

Sc. 119: Andy with the doctor. The scene of Andy demanding the neck
brace was shot but cut.

Sc. 120–121: Andy's folks think he's hurt. In our original draft, Mom and
Dad see Andy's accident on the news, then call him on the phone. Milos had us

move the scene to Memphis, backstage. The actors were terrific. But during editing, Milos worried that this moment was tipping off the Lawler reveal. So it all got cut.

Sc. 122–128: Andy milks his injury. This was all axed after the first draft, but we thought it was hilarious. In real life, Andy milked the neck brace for months. He totally blurred the line between art and behavior, refusing to admit he was okay. People said it went on so long that the neck brace became smelly from spilled food.

The moment where Ed watches Andy's injury frame by frame is stolen from Danny DeVito. Danny is actually the one who got hold of a tape and figured it out.

Sc. 129: George begs Lorne Michaels. Well . . . in our script you'll notice that the man's name isn't LORNE MICHAELS. It's SNL PRODUCER. That's because Michaels wasn't the producer of the show when Andy got torpedoed. It was Dick Ebersol. For the sake of dramatic unity, we combined the characters, but we didn't feel comfortable blaming Michaels for something he didn't do. So we made the character nameless. However, Milos eventually fast-talked Lorne Michaels into playing the part, so none of this mattered.

Sc. 132: *Saturday Night Live*'s election. We made up the connection between this event and Letterman. It's this re-ordering that creates an illusion of story.

The election itself was very traumatic for Andy. He didn't expect the results to be taken literally. Andy's family claims that he thought it was a gag—Andy assumed he'd be back next week, fighting his way onstage in a disguise.

Desperate, Andy shot an absurd 30-second commercial, where he asks viewers to pressure NBC into putting him back on the air. He was going to buy time on local stations around the country, trying to drum up grassroots support. But this ploy proved unreasonably expensive, so he gave up.

Sc. 134–139: Andy becomes born-again. This section is the last big cut. It made it to draft six—then got yanked. Andy's Christian misadventure was amusing, but it was one "Fridays" too many.

Structurally, we were trying something unusual. In the second half of the story, Andy's act became too unpleasant. The predicament was how to modulate his behavior. So we wrote two sequences where Andy was *falsely* acting sweet. The Christian routine (not shot) and the Improv heckling (shot but cut) were designed to give the audience a breather. Even though Andy was blatantly insincere, he was still calm and smiling.

Andy's "bride" Cathy Sullivan was a real gospel singer from the *Lawrence Welk Show*. She good-naturedly went along with the ruse, until her mother told her to knock it off.

Sc. 140: Andy is thrown out of TM. In the shooting script, the scene opens less busy. Andy simply leads a class.

Originally, we had tons more TM throughout the movie. It was a huge part of Andy's life, and he used to talk about it incessantly. Here's a nutty deleted scene, a true story, which shows how far his beliefs went:

```
INT. VOLKSWAGEN BUG - NIGHT

Little Wendy drives Andy home. He tries to cheer her up.

                    ANDY
          Hey! Did I tell you where I'm going this weekend?

                    LITTLE WENDY
          No...

                    ANDY
                (eyes twinkling)
          The TM levitation seminar!

Wendy is awed.

                    LITTLE WENDY
          They accepted you?!

                    ANDY
          Yeah, I had to write a personal letter to the Maharishi.
                (beat)
          And pay them eight thousand dollars.
                (beat)
          But it's worth it! I'm goin' to India, and they'll teach
          me how to fly!

                    LITTLE WENDY
          I've seen the pictures. Some students get six inches off
          the ground.

                    ANDY
          Nah, those're beginners. I'm gonna go WAY up! I'll use it
          as the finale to my concerts. I'll do foreign man...Elvis
          ...and then I'll soar out over the heads of the audience!!
          They'll look up, and I'll fly out of the building!!
                (totally caught up)
          Then people will leave and get in their cars, and I'll be
          up in the sky, waving goodbye!!
                (beatific)
          No one's EVER ended a show like that!

Wendy looks up at him, and laughs softly.

                    LITTLE WENDY
          Wow.
```

                                                  CUT TO:

(A few scenes later...)

INT. AIRPORT TERMINAL - DAY

INDIAN PASSENGERS in saris exit an airplane. Little Wendy and
Zmuda wait — she's giddy, he's bored.

                         LITTLE WENDY
          I wonder if he actually learned to fly?!

                         ZMUDA
          Dummy, if he learned how to fly, we wouldn't be waiting at
          the airport. He'd just show up at the house.

At that — Andy listlessly shuffles into view.

                    LITTLE WENDY AND ZMUDA
          HEY! Andy!

They run over and hug him.

                         LITTLE WENDY
          So how'd it go...??!

                         ANDY
                    (blasé)
          Did you know they don't have Häagen-Dazs in India? Boy,
          I'm dying for a Häagen-Dazs.

Beat.

                         ZMUDA
          Yeah...? But...what happened?

                         ANDY
          Oh, I got an overseas phone call from George. Guess I'm
          supposed to do Fridays next week.

Longer beat. Finally Zmuda EXPLODES.

                         ZMUDA
          Andy, STOP FUCKIN' AROUND! Can you fly, or CAN'T you???

Andy quietly sighs.

                         ANDY
          I can't levitate.

                              175

                          LITTLE WENDY
        Oh no...

                              ZMUDA
        I KNEW it was bullshit!
                               ANDY
                          (gently correcting)
        No no no... I could've done it. There are some people who can...
                          (pause)
        But there's too much of a price to be paid.

Zmuda rolls his eyes.

                              ZMUDA
        Yeah, right, whatever. Alright, let's get to the baggage
        carousel—

                               ANDY
        No, Bob, you don't understand!
                          (impassioned)
        There was a catch. If you wanna levitate, you have to
        cleanse your body with total purity and reverence.
                          (distraught)
        You can't screw.
                          (beat)
        FOR A YEAR!
                          (long beat; very soft)
        It's just not worth it.

Silence. The friends look at each other. Bob and Wendy feel bad for
Andy. This has been a crushing experience. Until — she smiles slyly.

                          LITTLE WENDY
        Do you really have to fly???

Andy laughs.

Sc. 141: Andy and Lynne in bed. This scene contains the key lines in the
movie: "You don't know the real me." "Andy, there *is* no real you." For this concept, we're eternally grateful to Lynne.

    On-set, Jim ad-libbed a tender singing of the old Slim Whitman tune "Rose-
Marie."

Sc. 145: Andy's cyst routine. We stumbled across this morsel on *Evening at
the Improv.* The bit was originally whimsical, but by inserting it at this point in the
movie, it touches on his artistic decline and self-loathing. The moment also fore-
shadows his sickness.

Sc. 146: Budd counsels Andy. This was shot but cut.

Sc. 147–150: Andy gets heckled. This was shot and turned out quite interesting, but it all got cut. The original routine was one of the most brilliant things Andy ever did—we found it on a *Catch a Rising Star* anniversary special.

This was a perfect example of editing out a good scene. Jim and Paul Giamatti were terrific. Danny's depressed reactions were right on. But when the rough cut was strung together, the heckling and cyst scenes seemed too similar. They read completely differently—the cyst is maudlin, while the heckling is a cerebral deconstruction of Andy's art. But on film they both played as sad, emotional beats. The movie needed only one.

Hopefully, this scene will turn up on the DVD.

Sc. 151–153: Andy disappears. These scenes were compressed to just Lynne, but it didn't get shot.

Sc. 154: Andy announces he has cancer. We wanted Andy's sickness to play as 90-percent sincere, 10-percent suspicious. So this scene was written that way, with a dollop of doubt.

Our entire third act had this balance. We feel sorry for Andy, we laugh at people not believing him—but perhaps we're not sure. To do this, we laced uncertainty throughout the script, as well as numerous references to Andy faking his death. We wanted the viewer off-balance until the final fade-out.

Ultimately, this struck Milos as an intellectual exercise—at some point it had to end. He disagreed on a key point: We weren't making an Andy Kaufman film, we were making a film about Andy Kaufman—meaning that this was the story of a man, and eventually, we had to take that man seriously. So as the final movie winds its way to the end, doubt drops away. It all plays real.

Sc. 157–158: The family at the hospital. These two scenes were combined. The family talks only to the doctor, not to Andy.

Sc. 160: George sees the Guru. In a zany piece of casting, the Guru is played by Johnny Legend.

Sc. 163: Andy plans the show. In the movie, the scene is extended. Milos wanted Andy to talk about Tony one last time.

Sc. 164: Andy with the doctor at Cedars. This was cut from the script. Too much cancer talk.

In a bizarre footnote, many years earlier, Andy and Zmuda had written a script called *The Tony Clifton Story*. It was a lavish enactment of Tony's life. Yet in this fictitious script, Tony dies of cancer at Cedars-Sinai. It's truly spooky, since that's exactly what happened to Andy.

Sc. 167: Andy backstage at Carnegie Hall. This was cut from the script. The "weakened star must go on" was probably too hammy for Milos.

Sc. 168-172: Carnegie Hall Show. This is our favorite lie. Everyone who knew Andy pinpointed this show as his greatest achievement. The concert, followed by milk and cookies, was hilarious, warm, and thrilling. The event felt like the culmination of Andy's career . . . so we made it our finale.

Of all the acts in the show, "raising the dead" seemed thematically the most appropriate. We also included Michael in the show, representing family, to help tie together different strands of Andy's life.

Sc. 173-175: Staten Island Ferry. This was cut from the shooting script. Like milk and cookies, it was gentle and sweet. However, Milos thought the sequence had too many endings. When two scenes in a row have similar emotions, it's hard to defend them.

Sc. 176: Andy and George. This was combined with Sc. 183. In the final script, the third act is condensed to make each point only once.

Sc. 177: Tony in the kitchen. This scene was our way of crystallizing a key Kaufmanesque concept: Andy is sick, but Tony's not. Andy joked about it, but never took the denial as far as we have in the script.

Milos once suggested an even crazier idea: The doctor tells Andy he has cancer. So Andy leaves and returns as Tony. The doctor examines Tony, then says he's perfectly healthy!

Sc. 178: Airport. This scene was in the script until the very last draft. We confronted Andy directly with his problem—nobody believes he's dying—then let him laugh at it. It made him strong.

The altercation with the paparazzo really happened. Once the picture showed up in the *Enquirer,* Andy knew he'd passed the point of no return.

Sc. 181: Zmuda fights with the administrator. This was shot but cut. It's unfortunate that this scene was lost—it moved Zmuda's character from being a wise guy to being a friend.

Sc. 184-188: Andy in the Philippines. This sequence was our biggest crapshoot: A three-page climax without dialogue. Creatively, it was daring, since our script was so talky up until then.

Everything is done visually. We take Andy from belief, to shock, to disappointment, to laughter . . . to his funeral. Nothing is overtly explained. After a test screening, we breathed a huge sigh of relief: The focus group was asked if they had any confusion about the scene—and they said no.

SC. 189: The funeral. This scene changed dramatically in the shooting script, and then even more on the set. Originally, we were going for total ambiguity. We heard so many stories about people peeking behind curtains and poking the body . . . and we wanted to capture that oddness. As a cheap movie device, we put the entire cast there, to experience it. Zmuda gets the key line: "It's a perfect Kaufman audience. They don't know whether to be sad, or angry."

However, Milos was strongly influenced by a tape we had shown him—a memorial service at the Improv where a touching video of Andy's song "Friendly World" had been played. As stated earlier, Milos felt strongly that the funeral was literal: Andy had clearly died. So he asked us to center the funeral on "Friendly World." Go with the emotion. We did that, but also kept the crowd's confused dialogue. In production, however, none of the dialogue got shot. So at Andy's funeral, Andy got all the lines!

Here is the final version:

INT. FUNERAL HOME - DAY

Andy lies at peace in a casket. He has died.

His expression is pleasantly bland. Almost Latka-like. But his face is caked with so much funeral-home makeup, it almost looks like a mask.

We slowly widen. The casket is surrounded by beautiful flowers. We TILT UP...and high above...is a MOVIE SCREEN.

On the SCREEN is a projection of Andy, silently staring at us. There's a gentle smile on his face. It's the image from the opening of this film.

ANDY'S POV: The chapel is filled with GRIEVING MOURNERS. All are in black. Everyone's quiet, in a state of shock.

Andy's family is huddled.

Lynne sits alone in a pew, crying.

George gives Zmuda a hug. Little Wendy comes over...and they comfort each other.

Everyone who ever knew Andy is there: *Taxi* cast, *Fridays* cast, TM followers, hookers, Jerry Lawler, Ed Weinberger, Budd Friedman, it goes on and on...

And — they all have odd discombobulated expressions. They stare up at the PROJECTED ANDY.

                    ANDY (ON FILM)
        Well...my show is over. I did my best, and I just want to
        say, until we meet again...please remember:
                         (he begins to SING)
        "In this friendly, friendly world,
        With each day so full of joy,
        Why should any heart be lonely?"

179

Some gathered people tentatively join in the SINGING.

> ANDY (ON FILM)
> So everybody! Put your arm around the person next to you,
> even if you don't like that person. Come on!
> (he resumes SINGING)
> "The world is such a wonderful place
> To wander through.
> When you've got someone to love,
> To wander along with you.
> With the sky so full of stars,
> And the river so full of songs.
> Every heart should be so thankful,
> Thankful for this friendly, friendly world."

The curtain behind the coffin OPENS, and the casket with Andy's
body slowly slides into the DARKNESS.

The curtain closes. The FILM ENDS.

And all goes silent.

Sc. 190–191: Tony's return. In the shooting script, these two scenes were combined. The Dudes represent all fans and the audience is us. Tony Clifton's reappearance was an incredibly strange event, and the media collectively freaked out when it happened. Most Kaufman fans believed he had come back, and this scene was designed to goose expectations. But in production, the club exterior spun out of control with extras, cars, and cranes, and the actors never got filmed.

Sc. 192: Tony onstage. This was always the ending of our script. Even when we knew nothing else, we knew we'd go out with Tony singing and Zmuda applauding. This scene left things funny and sad, serious and ridiculous, resolved yet open-ended. It hit the emotions we were striving for the entire movie.

As stated earlier, we had test screenings with and without Zmuda. This led to berserk Internet gossip about multiple endings. The weirdest rumors were: The movie ends with Andy getting plastic surgery to become Tony, or there's a final shot of Jim Carrey getting acting tips from the *real* Andy Kaufman. We deny these charges.

Of course, we think as a final post-post-punch line, a mysterious bandaged figure should show up at the *Man on the Moon* premiere. We'll let you know who it really is. . . .

In closing, we want to thank the movie's big supporters. At Universal, Ron Meyer, Stacey Snider, and Kevin Misher were huge advocates of the film. And at Jersey, Stacey Sher was our biggest fan, the self-appointed "guardian of the script" who always fought for what mattered. Thanks.

STILLS

Inset: Andy Kaufman as Elvis. *Above:* Jim Carrey as Andy Kaufman as Elvis.

Above left: Danny DeVito as George Shapiro. *Right*: George Shapiro.
Below left: Paul Giamatti as Bob Zmuda. *Right:* Bob Zmuda.

Above: Courtney Love and Jim Carrey as Lynne Margulies and Andy Kaufman.
Inset: Lynne and Andy. *Below:* Little Wendy plays herself in the movie.
Inset: Andy Kaufman and Little Wendy.

Above (clockwise): The Kaufman Kids: Michael, Carol, and Andy. Stanley Kaufman and the actor playing him, Gerry Becker; Melanie Vesey, who plays Andy's sister, Carol Kaufman Kerman; Michael Kaufman and his movie counterpart, Michael Kelly.
Below: Jerry Lawler plays himself in the movie.

Above: Tony Clifton being thrown off the set of *Taxi* in 1978. *Below:* Tony Clifton re-creating the same scene for the movie.

Andy Kaufman and Jim Carrey playing the bongos on stage.

Above: Andy Kaufman fights with Jack Burns, live, on set of *Fridays*. Michael Richards (pre-*Seinfeld*) is in the background. *Below:* Bob Zmuda plays Jack Burns and Norm MacDonald (in the background) is Michael Richards in the movie re-creation of the fight.

Above: Original photograph of Tony Clifton and Andy Kaufman appearing together on stage. *Below:* Tony Clifton and Jim Carrey appear together on stage at Harrah's Tahoe in the movie.

Above: Danny DeVito, Milos Forman, and Jim Carrey. *Below:* Actors Leslie Lyles (Andy's mom) and Gerry Becker (Andy's dad) with Jim Carrey after his wrestling "injury."

Andy Kaufman *(top)* and Jim Carrey *(below)* on stage at Carnegie Hall.

TALKING WITH

MILOS FORMAN
BY SCOTT ALEXANDER & LARRY KARASZEWSKI

Man on the Moon is the second collaboration between the writing team of Scott Alexander and Larry Karaszewski and director Milos Forman. Although their first movie, The People vs. Larry Flynt, *was also a biopic, here they were dealing with a much different central character and a very different film. In the late summer of 1999, when the film was almost in its final edit, the writers sat down with the director to discuss the making of the movie and what attracted each of them to Andy Kaufman. The interview that resulted is part question-and-answer and part free-for-all.*

LK: Now, is it true you actually saw Andy perform?

That's where it all started, in 1975 or '76. Buck Henry took me to the Improv. And then at two in the morning, this guy comes on the stage. There weren't that many people in the audience. And he had a little book, and he said, "I'm going to read you a short story about this guy whose name was this. And when he was this old, he went there and there and then he met this and that person and they did this and this and then they went there and there and did this and that." For ten minutes he's telling you what the story would be about. And so okay, okay, we're waiting. And then he opened the book and started to read in a very monotonous way the whole short story from beginning to end. And the first five minutes, I felt sorry for him, because the Improv is where new comedians try out. I said, oh my God, does this poor guy think he's going to be funny? I just felt sorry for him. He was pathetic, and everybody was sort of cringing. But then—after another five minutes, I was (and not only me!) on the floor *laughing*. And I didn't know why! Just suddenly, it started to work, and then I felt good about him.

After that, whenever I heard about Andy, or saw him on TV, it was like a magnet. I don't know how magnets work. I don't know what draws you, what draws the metal to the metal. I don't know the principle. But every time I got close to Andy, somehow I felt the pull. And then when I learned more details about his life, how his alter ego developed, I started to be very, very intrigued. This might be a story for a movie.

Especially in the beginning, I was thinking that if this guy learns or even feels that something is wrong with him, his life will be short. That's why he's developing the alter ego. That's why he's developing this character, Tony. And Tony has to be an arrogant man, because he has to live if Andy dies. And, of course, that's not true. But that was, for me, the dramatic engine.

Then, I was at Michael Douglas's birthday party in New York…and there's Danny DeVito, whom I hadn't seen for many, many years. But I remembered him as a wonderful guy. I worked with him on *Cuckoo's Nest*; he was a friend, a wonderful actor, and he worked with Andy. So I sat down and said, I would like to make a film about Andy Kaufman. And he was enthusiastic. Then I called you, and that's how it started.

SA: But as we began working on the project, we couldn't figure out why *you'd* want to direct it. Because all your other movies are very honest about what they're presenting. You don't withhold information. You present the truth naturalistically. However, this particular movie is all manipulation. It lies to the audience.

I don't see any conflict here. Because if you are naturalistic and real about this guy who is so unreal, then that unrealness will be even more real and interesting and fascinating.

LK: It's a movie about a magician.

And I don't mean it to be derogatory at all, but I think that this guy really lived only when he was performing. Not only on the stage, but in real life. When he was not performing, for the rest of the world, he seemed like a small, boring guy. I know a few people like that, not only comedians, but actors, dancers. And usually it's the most brilliant ones. They don't live unless they perform. And that's Andy.

SA: Danny talked about that during "Taxi." A few times he and Rhea invited Andy over to dinner, and a dull guy in a T-shirt would show up and just sit there hunched over and eat his food.

That's what I mean.

SA: He was trying to get close to Andy, and there was nothing there.

No, no, absolutely. When he says, "You don't know the real me," and she says, "There is no real you," the audience gets it. That's the line.

SA: Do you think differently of Andy now, than before you made the movie?

Yeah, I like him more. It's like somebody charms you, so you want to spend more time with him.

SA: As we structured the story, something we thought about a lot was that the movie needed the form of Andy's routines, because they were exciting when they were live. The movie needed this surprise and manipulation, so that your experience watching the film is like an audience experiencing Andy twenty years ago. Is that something you thought about while you were shooting?

Yes, but only in a sense that I realized how, more than any other film I ever made, the audience extras are important, because they really represent Andy's antagonist. His antagonists are not George, or Lynne, or Zmuda. His antagonist is the public.

SA: People paying to see him.

People paying to see him! So you have to make these people live on the screen. So that I, as an audience, can understand these people reacting to his act. That's me! That's my feeling about seeing Andy for the first time.

SA: Did you keep the extras in the dark that Tony was Jim? Did they know what was going on?

No, they didn't know. We never explained it to them in detail. They were just told, listen, this guy, Tony Clifton, is saying things which some of you will be offended by. Please feel offended and express it. Some of you will find them funny—please feel free to laugh. Some of you will find them totally uninteresting—so keep quiet. Whatever you feel.

SA: When you shot "Gatsby," were you actually boring the extras, by reading them the book?

Well, "Gatsby" was a little different, because it was Jim Carrey playing Andy. The audience knew. They loved Jim Carrey. Even those who didn't know Andy loved Jim. So they had to be told . . . no, no, no.

LK: Don't like this so much.

Yeah. Don't be so crazy about Jim Carrey. Here you will react this way, and here you will react that way.

LK: That's probably the biggest difference between the screenplay and the film— the character of the *audience*—which is something you really can't do on a page.

On the page you can't do it.

LK: It was all about the routine; it was about what was going through Andy's head. In the movie you just see the transformation of the people watching, like "What the hell is this guy about?!" Trying to figure him out.

I have to compliment David McGiffert [first assistant director], because the only thing I told him was, I want this film to be a kaleidoscope of American faces. And he was dealing not with hundreds, but *thousands,* of extras. So then he told me, that row over there, I picked you those faces, and that section over here, I picked some interesting ones.

SA: One of my favorite extras is a guy in Harrah's Tahoe. When Tony starts singing "I've Gotta Be Me," he sort of starts applauding, like he's being entertained.

Yeah, yeah, yeah!

SA: He paid good money to get in, he got a good table, and he's hearing the hits. I know that song!

LK: The extras' reactions were always changing. I've never worked on a film that was as liquid in the editing room. You seemed willing to try anything. Things would be thrown out, they'd come back, a scene would have a reaction shot for three screenings, then next time, there'd be a different take. Did this movie accommodate that more than your other films?

Yes, because the same number of options you are trying with the principals, here, it was important to try with the extras. And we had tons. You can't be behind six cameras and tell them exactly what you want to see, so you let them shoot. You just give them the general direction. And sometimes it's very difficult, because suddenly you have three options, and they are all good. And that's the worst—because it's easy to think that one of them is the best, let's go. But with that one, very often in editing you must experience it. You change something here and suddenly you realize, because of this change, you have to start changing things afterwards.

SA: At the test screenings, the reaction shots on Danny kept changing. There were things I'd gotten used to, and suddenly, there was a new face there.
LK: When you work on films, that so rarely happens. You lock yourself in.
SA: This was a very loose production. During shooting, you even let Jim re-create Andy's madness, bringing that experience onto the set.

Well, this film was more special than any other film I'd made, because every day I was dealing with a different leading man. Andy was very pleasant, but you had to treat Andy, I mean Jim as Andy, with more caution. Like a snail, when you touch the horns, they pull in; so you have to be careful not to touch them. But as long as you didn't, Andy was wonderful to work with.

SA: He created a level of chaos. It worked against the filmmaking schedule, but it was in the spirit of experiencing it like Andy would have.

Yeah, and you would have to accommodate, not try for him to accommodate *you*. You just have to accommodate yourself to his pace and rhythm and everything. On the other hand, Tony Clifton was a nightmare to deal with. You never knew if he was listening to you, so you never knew if he'd do what you asked him to do. You never knew if he'd antagonize the other actors. Now, Latka was the easiest. Latka was a puppy dog. Latka was great. Elvis was easy, because Elvis wouldn't let you talk to him. He knew his things, and he would do it and didn't give a damn what anybody wanted.

SA: Were there people on the production who dreaded Tony days? The AD's, the production manager, like, oh God, we have Tony tomorrow?

Yeah, but they didn't do it in a dismissing way. They dreaded it with a certain excitement. Because Tony was Tony.

SA: I love how you call them "Andy" and "Tony."

Oh, well, that developed somehow. You know, Jim is as good an actor as he is a comedian. And he's a brilliant comedian. And I can say now, that during the shooting, I never met Jim Carrey. I either met Andy Kaufman or Tony Clifton or Latka or Elvis or Foreign Man, whatever. And after a couple of days, we started to call him the character. In the morning, Andy came, so everybody called him Andy.

SA: Have you ever had that happen on a movie before?

No, not to this extent. I remember when Jack Nicholson came on the set in the morning. Before the first clap he was Jack. From the first clap to the last he was Mac. When I said cut, he was Jack again. But this guy, Jim, he was never there. In the middle of the shooting, one Saturday I had dinner with Jim, and I felt intimidated. I felt like I was dining with somebody I met for the first time.

LK: A stranger.

SA: Plus, you also had a lot of the real people on the set. You had the real George, the real Lynne, the real Bob. They were around while you're shooting this movie about their lives. Was that a problem?

No! As a matter of fact, I like to do these things very much. It gives me a kind of extra excitement, and pleasure, and fun, that this is the whole movie right from the beginning.

SA: But that never made it hard for you to focus? When you're trying to do a scene, and you have the real person standing in your eye line?

No, no, no. You are just like the racing horse who can see what's in front of you. No peripheral vision, once you start working.

LK: The only time you confused me in the movie was when Andy's real dad was sitting behind Andy's fake dad, at *Saturday Night Live*. And I don't know which one I'm supposed to be looking at.

SA: Andy's fake dad doesn't like the show, but Andy's real dad is laughing.

[Everyone laughs.]

LK: You even have people playing themselves, like Jerry Lawler, Lorne Michaels, Little Wendy. That must have been a totally different experience.

It makes it more special.

SA: But what was it like for Letterman and Lawler, re-creating this exact moment, twenty years later, but with a different Andy? I mean, were they huddling among themselves, saying, "Can you believe we're doing this?" It must have been strange for them.

Well, obviously, they had very, very fond memories of what they had done. They were happy to re-create the past, for the sake of memory.

SA: When you make this kind of movie, about real people, does it matter to you if something is exactly true or not?

It depends. Sometimes it matters. When I was working with Peter Shaffer on Mozart, very often I asked, is this true? Did this really happen? And Peter said, look, the story is a summary of facts. But drama is the summary of the *spirit* of the facts. So as long as we don't betray the spirit, you can change the facts.

SA: But aren't the rules different when you're doing *Amadeus*? They're all dead. You're not gonna run into Salieri. Do you feel more inhibited with *Larry Flynt* and this film because they're real people you might bump into in a restaurant?

It doesn't matter, because it doesn't make any difference. You know, Larry found things that were different. But he never objected to anything, because the idea or the spirit of the fact was true.

SA: I think Larry had an appreciation for myth. Larry could look at his own life objectively as drama and as a character in drama. He could separate his own life from the presentation of his life.
LK: He had been giving a presentation of his life for so many years.
SA: Bob Zmuda also has a bit of that. He's able to look at his own events as part of a three-act drama.
LK: I'd ask Zmuda a question and he'd say, "If I say yes to that, will I get another scene in the movie?!"
[He laughs.] That's great, that's great!

SA: Sometimes, when we were writing, we'd almost feel more of a freedom with a Zmuda scene than a family scene . . . because the family are real people living regular lives. And we're not sure what they're going to think of what we write. Whereas Zmuda, he's a performer himself.
He is creating his own life. Even if he is not living it!
[Everyone laughs.]

SA: He's a terrific performer. We quickly figured out, watching all the old tapes, that Zmuda's Tony Clifton is much better than Andy's Tony Clifton. Because Andy was trying to deconstruct the presentation and just make it bad for the sake of being bad. But Zmuda was shining, in the spotlight. Zmuda's Tony is hilarious.
LK: Andy used Tony as a way not to be entertaining. Zmuda's Tony is obnoxious, but he's trying to entertain.
It's interesting, that's almost the same thing in the film when Paul Giamatti does Tony.

LK: Well, Tony does that to you. Even when I'm imitating Tony, I become the entertainer.
SA: Does Tony get billing on the poster? Tony Clifton as himself?
On the poster, I don't know. I don't think so.

SA: Maybe he should. Like when they did *Sleuth*. The detective got billing, with a fake name.
No. I think we even took Tony's credit out from after the film, because it would just add to the confusion.

SA: It's weird, in the book we've got stills. And one of them is Tony Clifton at the Comedy Store. And usually you caption it, you know, "Paul Giamatti as Bob Zmuda," that sort of thing. But we didn't know what caption went under that picture, because we don't know who it is!

[Everyone laughs.]

That's funny.

LK: Both *Amadeus* and this movie are about guys that died young, but it seems like their lives had so much packed in. It's like they almost had a premonition, that they wanted to do as much as they possibly could so that their body of work would outlive their actual bodies.

There are many parallels. They both died at the same age, thirty-five.

SA: Really? I didn't know that.

Oh yeah. They were both fighting death.

SA: Well . . . Salieri and Tony are very similar.

[Laughs.] Very similar.

SA: They both hate that good-looking young guy. Stealing his act, getting all the credit.

Well, I think that Andy Kaufman's genius was, he was more than a people's comedian. He was a comedian's comedian. They loved him, and I think it's because every comedian feels he's a failure. And Andy was the first comic who conquered this fear of failure, by including failure in his act. So if people either applauded or booed, it was a success. The failure worked.

SA: You played with that a lot in the movie. Andy loved manipulating how long he could torture an audience. And we've learned that you love shooting stuff in real time and re-creating real time. And there's a lot of points in this movie where any other filmmaker but you—like Andy doing silence on *Saturday Night Live*—would have held for three seconds, then cut. But you're happy to really be true to who Andy is.

Andy is directing this movie. He knows better.

LK: I mean, that void in the beginning of the movie, the black leader . . . pushed a little too far . . .

Yeah, that's what I mean, that's what I'm talking about!

LK: You sit there, you sit there, you get a little bored, and then you laugh.

Well, this is an odd movie. But Andy was an odd guy. Did you know that you were writing an odd movie?

SA: Oh yeah. It's the only movie we've ever written where we didn't think we could write it.

Really?

SA: We gave up hope a couple times. It's such an odd story, it didn't seem to be a movie.

Everything is a movie. If you adapt it well. But the danger here was that it not come across as just a simple biography. Going from chapter to chapter . . .

SA: But Milos, Larry and I openly admit that we like doing "biopics." We've written three, two directed by you, and we're about to start another one. We like that genre. But when you talk about it, you always sort of distance yourself. You don't talk about it as just a biopic. Yet when I think about your body of work, you've done a lot of movies with real historical figures. In fact, since *Ragtime*, everything except *Valmont* is about real people. So you don't like approaching it as a biopic . . . but there's something there you like.

Oh, well, I think that "biopic" is an abstract term which doesn't have too much meaning for me. Because every film is a biopic, even if it's about a fictional character. Plus, you know how often you hear or witness a real story and you realize, my God, nobody would believe this. Life is really giving you the best stories. And so it's not a biopic—it's just a real story, besides being a fake story. I don't think we would be able to invent this character, Andy. He's better than many invented stories.

LK: *Larry Flynt* was a very odd film, too. You'd never structure the movies like this if they didn't actually happen. Somebody would learn a lesson.
SA: Or Althea lives.

I don't think I should admit this, but it's not as important for me what the film is about, as it's important for me to make a movie about people I enjoy, for whatever reason. It's like going to a dinner party. I don't know what the dinner party is about, but if I enjoy two hours with these people, it's great. You know what I mean? If we happen to be true, it will be about something. Because it will be about life, and life is always about something.

SA: Yeah, but you go to dinner parties with Buck Henry and Henry Kissinger. You have the cream of the crop. Not like the ones I go to.

Well, the oddest thing is that usually when you do a biographical or semi-biographical movie, the purpose it serves is to illuminate the characters. So that at the end, you know more than you knew before. But I think in this case, in the end you know less!

[Everyone laughs.]

SA: And you *know* that you know less!

But I do hope that people will experience what everybody who knew Andy experienced after his death. That now, you start to think, who was that guy? Who really was he? After they see the movie, only then will they start to try to fully figure out who the guy was.

CAST AND CREW CREDITS

UNIVERSAL PICTURES and MUTUAL FILM COMPANY Present

A JERSEY FILMS / CINEHAUS Production

In Association with
SHAPIRO / WEST PRODUCTIONS

A MILOS FORMAN Film

MAN ON THE MOON

JIM CARREY   DANNY DEVITO   COURTNEY LOVE   PAUL GIAMATTI

VINCENT SCHIAVELLI   PETER BONERZ   JERRY LAWLER   GERRY BECKER   LESLIE LYLES

Directed by MILOS FORMAN	*Director of Photography* ANASTAS MICHOS	*Score Produced by* PAT MCCARTHY
Written by SCOTT ALEXANDER & LARRY KARASZEWSKI	*Production Designer* PATRIZIA VON BRANDENSTEIN	*Music Supervisor* ANITA CAMARATA
Produced by DANNY DEVITO MICHAEL SHAMBERG STACEY SHER	*Edited by* CHRISTOPHER TELLEFSEN LYNZEE KLINGMAN, A.C.E.	*Costume Designer* JEFFREY KURLAND *Associate Producers* SCOTT FERGUSON PAMELA ABDY
Executive Producers GEORGE SHAPIRO HOWARD WEST	ADAM BOOME *Casting by*	*Unit Production Manager* MICHAEL HAUSMAN
Executive Producer MICHAEL HAUSMAN	FRANCINE MAISLER, C.S.A. KATHLEEN DRISCOLL- MOHLER, ASSOCIATE	*First Assistant Director* DAVID MCGIFFERT *Second Assistant Director* STEPHEN HAGEN
Co-Executive Producer BOB ZMUDA	*Music by* R.E.M.	

CAST
(In order of appearance)

Andy Kaufman	JIM CARREY	Meditation Students	MATT PRICE
Stanley Kaufman	GERRY BECKER		CHRISTINA CABOT
Little Michael Kaufman	GREYSON PENDRY	Richard Belzer	HIMSELF
Baby Carol Kaufman	BRITTANY COLONNA	Carol Kaufman	MELANIE VESEY
Janice Kaufman	LESLIE LYLES	Michael Kaufman	MICHAEL KELLY
Little Andy Kaufman	BOBBY BORIELLO	SNL Assistant	MILES CHAPIN
Mr. Besserman	GEORGE SHAPIRO	NBC Executive	DR. ISADORE ROSENFELD
George Shapiro	DANNY DEVITO	Maynard Smith	VINCENT SCHIAVELLI
Budd Friedman	HIMSELF	Maynard Smith's Assistant	MOLLY SCHAFFER
Wiseass Comic	TOM DREESEN	ABC Executives	HOWARD WEST
Improv Piano Player	THOMAS ARMBRUSTER		GREG TRAVIS
Diane Barnett	PAMELA ABDY		MAUREEN MUELLER
Little Wendy	WENDY POLLAND	Mama Rivoli's Angry Guy	PHIL PERLMAN
Yogi	CASH OSHMAN	Tony Clifton	HIMSELF

Mama Rivoli's Diner ....JESSICA DEVLIN
Bob Zmuda ....PAUL GIAMATTI
Andy's Stand-In ....JEFF THOMAS
Randall Carver ....HIMSELF
Ed Weinberger ....PETER BONERZ
Taxi Marching Man ....HOWARD KEYSTONE
Howdy Doody ....HIMSELF
Heavyset Technician ....BRENT BRISCOE
Blue Collar Guys ....RAY BOKHOUR
                                  PATTON OSWALT
Sorority Girl ....CAROLINE GIBSON
College Promoter ....CONRAD ROBERTS
College Student ....JEFF ZABEL
Madame ....MARILYN SOKOL
Hookers ....ANGELA JONES
                                KRYSTINA CARSON
Taxi AD/Stage Manager ....GERRY ROBERT BYRNE
LA Times Reporter ....MARK DAVENPORT
Taxi Security Guards ....BERT F. BALSAM
                                LONNIE HAMILTON
                                  RON SANCHEZ
                                  BILLY LUCAS
Ed Weinberger's Secretary ....PATRICIA SCANLON
Harrah's Booker ....MAX ALEXANDER
Harrah's Conductor ....ED MITCHELL
Mimi ....REIKO AYLESWORTH
Merv Griffin ....MICHAEL VILLANI
Lynne Margulies ....COURTNEY LOVE
Irate Merv Spectator ....MARIA MAGLARIS
Merv's Guest Coordinator ....HEATH HYCHE
Boxing Trainer ....ROBERT HOLEMAN
Wrestling Commentator ....JAMES ROSS
Jerry Lawler ....HIMSELF
Foxy Jackson ....TAMARA BOSSETT
Foxy Jackson Referee ....GENE LEBELL
Jack Burns ....BOB ZMUDA
Friday's Announcer ....BRIAN PECK
Friday's Melanie ....CAROLINE RHEA
Friday's Mary ....MARY LYNN RAJSKUB
Friday's Tech Director ....PHIL LENKOWSKY
Friday's Control Booth Tech ....ROB STEINER
Friday's Floor Director ....CLAUDIA JAFFEE
Jerry Lawler Referee ....MANDO GUERRERO
Ring Announcer ....LANCE RUSSELL
Stadium Photographer ....LADI VON JANSKY
Memphis Paramedics ...................K.P. PALMER
                                  MARK MAJETTI
                                DEANA ANN ABURTO
TM Administrators ....MEWS SMALL
                                DAVID ELLIOTT
Bland Doctor ....FREDD WAYNE
National Enquirer Editor ....TRACEY WALTER
National Enquirer Reporters ....DAVID KOECHNER
                                JEANINE JACKSON
Wild-Haired Guru ....JOHNNY LEGEND
Eleanor Gould ....DORIS EATON TRAVIS
Carnegie Hall Conductor ....GREG SUTTON
Crystal Healer ....SYDNEY LASSICK
Jun Roxas ....YOSHI JENKINS
Comedy Store Patron ....LANCE ALARCON
Comedy Store Waiter .................D.J. JOHNSON
Comedy Store Waitress ....MELISSA CARREY

New York City Rockettes ....DANIELLE BURGIO,
KAREN MARTIN, LINDA CEVALLOS, TABATHA MAYS,
BETSY CHANG, KATIE MILLER, JENNIFER CHAVARRIA,
JESSICA MOORE, SHIRRY DOLGIN, TARA NICOLE, LISA
EATON, MIA PITTS, MELANIE GAGE, KELLY SHEERIN,
CATHERINE HADER, ALISON SIMPSON, BETSY HAR-
RIS, MELINDA SONGÉR, KELLY JONES, MICHON
SUYAMA, TRICIA LILLY, MICHELLE SWANSON, NATALIE
WEBB

Tony Clifton Dancers ....JACQUELINE CASE,
NATALIE MILLS, KAREN BLAKE CHALLMAN, APRIL
NIXON, TERESA CHAPMAN, TIFFANY OLSON, KELLY
COOPER, KATHRYN ROSSBERG, PENNY FISHER,
KARISSA SEAMAN, EVA JENICKOVA, LEA SULLIVAN, LIND-
SAY LOPEZ, AMY TINKHAM, KRISTIN K. WILLITS

Stunt Coordinator ....BUDDY JOE HOOKER

Stunt Double for Jim Carrey ....PAT BANTA

Stunts ....GEORGE AGUILAR,
HELENA LE COUNT, LESLEY ALETTER, MIMI LESSEOS,
ELLE ALEXANDER, BILLY LUCAS, BOBBY BASS, KENT
LUTTRELL, TAMARA BOSSETT, FRANCINE MORRIS,
JANET BRADY, MICHIKO NISHIWAKI, CHARLIE BREWER,
RALPH ODUM, TROY BROWN, SHAWN ODUM, EDITA
BRYCHTA, CYNTHIA PROUDER, HEATHER BURTON,
SUZANNE RAMPE, JENNIFER CAPUTO, CHERYL RUSA,
STEVE CHAMBERS, LYNN SALVATORI, ALISA CHRIS-
TENSEN, DIANE GRANT SCHOTT, CARON COLVETT, SUE
SEXTON, CHRISTY COTTON, GAYLE SHERMAN,
RICHARD DROWN, RON STEIN, ANNIE ELLIS, LISA
STOVER, MANDO GUERRERO, CINDY THOMPSON, ACE
HATEM, DAVID WELCH, JOEL KRAMER, SPICE WILLIAMS,
GENE LEBELL, DICK ZIKER

Tony Clifton Bikers ....DOUG FORD
                        BILL REID, CHUCK ZITO

SNL Band ....THOMAS BARNEY,
CHERYL HARDWICK, LEWIS DEL GATTO, VALERIE
NARANJO, ALEX FOSTER, SHAWN PELTON, EARL GARD-
NER, LEON PENDARVIS, LUKASZ GOTTWALD, LEONARD
PICKETT, STEVE TURRE

Mama Rivoli's Band ....FRANK DEVITO,
TONY GALLA, FRANK MAROCCO, PAT SENATORE

Harrah's Band ....HAL BLAINE,
NORMAN MAMEY, CHARLIE BRISSETTE, JOHN
MITCHELL, EVAN DINER, ROBERT O'DONNELL, TIM
DIVERS, GREG PRECHEL, PHILLIP FEATHER, JAMES
SAWYER, ALEX ILES, DAVID THOMASSON, JAMES LUM,
STEVEN WILLIAMS, JOHN YOAKUM

Letterman Band ....ANTON FIG,
WILL LEE, SID MCGINNIS

Comedy Store Band ....ROBERT EMMET,
MICHAEL LUFKIN, JAMES MCCARTY, DAVID THOMAS-
SON, THOMAS VERDONCK

CREW

Production Supervisor &
Post Production Supervisor ......GERRY ROBERT BYRNE
Unit Supervisor ....HENNING MOLFENTER
Creative Consultant ....LYNNE MARGULIES
Art Director ....JAMES TRUESDALE
Set Decorator ....MARIA NAY
Assistant Art Directors ....JOHN BERGER
                                ANDREW MENZIES
Assistant Set Decorator ....LIZ CHIZ

Property Master ....EMILY FERRY
Assistant Property Master ....JOY TAYLOR
Property Assistant ....NEIL GONZALES
Leadman ....JASON BEDIG
Graphic Artist ....STEVE SAMANEN
A Camera Operator ....MITCH DUBIN
B Camera Operators ....KIM MARKS
                                SCOTT SAKAMOTO

First Assistant Camera . . . . .PAT MCARDLE
ROBIN MELHUISH
Second Assistant Camera . . . . .KATE O'NEILL
ERIC AMUNDSEN
Camera Loader . . . . .ANDREW OSBORNE
Production Sound Mixer . . . . .CHRIS NEWMAN
Boom Operators . . . . .MARC-JON SULLIVAN
GREGG HARRIS
24 Frame Video Playback . . . . .JOHN MONSOUR
Video Assist . . . . .STAN HARRISON
Gaffer . . . . .JACK ENGLISH
Best Boy . . . . .JAMES BABINEAUX
Electricians . . . . .ERIK ERICHSEN,
BLAKE HILL, JUAN MORSE, STEVE THORP, BEN ZURA
Dimmer Operator . . . . .GENE HARA
Key Grip . . . . .CHRISTOPHER CENTRELLA
Best Boy . . . . .DEAN KING
A Dolly Grip . . . . .BRAD REA
B Dolly Grip . . . . .BILL SUMMERS
Grips . . . . .RON GLENN,
KEN KING, HUGH MCCALLUM, TOMMY NOROIAN
Rigging Gaffer . . . . .CHRISTOPHER LYONS
Best Boy . . . . .GLENN MORAN
Rigging Electricians . . . . .MARK LINDSEY,
JEROME PONDELLA, MARK SADLER, JEFF WILD,
CHRISTOPHER ZWIRNER
Rigging Grip . . . . .JEFF KLUTTZ
Best Boy . . . . .OSCAR GOMEZ
Rigging Grips . . . . .JOE BATES
HILLIARY KLYM, TOM WAZNEY, IGNACIO WOOLFOLK
Special Effects Coordinator . . . . .LARRY FIORITTO
Special Effects . . . . .VIRGIL SANCHEZ
Assistant Costume Designer . . . . .BOB WOJEWODSKI
Costume Supervisor . . . . .ELAINE MASER
Key Set Costumer . . . . .TRICIA BERCSI
Set Costumer . . . . .SHOSHANA RUBIN
Mr. DeVito's Costumer . . . . .COREY BRONSON
Mr. Carrey's Costumer . . . . .CINDY EVANS
Costumers . . . . .JANIS MEKALIAN
KARO VARTANIA
Makeup Department Head . . . . .VE NEILL
Key Makeup . . . . .BILL CORSO
Mr. Carrey's Makeup . . . . .SHERYL PTAK
Original Tony Clifton Makeup Designed by . . .BOB ZMUDA
Hair Department Head . . . . .YOLANDA TOUSSIENG
Key Hair Stylist . . . . .KATHE SWANSON
Hair Stylist . . . . .LEE ANN BRITTENHAM
Script Supervisor . . . . . .WILMA GARSCADDEN-GAHRET
Location Manager .JIM MACEO
Assistant Location Managers . . . . .RANDY FLOSI
FRANK H. WOODWARD
Production Accountant . . . . .JACKIE BAUGH
Payroll Accountant . . . . .DAVID C. ROMANO
Key Assistant Accountant . . . . .KAYE MCCALL
Assistant Accountants . . . . .KATIE ZASLAW
NICOLE GALLARDO
MICHELE KENNEDY
Production Office Coordinator . . . . .JACQUI POPELKA
Asst. Production Office Coordinator . .MARCI ROSENBERG
Production Office Secretary . . . .ELIZABETH A. MEREDITH
2nd 2nd Assistant Directors . . . . .TIM ENGLE
MICHAEL RISOLI
Art Department Coordinator . . . . .KARLA TRISKA
Casting Associates . . . . .KATHRYN EISENSTEIN
JON STROTHEIDE
Extras Casting . . . . .CENTRAL CASTING
CENEX CASTING
TONY HOBBS
Crowd Promotion . . . . .AUDIENCE ASSOCIATES
Unit Publicist .SPOOKY STEVENS
Still Photographer . . . . .FRANCOIS DUHAMEL
Executive Assistant to Mr. Carrey . . . . .LINDA FIELDS-HILL
Assistant to Mr. Forman . . . . .MAX HUNT

Assistants to Mr. DeVito . . . . .JULIAN ANDRAUS
IAN HARRINGTON
LAURIE RECORD
Assistant to Mr. Shamberg . . . . .WINFIELD HAN
Assistants to Ms. Sher . . . . .ADRIENNE BIDDLE
NATASHA CUBA
Assistant to Mr. Shapiro . . . . .AIMEE HYATT
Assistant to Mr. West . . . . .AMY MACNOW
Assistant to Mr. Zmuda . . . . .RANKO MASUYAMA
Conceptual Storyboard Artist . . . . .TOM SOUTHWELL
TV Sitcom Tech Advisor . . . . .PETER BONERZ
Choreographer . . . . .JAYMI MARSHALL
Stock Footage Researcher . . . . .DEBORAH RICKETTS
Additional Research . . . . .TAKE AIM PRODUCTIONS
Key Set Production Assistant . . . . .JOHN SAUNDERS
Set Production Assistants . . . . .DAN BERKOWITZ,
TAMMY DICKSON, KARIS JAGGER, JOHN NASRAWAY,
TRAVIS STEWART, PHILLIPPA WEAVER
Office Production Assistants . . . . .JON BORCHERS
RICH JONES
SHAUN MERRIMAN
Art Dept. Production Assistants . . . . .MICHAEL TRUESDALE
POLLY WALTER
KATE KEADY
Camera Production Assistant . . . . .WILLO HAUSMAN
Extras Coordinator . . . . .TAYLOR BERNARD
Construction Coordinator . . . . .DAVID ELLIOTT
General Foreman . . . . .MICHAEL CROWLEY
Propmaker Foremen . . . . .REYES RODRIGUEZ,
TODD WATSCHKE, JOSHUA KING, R. LUCAS STEWART,
DAVID DAVERN
Welding Foreman . . . . .CHRIS M. ALVAREZ
Construction Buyer . . . . .CYNTHIA MARTINEZ
Labor Foreman . . . . .EDWARD A. REGAN
Head Painter . . . . .JOHN SNOW
Paint Foremen .CHRIS BARNES
JEFF CAHILL
Paint Gang Boss . . . . .BOB FOX
Sign Painter . . . . .THOMAS MOFFITT
Stand-by Painter . . . . .CHARLES W. ESKRIDGE
Drapery Foreman . . . . .BOB BAKER
Draper/Set Dresser . . . . .DON GOODMAN
On Set Dresser . . . . .MARA MASSEY
Set Dressers .DALE ANDERSON
BROOKE BACON, BRENT BLOM, BROOKE SARTORIUS
Mr. Carrey's Stand-In . . . . .KERRY HOYT
Ms. Love's Stand-In . . . . .CASSANDRA WESSLE
Mr. DeVito's Stand-In . . . . .FREDDIE SCIALLA
Mr. Carrey's Security . . . . .DOTAN BONEN
Transportation Coordinator . . . . .JAMES TAYLOR
Transportation Captain . . . . .DAVID JERNIGAN
Set Captain . . . . .RICK CHOUINARD
Mr. Forman's Driver . . . . .KELLY ALDRICH
Mr. Carrey's Driver . . . . .JERRY MCMULLEN
Mechanic . . . . .DON HARBACK
Caterer .FOR STARS CATERING,
FRANK WOODWARD, MICHELLE WOODWARD
Craft Service . . . . .CHARLIE SCOTT
Security . . . . .CAST SECURITY
VINCE CORTEZ
Mr. Carrey's Masseuse . . . . .LINNEA LIGHT HARRIS
Set Medic .TODD J. ADELMAN

NEW YORK CREW

Art Director . . . . .RAY KLUGA
Set Decorator . . . . .KARIN WIESEL
Assistant Set Decorator . . . . .DIANE LEDERMAN
Set Buyer .ALEXANDRA MAZUR
Property Master . . . . .KEVIN LADSON
Assistant Property Master . . . . .TYLER KIM
Prop . . . . .VICTOR LITTLEJOHN
Leadman . . . . .TIM METZGER
B Camera Operator . . . . .TOM WESTON
B Camera 1st Assistant . . . . .JIM BELLETIER

2nd Assistants ....LEE KAZISTA	Assistant Editors (NY) ....SONIA GONZALEZ
ROD CALARCO	BEATRICE SIŠUL
Camera Loader ....BRADEN BELMONTE	Editing Room Apprentice ......SAMARA LEVENSTEIN
24 Frame Video Playback ....HOWARD WEINER	Assistant Editors (LA) ....MICHAEL HOFACRE
GARY M. PARKER	JUDITH ANN WESLEY
Video Assist Operator ....BOB BALZARINI	Editing Room Apprentice ....CHRISTINE KIM
Gaffer...............................BOB CONNERS	
Best Boy ....JAY FORTUNE	Re-Recording Mixers ....MICHAEL BARRY
Generator Operators ....RAY FORTUNE	RON BOCHAR
LEON VERCRUSE	Supervising Sound Editor ....RON BOCHAR
Key Grip ....EDWIN A. QUINN	Dialogue Editors ....NICHOLAS RENBECK
Best Boy ....EDWARD J. EGAN, III	PHIL STOCKTON
Rigging Gaffer ....JIM MALONE	
Rigging Key Grip ....THOMAS GILLIGAN	Supervising ADR Editor ....HAL LEVINSOHN
Men's Costume Supervisor ....BENJAMIN WILSON	ADR Mixer ....DAVID BOLTON
Women's Costume Supervisor ....MELISSA STANTON	Background Vocals ..DAVID KRAMER'S LOOPING GROUP
Key Makeup ....MARIANNE SKIBA	Sound Effects Editors ....LEWIS GOLDSTEIN
Key Hair Stylist ....PATRICIA GRANDE	BEN CHEAH
Location Manager ....TOM WHELAN	Foley Supervisor ....KAM CHAN
Assistant Location Manager ....LYNN POWERS	Foley Editors ....JENNIFER RALSTON
Location Scout ....LAUREN KEANE	TIM O'SHEA
Production Accountant ....CARLA SCHORR ROSE	Foley Engineer ....GEORGE A. LARA
Assistant Accountant ....JOANNA ZORCIK	Foley Artist ....MARKO COSTANZO
Payroll Accountant ....DARRYL A. SMITH	Assistant Sound Editors ....WYATT SPRAGUE
Production Office Coordinator ....CHRISSIE DAVIS	CHRIS FIELDER
Assistant Production Office Coordinator ....KATHERINE M.	IGOR NIKOLIC
COHN	Apprentice Sound Editor ....RUTH HERNANDEZ
2nd 2nd Assistant Director ....MICHAEL I. SMITH	Sound Intern ....ALICE BYRNE
Extras Casting ....KEE CASTING	Re-Recording Assistant ....TERRY LAUDERMILCH
Set Production Assistants ....AUGIE CARTON	Dolby Consultant ....GEOF LIPMAN
MATT POWER	
Office Production Assistant ....VINCENTE STASOLLA	Wescam Provided by ....WESCAM, INC.
Art Department Production Assistant ....BETH DARY	MICHELLE CISNEROS
Locations Assistants ....STEPHEN CARR	
JON M. JOHNSON, JIMMY PRICE, JULIA RYDHOLM	Front Screen Projection ...HANSARD ENTERPRISES, INC.
Construction Coordinator ....MARTIN BERNSTEIN	
Construction Foreman ....MICHAEL CURRY	Opticals ....BALSMEYER & EVERETT, INC.
Key Construction Grip ....ARNE OLSEN	THE EFFECTS HOUSE
Construction Grips ....RALPH FRATIANNI	Negative Cutter ....GARY BURRITT
ARNE OLSEN, JR.	Color Timer ....JIM PASSON
Greensperson ....WILL SCHECK	Title Design & Visual Effects Produced by ....
Scenic Charge ....JON RINGBOM	BALSMEYER & EVERETT, INC.
Scenic Foreperson ....JUNE DECAMP	
Camera Scenic ....PETER HACKMAN	Visual Effects Supervisor ....RANDALL BALSMEYER
Scenic/Shop Manager ....JOYCE LEIFERTZ	
Construction Shop P.A. ....SANJIT DE SILVA	Music Editor ....SHARI SCHWARTZ JOHANSON
2nd Dresser ....HARVEY GOLDBERG	Associate Music Editor ....MISSY COHEN
On Set Dresser ....JOE TAGLAIRINO	Associate Music Supervisor ....KAYLIN FRANK
Transportation Captain ....THOMAS LEAVEY	Ms. Camarata's Assistant ....CARI COHEN
Transportation Co-Captain ....MIKE BUCKMAN	Live Recordings Engineered & Mixed by ....JOEL MOSS
Caterer ....COAST TO COAST CATERING	Additional Engineers ....JIMMY HOYSON
Craft Service ....JOE FACEY	FRED VOGLER
MELINA C. PAVLIDES	RIC WILSON
Aerial Coordinator ....GERRY ROBERT	Live and Pre-Recordings Produced by ....ED MITCHELL
LAKE TAHOE AERIAL UNIT	Score Produced by ....PAT MCCARTHY
Helicopter Pilot ....DIRK VAHLE	
Aerial Cameraman ....STAN MCCLAIN	
Aerial Asst. Cameraman ....MARK LEINS	Recorded & Mixed by ....PAT MCCARTHY
Wescam Technician ....STEVE WINSLOW	and JAMIE CANDILORO
	Orchestrations .....ALEXANDER JANKO, EDDIE HORST
BAGIO CITY AERIAL UNIT	Music Preparation ......JO ANN KANE MUSIC SERVICES
Beech 18 Pilot ....SKIP EVANS	Music Contractor ....DAVID LOW
DC-3 Pilot ....GARY DOURIS	Recorded at ....CELLO STUDIOS, ROYALTONE,
DC-3 Co-pilot ....DIRK VAHLE	SONY SCORING STAGE, THE MONASTARY
Post Production Coordinator ....REBECCA L. MURRAY	Mixed at ....O'HENRY STUDIOS
Post Production Accountant ....LISA COFINI	
Post Production Assistant ....JERRY CARITA	
First Assistant Editor (NY) ....MARTIN LEVENSTEIN	

BIOGRAPHIES

SCOTT ALEXANDER AND LARRY KARASZEWSKI wrote *Ed Wood,* for which they were nominated for Best Screenplay by the Writers Guild. They followed this with *The People vs. Larry Flynt,* for which they won the Golden Globe Award for Best Screenplay, as well as a special Writers Guild Award given in recognition of work done for civil rights and liberties. They are currently writing and directing a screwball comedy for Universal Pictures. Collaborators since their senior year at USC's School of Cinema, they began their careers with the box-office hit *Problem Child* and its sequel. They live in Los Angeles.

MILOS FORMAN was born in Czechoslovakia in 1932. After being orphaned during the war, he studied screenwriting at the university in Prague. His first films were *Competition* (1963); *Black Peter* (1963); *Loves of a Blonde* (1965); and *The Fireman's Ball* (1967). In 1971 he made his first American film, *Taking Off.* Milos Forman has won two Academy Awards for Best Director and Best Picture, for *One Flew over the Cuckoo's Nest* (1975) and *Amadeus* (1984). His other films include an episode of David L. Wolper's production of *Visions of Eight* (1973); *Hair* (1979); *Ragtime* (1981); *Valmont* (1989); and *The People vs. Larry Flynt* (1996).

JERSEY FILMS is a motion picture, television, and record company owned by Danny DeVito, Michael Shamberg, and Stacey Sher. In addition to *Man on the Moon,* Jersey will also release *Erin Brockovich,* starring Julia Roberts, in the year 2000. Other Jersey productions include *Living Out Loud*; *Out of Sight*; *Gattaca*; *Reality Bites*; *Pulp Fiction*; *Get Shorty*; *Matilda*; *Hoffa*; *Sunset Park*; *Feeling Minnesota*; *Fierce Creatures*; and *8 Seconds.* Jersey also produced *The Pentagon Wars* for HBO, and the television division signed a production agreement with Twentieth Century Fox. Jersey Records has produced soundtrack releases for the motion pictures *Sliding Doors*; *Out of Sight*; *Living Out Loud*; and *Man on the Moon.*